SERILDA'S END

Serilda wiped the rain from her eyes. Or were they tears? "You were the king's most trusted advisor, his friend and confidant. You had wealth, status, power. His love. Anything you wanted was yours. You betrayed and killed the royal family, and in the end it gained you nothing."

Behind her, above the pounding rain, Serilda heard the clatter of boots but didn't dare turn to see if friend or foe approached; Roark would seize such an advantage and make her pay. But as she stepped forward, her feet slid on the slick stone and she struggled to regain her balance. Her sword dipped. Roark lunged.

"No!"

Serilda heard Donoval's anguished cry. She looked down. Roark's sword protruded from her chest.

Other *Love Spell* books by Elysa Hendricks:

STAR CRASH

THE
Sword
AND THE Pen

ELYSA HENDRICKS

LOVE SPELL   LOVE SPELL   NEW YORK CITY

For Gerrie, a true warrior woman.
If the pen were mightier than the sword
I'd write you back to life.

LOVE SPELL®

May 2009

Published by

Dorchester Publishing Co., Inc.
200 Madison Avenue
New York, NY 10016

ISBN 10: 0-505-52817-7
ISBN 13: 978-0-505-52817-9
E-ISBN: 978-1-4285-0678-7

The name "Love Spell" and its logo are trademarks of Dorchester Publishing Co., Inc.

Printed in the United States of America.

10 9 8 7 6 5 4 3 2 1

Visit us on the web at www.dorchesterpub.com.

ACKNOWLEDGMENTS

As always I have to acknowledge my darling husband who through the years has supported me in my quest to write, both emotionally and financially. Without him I'd be too busy and tired from working a nine-to-five job to write.

THE Sword AND THE Pen

Serilda

*"Choices determine destiny.
Choose wisely."*
—Brother Eldrin, Order of the Light

Chapter One

While outside a storm raged, Brandon Alexander Davis wrote the final chapter of what he hoped would be his last Warrior Woman book:

Inch by inch Serilda fought her way forward. Lightning streaked across the rolling black clouds, darkening the midday sky. In the brief light, her sword flashed crimson. Thunder crashed, drowning the screams of the men dying around her. The stench of death and gore stung her nostrils. Bits of flesh and bone along with a generous amount of blood spattered her face and body.

Despite Hausic's wise counsel, she'd launched a frontal attack against Andre Roark's army. She could see him. A few yards more and she'd break through his guard and cut him down. Arms burning from the strain of fighting for hours, she swung again and . . .

* * *

Lightning touched the tip of my upraised sword. A jolt of energy shot through my body. Stunned, I slipped on a puddle of blood and tumbled backward. My sword flew out of my hand. A blade swept downward toward my neck, and I faced death.

Doubts and regrets about my chosen life aren't something I often consider, but at that moment, I regretted my failure to reach my goal—burying my blade deep in Roark's heartless chest—before I died.

Though I kept my eyes wide—it was better to embrace my demise and face my reward or punishment for my sins—I didn't die. Instead, nothingness surrounded me. I blinked to clear the misty haze, but Roark, my troops, and the battle that raged around me vanished. Other than my body, I could neither see nor feel anything. Fear faded. Time stretched endlessly. How long I existed in that limbo I don't know. As I waited, my irritation grew.

Had a great wizard plucked me from my world? Since Roark, my belief in magic had been fading. If magic still existed, I'd experienced little good from it. Was this a place of safety? A place of death?

A place of judgment?

Though my path has always involved death, I choose with discretion. I take only righteous commissions, and those I hunt are always given the opportunity to surrender. It isn't my fault they rarely do so. Neither do I harm or kill innocents. I'm a mercenary with a solid code of ethics. I fight only for justice and freedom. If I was dead, surely my few slips wouldn't condemn my soul to . . .

Damn it, woman. The voice in my head spoke without real heat, just resigned frustration. I liked his strange accent. Deep and even, this voice hinted at long nights spent between the sheets.

Why won't you ever do what I tell you to?

"To whom do you speak?" I tried to shout, but no sound came from my throat.

I had Hausic counsel you to stage a sneak attack from the rear, not make a frontal assault on Roark's fortress. But no, you had to do it your way. Three weeks' work and outlining wasted.

A frontal assault? How did this stranger know of my chief counsel's arguments against my plan? Our conversation had been private . . . or so I thought. What spy of Roark's had been listening?

The voice I heard in my head gave me my first clue as to where I was and what I had become: *It's my own fault for giving you a conscience, a sense of fair play, and a stubborn streak.*

I bristled at his assumptions. The monks that took me in after my parents died at Roark's hands were to blame for my conscience, not this disembodied voice. My sense of fair play came from my father, and my stubbornness from my mother. Or so I believed. Unease slid down my spine.

If I didn't have other plans, I swear I'd let that barbarian take your head off right now. Let's go back and get it right.

I wanted to argue. To tell him I *had* gotten it right. The frontal assault was working fine. I'd drawn Roark from his fortress. He was nearly within my reach. It wasn't my fault I'd slipped on the gore left from the battle, was it? But at that point, I had no voice—at least none my tormentor could hear.

And this time we'll do it my way.

Before I could blink, I found myself back in my tent a week earlier, Hausic repeating his arguments against a frontal assault. He spluttered when I pushed past him and out into the night. Sword drawn, I slipped around the tent but found no strangers lurking. The guards stared at me in confusion.

Back in the tent, I slumped on my cot, sword dangling between my knees. Hausic pestered me with questions about my unusual behavior until I sent him away, plans for the attack still unresolved. Perhaps a sneak attack *was* more prudent. Roark's troops had been ready for the frontal assault—unless I had dreamt the last week? I would have considered that the only possibility, gone on with my life if the sultry voice of my wizard tormentor had not then asked, *What is it now, woman? I'm already past my deadline on this damned book!*

I searched the small tent, but I knew the voice came from inside my head.

Donoval may be more brawn than brain, but I never had this much trouble with his *books.*

King Donoval of the kingdom of Shallon was my onetime lover: beautiful as an angel, strong as a bull . . . and as dense as a rock, at least in matters of the heart. With more than a twinge of regret, I'd kicked Donnie out of my bed and life several years ago. For all his faults, he was spectacular to look at, honorable, and a dedicated lover. But his demand that I choose between fighting for my country or becoming his bondmate was more than I could stomach. Marriage was too final a commitment for me.

Cooperate, or I swear I'll write you out of existence in the most painful way I can dream up.

Write me out of existence? The possible answer to what was happening was beyond my ability to believe, but once imagined, the idea wouldn't leave. My breath stilled. Was I indeed some wizard's creation?

Brandon Alexander Davis scratched his stubble with a weary hand. After ten years and ten books, he'd thought he was beyond writer's block. But finishing this book and this series was giving him nothing but grief. He should have stayed with the Donoval series. But no, he'd had to create Serilda. And though fictional, the woman had taken over his life.

When he'd first begun writing fantasy stories, his grandmother, the woman who'd raised him from the age of ten, warned him that words held powerful magic—magic that could consume him, magic that would demand he sacrifice everything, magic that would destroy him if not carefully controlled. At the time, he'd laughed. Nonsense! He loved her, but it was just another of her bizarre stories. Once she'd told him they were descendents of an ancient race of sorcerers from Atlantis! The one time he'd asked about his father, who'd vanished before Brandon was born, she'd said he disappeared into a fantasy world of his own creation. After that, Brandon avoided such subjects. Though his grandmother had been a better parent than his mother, in many ways she was just as crazy.

Or, so he'd always thought. But his fictional world was indeed becoming too real. Face it, he talked to his characters, and at times, it even felt like they talked back. Maybe this world and magic really *was* devouring him.

The parallels between Serilda's life and his own were disturbing. Orphaned at a young age, raised by wise elders, then left alone again . . . The truth was, in creating Serilda and her quest, he'd found an outlet for the anger and pain inside himself; but as much as he loved the world he'd created, it was time for him to reconnect with reality. This was Serilda's last quest. It was time to make a clean break. It was time to kill off Serilda. It was time for him to be reborn.

His phone rang. He ignored it, but he couldn't ignore his agent's shrill voice through his answering machine.

"Brandon? Pick up, I know you're there. You're always there. You need to get a life. At least move out of that hick town to Chicago." She paused.

Interesting that her thoughts echoed his.

"Attend the Sci-con exhibition at the mall. Sign some books. Judge the cover model contest. Get your face out there for your fans."

He smiled at what she considered a life: attending fantasy and sci-fi conventions, doing book signings, and judging some cheesy book cover model contest. Hell, no! Especially not the contest. Though he was killing her off, Serilda was his creation. No real woman could match the image in his mind. He wouldn't watch wannabes make the attempt.

Hillary gave a dramatic sigh and continued, "You're already three months past your deadline. The publisher is starting to talk lawsuit, and the movie producer is going to cancel his option if the next Warrior Woman book isn't released on time. You've got to strike while the iron's hot. Make hay while the sun shines."

He cringed at her clichés, something he prided himself on avoiding in his novels. Hillary Raymond was past the cajoling point. She'd reached the demanding and trite stage.

"What's going on with you? You never had these problems with Donoval. Now *there* was a hunk." Her sigh held a wealth of meaning.

He'd never had problems writing Donoval because Donoval was never a real person to him the way Serilda was. Donoval was simple. Brandon had written him without any deep emotions. Brain and brawn, but no heart—at least not compared to Serilda. Was that another reflection of his own life? Yeah, probably. At the time, Brandon had just buried his grandmother and didn't want to feel.

When he'd first signed with the Raymond Agency, Hillary had assumed that because Brandon looked like Donoval—tall, blond, and muscular—that he was *like* Donoval, and she'd thought they could have a physical relationship as well as a business one. Brandon had soon quashed that idea. Hillary was a shark, handy to have on his side in business but uncomfortable as a bed partner. He'd known from the first that she'd eat him alive if he made the mistake of responding to her offer. He might be a physical model for his character—aside from the long hair, iron-hard muscles, and fighting skills—but inside they were nothing alike. Donoval was honest and honorable. Physically and emotionally secure in his own power. Fearless in the face of death. Kind to small children and animals. A legendary lover. Brandon was the exact opposite.

Well, almost opposite. He wasn't flabby. He ran and worked out regularly to keep in shape, but he didn't have Donoval's sculpted physique. No real men did, did they? And he wasn't dishonest. He wrote his own books, paid his bills, and tried not to cheat people. But was he honorable? In today's world, what did that really mean? And fearless? Not. He had more phobias than he cared to think about. He abhorred physical violence. Large crowds made him cringe. Insects sent him running from a room. Animals of any size gave him the shudders, and he ranked children along with animals: creatures better left alone.

As for being a legendary lover? His limited understanding of real women—a failed marriage was proof of that—had left him wary of the trap of sex. The few minutes of physical gratification women provided weren't worth the cost in time, money, or emotion. His failed marriage had even caused him in his fictional world to make marriage a permanent condition. Divorce wasn't an option, so his characters thought long and hard before making that true 'til death do you part commitment. As true as he realized they were, his ex-wife Wanda's scornful comments about how he'd avoided her by living in a fantasy world still stung. Thank goodness his marriage ended long before he started making any money.

Actually, it surprised him Wanda hadn't turned up on his doorstep looking for a piece of his success. Or maybe he was just too well hidden. Being a recluse had its advantages. Although, a direct assault wasn't her style. When she turned up, and he was sure she would eventually, it would be a sneak attack—something his infuriating creation seemed to be refusing to consider. Damn Serilda!

He tuned back in to Hillary's tirade.

"Maybe you can avoid your fans and the press by rusticating in that hick town, but you can't hide from me," his agent continued. "I'll be there a week from Monday. That gives you a little over a week. I want to see the end of this book and at least the first three chapters of the next. Or else!"

Brandon winced at the sound of her slamming down the phone. The answering machine beeped, and he turned back to his computer screen. The cursor blinked at him in mockery.

Telling Hillary that he wasn't writing any more Warrior Woman books wasn't going to be easy, and she wasn't going to be happy with the ending of this book. But he could do it. He'd written many, many books before, and he'd finished them all. While Serilda was his creation, a warrior woman of amazing beauty and skill, after one more chapter, book seven, her last, would be done. All he had to do was keep her from killing Roark outright in this scene. But he had to have the villain escape without making her look stupid or incompetent.

Not possible.

He groaned. In the three months since he'd decided to kill off Serilda and end the series, he'd been hearing a sultry, sarcastic female voice in his head. The voice was the reason he was behind schedule. The voice fought his every decision, arguing for scenes to go her way. He'd fought and won every battle, but the resulting scenes seemed flat and forced.

He'd written and rewritten Serilda's death scene a dozen different ways. Though none felt quite right, he'd have to choose one soon.

He'd heard of authors who claimed their characters were real people who managed to take control of their stories, but he'd never had that problem. He was a realist. Despite his grandmother's fanciful warnings, characters were fictional creations, figments of the imagination, not real. He controlled them in a way he'd never be able to control real people. That was half of their appeal!

Or at least he had controlled them until this book, until that sultry voice began whispering in his ear.

As satisfying as it might be to just kill her off, he started rewriting the book's climactic scene so she didn't die:

> *Serilda placed the tip of her sword against Roark's throat. Blood trickled from the tiny cut her blade made. She pressed forward, and Roark's dark eyes widened in fear.*
>
> *"Would you kill me, your . . ."*

Brandon stopped for a moment. Before Serilda's final deadly confrontation with Roark, she would learn the truth—that she was Roark's daughter—but that came later. It couldn't happen yet. Brandon continued typing.

> *The would-be king paused and seemed to think better of what he was about to say.*
>
> *"Would you kill an unarmed man?" He spread his arms wide and gave her a small smile of defeat, but his body stayed tense and ready.*
>
> *Serilda took a step back. "Pick up your sword." She motioned to the blade lying at his feet. "I'll kill you in a fair fight."*

"Yeeek!"

At first Brandon thought the shriek was an electronic whine that came from his computer. Panic threatened. When was the last time he'd backed up his files? It had been during that bad electrical storm three months ago when he'd almost lost everything, the same time his writing troubles began. Fortunately the freak power surge from a lightning strike only fried his monitor; his computer hadn't been harmed. He should have learned from the experience, but writer's block had driven him past rational thought. The idea of losing what little work he'd managed to accomplish these last few weeks made him choke in fear. He scrambled to hit Save.

"Hell, no! Roark doesn't deserve a chance to defend himself. And even if he did, I'm not stupid enough to give him the opportunity to skewer me. That's something Donoval the Honorable would do."

At the sound of the familiar yet condemning voice behind him, Brandon whirled. He slipped off his chair and landed hard on his tailbone. Pain shot up his spine and blurred his vision.

"What? How did you get in here? And who the hell are you?" He stared up at the woman and gulped. The sword in her hand pointed straight at his heart.

"You know damned well who I am."

The woman didn't sound happy—and didn't look sane. She loomed over him. Her attire—a short, tight leather skirt, a leather bra, and knee-high boots—left a lot of skin exposed to his view. The smell of leather, fresh air, and warm woman teased his nostrils.

"What are you?" She poked him in the arm with the tip of her sword.

"Ow!" He scooted back, nearly under his desk.

"Warrior? Priest? Sorcerer?" She crouched down to rest on her heels and stared at him. The position put her full breasts nearly in his face. "Definitely not a warrior." She pinched his arm. "You have muscle, but not enough to wield a sword in battle. No courage, either. Priest? Unlikely. They don't fear the sword. Only their god makes them cower. Wizard? Perhaps, but not one of any power, or else I'd be at your feet. So . . . you're the wizard's assistant most likely." As if satisfied with her conclusion, she rose to her feet.

"Get up. I'll not harm you. I wish to speak to your master. He and I have business to discuss."

Brandon eyed the woman warily. Though her speech and clothing were odd, she sounded and looked extremely familiar. Why? Was she a crazy fan he'd somehow communicated with before?

To be honest, she bore a striking resemblance to Serilda, if shorter. She was five feet seven or eight inches, rather than six feet, and she was less buxom and had softer features than the character he'd ultimately developed. Actually, this woman was more like how he'd envisioned Serilda originally, when he'd introduced her in Donoval's second book: an extremely feminine woman forced to survive in a harsh world by denying her nature. Hillary had convinced him that in her own books Serilda needed to be stronger and have more sex appeal, hence the height and the bigger chest. The change hadn't sat well with him, but the public—men *and* women— loved her, and the books had hit all the bestseller lists. As a result, he had a thriving series, a pending movie deal, and cash in his once-empty bank account. Success was hard to argue with.

Despite the trampy clothing and hard scowl, she was attractive. Short reddish blonde curls framed an elfin face. Dark lashes fringed large, catlike green eyes. Sun-kissed skin covered high cheekbones, and her lips, though currently set in a hard line, were full and red.

"I said get up!" She grabbed his arm and hauled him to his feet.

He was surprised that, when he stood, he topped her by a good six inches and probably outweighed her by sixty pounds. That size difference gave him a bit of confidence, but the nasty-looking sword she held with such self-assurance negated it. One could never trust the actions of a crazy person.

"Who are you?" She looked him up and down, then seemed to dismiss him.

He pulled himself to his full height and stared down at her. "Brandon Alexander Davis. This is my home."

Unimpressed, she laughed. "Brandon? What kind of name is that? Bran is what I eat to ease my bowels."

Heat crept up Brandon's neck. Being compared to a laxative made him angry, which helped push fear away. "Who the hell are you? And what are you doing here in that ridiculous costume?"

"Who I am and"—she paused, and two spots of color stained her cheeks—"what I wear is a matter I will discuss with your master. Where is he? Has he run to hide from me? It will do him no good. I'm determined to find him and solve this."

"I don't have a master. I live here alone." Damn! Why had he told her that? He eased back from the lunatic toward the phone. Could he hit speed dial for 911 before she skewered him? Then what? Even if he succeeded, it would take the police a good fifteen to twenty minutes to reach his isolated home. Could he wrest the sword away from her before then?

His size would be an advantage, but even standing at ease, the woman radiated strength and skill. The odds seemed against him. To win he'd have to hit her—hard—and he doubted he could bring himself to do so. The lessons of chivalry his grandmother had taught were too deeply ingrained. In that way, he and Donoval were of one mind. No matter how greatly provoked, men didn't hit women.

Although, the thought of wrestling with this woman was appealing.

"No master? Do not lie to me." The lunatic's fingers flexed around the hilt of her sword.

"Why would I lie?" he snapped. "It's obvious your beef is with someone else. If I knew who and where he was, why would I protect him?"

"Because you're a coward. A powerful sorcerer inspires fear if not loyalty in his minions. But you should fear me more than him," she warned.

"There is no him! I'm the only one here. And I'm not a coward." Being called one triggered something inside him. Having phobias about crowds, insects, and small furry animals didn't make him a coward. Not really.

She gave him a thoughtful look. "Is it possible? Are you the one?"

"The one what?"

She ignored his question and studied him. Her intense perusal made him squirm.

"Why didn't I see the resemblance?" she murmured.

"What resemblance?" He didn't like the turn of this conversation. Come to think of it, he hadn't liked the original direction either.

"To Donoval. You are him—in form at least." A bit of fear crossed her features, though anger quickly erased it. "I'm loath to believe it, but you are the wizard. Did you construct me so you could play God in my world? Does it give you pleasure to toy with me?"

"What the hell are you talking about? Play God? I'm just a writer trying to make a living. I write stories for people to read and enjoy. It's just entertainment."

A writer? A scribe, perhaps, a scribbler of words? No, he meant more like a bard or a troubadour. But . . . impossible. I'd almost come to terms with the idea I'd been brought into existence by a wizard, but I hadn't imagined that my whole world, everyone and everything in it might also be his creation. If nothing of my past or my world was real, what did that mean for my quest to destroy Roark? If they never truly existed, was I yet bound by the vow I'd made at my mother's and father's gravesides?

Stunned, I sank into a chair. In my distress, its comfortable quality barely registered. My sword dropped between my knees.

I must have gone pale, because my tormentor looked concerned and said, "Are you okay? Is there someone I can call for you?"

"Call?" My whole reality was in question, and he wanted to yell out the window? I could hear no servants in this dwelling, and he'd said he lived alone. "No, there's no one." It was true, even if I *were* real and back in my own world, there was no one—no family, few friends, no lovers . . . Roark had seen to that. I was as alone there as I was here.

"Stay put. I'll get you a drink." He hurried out of the room.

Yes, a good strong drink would be nice. Something to wash away this nightmare I'd fallen into.

He came back with a tall glass filled with a colorless liquid. Whatever else he might be, he was wealthy. Only the very rich could afford glass of such purity and craftsmanship.

My hands trembled as I took the container, lifted it to my mouth, took a swig . . . and spat.

"Do you try to poison me?" I shouted, jumping to my feet and throwing away the glass. It shattered. The tip of my sword pressed against the villain's chest.

He used his fingertips on the flat of the blade to push it aside and spluttered, "W-what are you talking about? It's just water."

I stalked forward, tipping the blade upward and dropping my hand so that the point touched just below his chin. He scrambled backward into a piece of furniture. "Exactly. You would see me sicken and die in agony from the drinking of water. If you seek to kill me, I would prefer an honorable death. In battle."

He gave a quick nod and winced as my blade nicked his skin. "Oh, I forgot, in book two Roark polluted your country's water supply. It needs to be mixed with strong wine to kill the germs. It was a mistake. The water here is clean. I promise it won't make you sick."

"If you've created everything in my reality, how could you forget this?" Part of me still wanted to believe that my world had an actuality beyond this man's sorcery, that only I was his creation. There was some solace in that thought.

"There are a lot of details that go into world-building when you're writing a fantasy novel. It's hard to keep them all straight, especially when one of your characters is holding a sword to your throat. Do you mind?" He grunted.

I felt the pressure of his hand against my blade. A small bead of blood welled on his skin, and I let my sword drop. If I killed him, would I cease to exist? More important, what of my world and all those who resided there? Though I wasn't yet sure of the truth of his words, I wouldn't take any chances.

He grimaced as he dabbed at the blood on his chin with a piece of soft white paper he pulled from a box behind him. "Do you think you might stop waving around that sword before somebody—namely me—gets hurt? Or are you all about the chop-chop?"

Though frightened, he remained sarcastic. I found myself smiling. Lack of humor had been one of Donnie's flaws; he never saw the funny side of things or made jokes. And this stranger's words resonated with something else I believed. *Knowledge is more powerful than any sword, my child. Often it is better to listen and learn than to slash and kill.* Though long dead, killed by Roark along with the other monks who'd raised and educated me, Brother Eldrin's words were wise. I sheathed my sword and sat.

A thought occurred to me. If all this man claimed was true, then I was finally free. Free of my past. Free of my vows. Free of the guilt that dogged my steps. I'd been a puppet dancing on another's string. Nothing I'd done was ever of my own free will, but it could be now.

Strangely, if there was freedom, it felt false. My mind might accept these new possibilities, but my heart could not. I felt real. My world felt real. The death of my loved ones felt real. The past blood staining my hands and soul felt real. This man's mere words couldn't wash it all away.

And yet, my mind believed him. Everything I was, everything I knew, and everything I'd done, he said he'd created as a form of entertainment for his people.

Suddenly, real or not, I wanted more than anything to be home. Back with Hausic, my wizened and wise fussy old war counselor. Back to Mauri, the little slave girl I'd liberated from an abusive owner by liberating said owner's head from his shoulders. Though she was free, she'd insisted on remaining at my side. She cooked my meals—admittedly badly—mended my clothing—also badly—and if I were interested, she'd share my bed. (There I'm sure she'd do quite well.) I wanted to be back with Jole, the lad who cared for my weapons and horses and made me smile with his quick wit and loyalty. I even wanted to be back with Donoval, the big lug. Though I no longer shared his bed and he refused to send troops to help in my campaign against Roark's reign over my country, I yet considered him a comrade.

My heart cried out in denial. The people in my world couldn't all be fictional. I'd touched them, watched them laugh and cry, bleed and die. And what was reality if not the ability to think and feel? Was I not real, no matter my origin?

I looked up at my tormentor. "Why and how have you brought me here? What do you want with me? And why, with all your power, do you allow me to defy and threaten you?"

"Even a rabbit will fight when cornered."
—Brother Eldrin, Order of the Light

Chapter Two

Brandon didn't answer; he simply watched all fight drain out of the woman. Sitting forlorn in his desk chair, she looked lost and alone. In his books Serilda rarely had a moment of fear or doubt. Her single-minded pursuit of justice against Roark for his murder of her family and subjugation of her country was what made her so popular with her audience.

Serilda? What was he thinking? He really was losing touch with reality if he could entertain this lunatic's wild claim. She obviously wasn't Serilda. Maybe she was a wacko fan or a friend's practical joke, but not Serilda. Serilda didn't exist anywhere outside of his head or on the printed page! Heaven help him if his characters started to appear in the real world. Roark came to mind as one horrible possibility. Handsome, charming, and immoral, the man would most likely end up taking over the world.

But whoever—or whatever—this woman was, she needed help. He edged toward the phone. Whom to call? The police? No, the local police would haul her off to jail. Somehow Brandon knew she wouldn't go peacefully, and he didn't want anyone to get hurt. Who, then?

Hillary. Used to dealing with crazy writers and psycho fans, his agent would know how to handle the situation.

The lunatic didn't stir as he grabbed his cordless phone and retreated into the kitchen.

"Hillary Raymond. Leave a message." Like the woman herself, her message didn't mince words.

"Hillary, this is Brandon. I've got a problem. Can you—"

"Problem? What problem?" Hillary came on the line. "I swear, Brandon, if you weren't so damned talented and your books didn't sell like hotcakes I'd drop you like a hot potato. What's the trouble now?"

"Well, ah, it's . . ." How did he explain the woman in his living room? And what exactly did he want his agent to do about it?

"Spit it out, boy. Unless you have some chapters for me, I don't have time to hold your hand. I have other clients."

Boy? Angry at the insult and also at his cowardice regarding the Serilda wannabe in the next room, he lashed out. "What other clients? Until I came along, you weren't making enough to pay the postage on the rejection letters you were getting." He exaggerated. She was a good agent, and a loyal one. Once she accepted a client, she fought for them, though until he came along none of her clients had earned her more than a comfortable living. His success was her success. She still worked with her old authors, but the bulk of her income came from him. "We both know I'm your number-one meal ticket."

Hillary's chuckle doused his flare of rage. Blunt herself, she didn't take offense. "That's my boy. I knew anyone who writes the way you do, with such fire and passion, had to have some spunk. So, what's the problem?"

"I have an unwanted houseguest."

"Your ex-wife tracked you down?"

Brandon shuddered. "No, Wanda I could handle." Maybe. "A few dollars and she'd be on her way. This woman is different."

"What woman? Different how?"

He could hear the curiosity growing in Hillary's voice. Even though he'd turned her down, her interest in his love life hadn't dimmed. His hermitlike lifestyle and refusal to participate in the promotional hype surrounding the success of his books was a constant irritation to her.

"She thinks she's Serilda," he blurted. "This woman showed up in my house decked out in the same outfit as on the cover of *Warrior Woman: Serilda's Quest*."

Total silence.

"Hillary? Are you still there?"

"Y-yes."

He heard her choked laughter. "This isn't funny! The woman's got a mile-long sword that she keeps waving around. If something isn't done, someone's going to get hurt. Probably me."

"I-I'm sorry, Brandon. You just caught me off guard. So you've got an overly enthusiastic fan on your hands. What do you want me to do about it? I'm halfway across the country. Call the police."

It was his turn to be silent.

After a minute she said, "You don't want to do

that, do you? Something about this woman has you intrigued. Tell me."

"You're right. There's nothing you can do. I'll take care of it." Serilda's flashing green eyes and wild claims challenged him in an entirely new way, while her womanly curves steered his thoughts in a different direction—a direction that, after his disastrous marriage to Wanda the Man-Eater, he'd been slow to venture. Until this moment, the promised reward just never seemed worth the effort. Still, the thought of *taking care* of his intruder no longer felt like a chore.

"No, wait! Brandon, don't you hang up on—"

He hit the End button and put the phone down. Speaking to Hillary made him realize how isolated he'd become since he'd bought this house three years ago. Aside from the weekly delivery boy from the local market, he often didn't see another person for weeks on end. He rarely went into town, taking his daily runs along little-used back roads, and none of his neighbors came by to visit. If he disappeared or something happened to him, it would be days or even weeks before someone noticed.

The kitchen door creaked open. He looked up. The Serilda wannabe stood in the doorway. Late afternoon sunlight turned her hair to flame.

"To whom did you speak? Another wizard?" She eyed the phone with a mixture of dread and admiration, clearly believing it to be a magic device.

He ran a hand around the back of his neck. "For the last time, I'm not a wizard, witch, or sorcerer. I'm just a writer."

She looked doubtful. "In my world, people created on paper do not come to life. It takes a person of great power to conjure a being into physical existence. Though I am loath to admit it, the only explanation for my current state is that I am your creation and you have, though I know not for what reason, summoned me into your world. At first I thought I could force you to return me to my world, but I now realize the strength of my sword is no match for the force of your words." She dropped to one knee and bowed her head. "Please, send me back."

The set of her shoulders and flash in her green eyes before she lowered her lids warned Brandon that acting humble and submissive didn't come easy to her. The Serilda he'd created would never bow to another. Her stubbornness and arrogance were both her greatest strength and fatal flaw. In real life those traits would have gotten her killed a dozen times over. In fiction she had the greatest power in the universe guiding her and watching her back: the writer, namely himself. Of course, of late she hadn't been listening too well.

"Oh, for Pete's sake, get up." He took her arm and tugged her to her feet, but she didn't raise her face to his.

"As you wish, my lord. But who is this Pete? Your familiar? Another wizard?" She tilted her head and peered at him from beneath sooty lashes.

The phone rang, the sound harsh. Before he could react, the lunatic's sword flashed and split it in two. The phone gave a last gurgling ring, then fell silent.

Open-mouthed, he stared at the pieces of plastic and wires now littering the floor. "What the hell did you do that for?"

"I beg pardon for my error. The noise startled me. I didn't mean to destroy it."

She didn't sound contrite, however, and he didn't believe for a minute she'd been startled. Brandon doubted this woman ever did anything without forethought. In his books Serilda always had a reason for what she did. She'd damaged the phone beyond repair but hadn't left a scratch on the table, an indication of careful control. What was she up to now? For that matter, what was she up to period?

His books were a success, and he was making good money, but he was hardly worth the trouble of tracking down to kidnap—and if kidnapping was her goal, why such a bizarre method? He'd managed to keep a fairly low profile as an author. So far, his fans had been more interested in his books than in him. What was she after? And how could he catch her up in her little charade? What did he know about Serilda that no one else could possibly know? The answer came to him, and he chuckled. Now, to wait for the right moment to confront her.

She slid the sword back in its sheath. There was no denying the curiosity and growing confusion in her eyes as she looked around his neat, modern kitchen.

"Are you hungry?" His question surprised him. He should be hustling her out the door. Instead, he found himself offering her lunch.

"Yes, please."

"Good. You can wash up at the sink and sit down while I throw something together." He opened the refrigerator and pulled out some eggs, cheese, and ham. "How's an omelet sound?" With practiced ease, he whisked the eggs together and heated the skillet. In minutes the tantalizing smell of sizzling butter and cooking eggs filled the air.

When she didn't answer, he turned. She stared at him with wide-eyed awe.

"What's wrong?"

"With a flick of your wrist you command fire. You've trapped light and cold inside a box. I never imagined such power existed."

He threw back his head and laughed. Even if her actions were entirely an act, being called powerful for owning a fridge and an oven struck him as funny. He caught sight of the anger building on the woman's face. No one appreciated being the butt of someone else's joke. God knows he'd been on the receiving end enough times. A sickly childhood spent with an overprotective, controlling single mother had left him with more than his share of insecurities. Deciding he'd play along, he smothered his laughter. Eventually he'd figure out what she wanted.

"Relax. Sit down. These powers don't belong to me. They come from ComEd and Nicor. I merely pay for the use of them." He felt her eyes on him as he finished the omelets and served them.

Perched on the edge of the chair, I eyed the wizard warily and poked at the food he'd provided. It smelled delicious, but my appetite had fled. To keep him from summoning another wizard to his aid, I'd destroyed the object into which I'd overheard him speaking. I'd thought I could lull this wizard into believing I was cowed into submission, but his power was far beyond what I'd first judged. And he had accomplices: ComEd and Nicor. How could I fight three great wizards?

And what exactly did I fight for? To go back to

my world, fictional though it might be? Did I truly
want to return to the life I'd known there, a life of
constant warfare and danger, where children were
left orphans so men could fulfill greedy ambition?
A world of strife and vengeance?

Yet, what else was there? Would I be forced to
remain here? What did I know of this world? Was
it better than the one I came from or worse? Why
had this wizard summoned me? His surprise and
confusion about my appearance didn't bode well.

"Eat," he urged. "Things seem less difficult on a
full stomach, or so my grandmother always said.
I've found she was right. I can think better if my
stomach isn't growling."

I forced myself to take a bite. Wonderful tastes
exploded on my tongue and renewed my appetite.
Though my soldiers and I were supplied with ra-
tions adequate to support life, the meat was dry
and tough, the bread coarse and filled with chaff
and grit, fruits and vegetables were withered or rot-
ten, and dairy products were a rare treat. It had
been years since I'd eaten anything as delicious as
this simple meal. It took every ounce of self-control
drilled into me by the monks not to shovel the food
into my mouth all at once.

Despite my efforts to prolong the meal, I finished
in minutes. I sat back with a sigh of pleasure and
summoned a loud belch of appreciation.

Brandon's fork clattered on his plate. "Why did
you do that?"

"Do what?" I asked.

"Belch."

"To express my gratitude for the meal you prepared."

"How could you know? I never included that custom in my final drafts. Not even my agent knows. No one does."

"It is an old custom. One no one has used in years, but the monks insisted. If it offends you, I will not do so again."

He stood. "No, that's not it. It's just . . ." He stopped and stared at me.

His lengthy appraisal made me uncomfortable. Training and instinct told me I should be wary of this man; he held my existence in his hands. But long weeks of sleepless nights and waking nightmares along with battles gone badly had drained my energy. Now a stomach full of delectable food left me feeling sleepy. Besides, I still had yet to decide what action to take. Better to rest and study the situation before I did anything.

I watched through heavy eyelids as he paced the floor muttering, "It's not possible. I'm losing it. You can't be Serilda."

"It may not be possible, but here I am. Whether you wish it or not, I am Serilda—apparently your creation."

A yawn caught me off guard. I forced my eyes open. This man might not look or act the powerful wizard, but he'd brought me from my world into his. I'd do well to remain alert.

He stopped in front of me, leaned down, and placed his hands on the arms of the chair I sat in. His face hovered inches from mine, his breath warm against my cheeks and scented with citrus from the orange drink he'd poured for us. Instead of pulling away in anger, my usual reaction when anyone invaded my personal space, I found myself wanting to draw closer, to find comfort in his embrace. This longing for something I'd never had startled me.

His aqua-green eyes locked on me. Unable to hold his intense gaze, I studied his face.

On closer inspection, his resemblance to King Donoval the Golden faded. The color of the ocean, the wizard's eyes held depths Donoval's lacked. They changed color with his mood. Despite his greater masculine beauty, Donoval's face didn't fascinate me as the wizard's did. Though they were both handsome, this man's features revealed more character. The lines bracketing his mouth and fanning out from his eyes gave a physical record of his life's challenges.

I resisted the urge to raise my hand and smooth the frown from his brow. A faint stubble of beard covered his cheeks. Like Donoval's, the wizard's facial hair was a few shades darker than the golden blond hair on his head. I wondered what it would feel like against my skin. A sudden heat coursed through my veins.

"There's one way you can prove to me who you are." He leaned closer. "Tell me your enchanted name."

His whispered demand chilled my blood. "No." I shook my head. "I cannot. I will not." No one but me knew the name I'd chosen when I reached the age of awareness at seven. With knowledge of my enchanted name, even one with little magic in them could control my every action.

Members of the royal family had been blessed with great magic. Until their foul murders, they'd wielded that power to the benefit of all Barue. Roark used deceit to get close to the royal family and his small magic ability to kill them. Their deaths threw Barue into civil war, a war that yet raged. Since then, use of magic had fallen into disuse. Each year that passed, fewer people took enchanted names and even fewer continued to believe in magic. I now had proof it existed.

"You will tell me!"

The wizard's façade of patience crumbled. He grabbed my arms and yanked me to my feet. I didn't know this man. His gentle demeanor had blinded me to the strength and power contained in his body. Gone was the clumsy oaf who stumbled over his own feet to escape my attack. Gone was the charming host who fed and cosseted me. In their place stood a fierce warrior determined to claim what he believed was his by right.

"As my creator you already know my enchanted name, but unless I speak it aloud you cannot use it against me." Or could he? Did the rules of my world apply here?

"I have to know the truth." His grip gentled along with his tone. "Are you really my creation? Or are you just a figment of my imagination, a result of isolation and writer's block? I may be crazy, but I know I'm not delusional. Serilda's enchanted name exists nowhere but in my mind. I've never written it down or told anyone. If you know it . . ."

"No!" I twisted free of his hold. Arms wrapped around my middle, I backed away from him. "I'll not say it. Not even Roark's master torturer could make me speak it. Kill me. Write me out of existence if you will, but I'll be no man's slave."

At that moment, he looked more horrified than I

felt. He took a step back and held up a hand in a conciliatory gesture. "All right. Either you're mad or I am. You're either an Oscar-award winning actress or, God help me, you're Serilda. In my thirty-five years, I've inspired affection or aversion, respect or contempt, but never terror. I don't much care for the feeling. Relax, I'm not going to hurt you."

Shame at my fear made me lash out. "As if you could."

The guilt in his eyes faded, replaced by anger. "You forget, if you really are Serilda, I can make you grovel with a stroke of my pen."

I pulled my sword. "You'll have a hard time using a pen with no hands."

His bark of laughter caught me off guard. The man didn't have normal reactions!

"I guess we have a bit of a standoff. You can cut me down with your sword, or I can cut you down with my pen." He cocked his head. "You know, someone once said, 'The pen is mightier than the sword.'"

The sight of his crooked half smile drained my anger, and I snorted. "Perhaps if the sword is very short and the pen is very sharp." With a mere flick of my wrist I could sever the hand he stretched out to me. Instead, I sheathed my sword.

He laughed again and nodded to his hand. "Agreed. Shall we call a truce? I won't write anything to hurt you, and you won't do anything with that sword of yours to hurt me. Deal?"

"Truce." I clasped his hand in mine. Though the skin of his fingers and palms was smooth, his grip felt firm and sure. A strange tingle traveled up my arm. I snatched my hand back and rubbed it against my thigh. "What do we do now?"

He shrugged. "Without your enchanted name I really can't be one hundred percent sure you're a character out of my imagination."

I went stiff.

"Relax, I'm not going to insist you say it."

"Insist all you like, I will not," I growled.

"Okay, I got that. I'm just saying I still have my doubts about you being one of my fictional characters come to life. It's too farfetched even for this fiction writer. I suppose I'd rather think that you're the insane one, not me. But if you're crazy, what am I going to do with you? I don't guess that you'd like to take a trip into town to see the local head doctor or the chief of police?"

I shook my head. Despite his previous words, his tone screamed disbelief.

"Let's go into the other room and sit down. Maybe we can sort out this mess." He opened the door and motioned me through. The feel of his gaze on my back made my stomach lurch. We seated ourselves; he lounged on the overstuffed couch facing a large fireplace, while I perched on a chair.

For several minutes he sat and looked at me until I felt like I had when called to task by Brother Eldrin for some minor infraction of a monastery rule. Finally he asked, "What do *you* suggest we do next?"

I shrugged. "How should I know? You brought me here."

"I told you, I didn't."

"You are inept for a wizard. Do you always practice magic without regard for the consequences?"

"That's the point! I don't practice magic. I'm a writer. I write stories!"

"There is magic in words, of course, especially

when put to paper. Brother Eldrin and the other monks believed the power of the written word was without limit. But they never used it as you have. Nor"—a shadow of grief made me pause—"did it save them from Roark's sword."

He leaned forward. "How do you keep doing that?"

"Doing what?"

"Keep saying things about my books that I only had in my head, backstory that I never revealed. You must have studied them intensely to remember all the details and to glean the meaning behind the characters' actions. But the real question is why? What do you hope to get out of this little charade? I'm comfortable, but I don't have enough money to make whatever you're doing worth all this time and effort. And despite your bizarre entrance into my life, somehow you don't strike me as being a real nutcase. So what's the hook here? What do you want?"

He'd asked the one question for which I had no answer. *What did I want?*

*"Dreams are the wishes of our
subconscious minds. In them lie the answers to
tomorrow's questions."*
—Brother Eldrin, Order of the Light

Chapter Three

Brandon leaned his elbows on his knees and scrubbed his hands over his face. What to do? He knew he should call the authorities, but with what? Serilda—no, the *lunatic*—had destroyed his phone. He had to stop thinking of her as Serilda. That way led to madness.

Once again he remembered his grandmother, her tales of sorcerers who created worlds with the power of their minds. She'd meant them as warnings, but those fanciful stories had inspired him to write. But, he'd never *believed* them. Fictional characters just didn't come to life.

Yet he couldn't seem to dismiss her dire warnings about what happened to the sorcerers in her stories, either. When the worlds they created took on lives of their own, when they obtained a reality beyond the sorcerer's imagination, the sorcerers were destroyed. Like his father had been?

He shook his head. Nonsense! Utter nonsense! Real was real. Fiction was fiction. And this woman was as real and solid as a person could get. He just had to figure out what to do about her.

Because he couldn't get reception in his area, he'd never bothered to get a cell phone. Even his Internet connection was erratic at best. Still, once he decided what to do about her, he'd give that a try.

"Perhaps if you show me what you're writing about me and my world, we can figure a way for me to return there."

He looked at her. As crazy as it made him, he found himself wanting to buy into her delusion. Besides, he didn't think she'd be thrilled with the direction her story had taken. "That's part of the problem. I haven't been able to write. Ever since lightning struck the house and fried my monitor, I've been suffering from a major case of writer's block."

"Monitor?" Her brows pulled together in a puzzled frown.

"You really do have your act down pat. If I didn't think it would make me as nuts as you, I'd almost believe it."

"Nuts? What do nuts have to do with this? Believe what you like, but I speak the truth. I understand most of the words you say, but sometimes the meaning of your phrases is lost."

"Okay, for now I'll play along. What do you want to know?"

She looked thoughtful for a minute. "What is this 'writer's block'?"

Her question confused him. How could she not know what writer's block was? "It's an ailment that afflicts authors from time to time."

"Do you suffer from it often?"

Damn, if she didn't sound concerned, too! "Actually, writer's block has never been a problem before. I'm considered a fairly prolific writer. In the last ten years I've had ten books published, six of them Warrior Woman books. Usually my writing just flows. Until this latest book, I've never had any trouble. Writing's always been my way of coping. When the real world gets to be too much, I escape into a simpler world, a world I control with my keyboard and mouse."

It surprised him how easily he opened up to this woman. How much he revealed both to her and to himself, more than he had to Wanda in their two long years of marriage. Had his desire to change the direction of his writing and life given rise to the block? Almost as if the world and characters he created objected. He didn't know.

"You have a mouse as a familiar?"

He laughed at the shocked look on Serilda's face, then sobered. He really had to call her something else. He'd only go so far in humoring her. "Do you have a nickname? Something you like to be called other than Serilda?"

"Mauri sometimes calls me Seri."

Her eyes softened at the mention of the little slave girl. Brandon smiled. The eager but inept Mauri had been a delight to create.

He mentally shook himself, trying to remember that she wasn't what she claimed; she was just some wacko fan. But equal parts of relief and disappointment left him feeling dizzy. Why should he be disappointed? There was no way this woman was his creation. What would be the point? If he decided to create a woman for himself, she wouldn't be anything like this. She'd be . . . Well, he had no idea what she'd be like. Since Wanda left, women hadn't really been a factor.

"What will happen to Mauri, Jole, and the others in my world? Do they live, or will they cease to be?" Serilda asked.

Seri, he reminded himself. He had to make a distinction.

The look of longing in her eyes tugged at Brandon's heart. Whoever this woman really was, she was lost. Though he knew he should turn her over to the police, or at least take her to a doctor, he also knew he wouldn't. In a strange way, he felt responsible for her and didn't want the harsh world to beat her down. Her delusion sprang from his writing.

"I haven't planned out their entire lives, but I don't intend to kill them off." Disturbed by a pang of guilt, he glanced away from her, unwilling to reveal just who he *did* plan to have die.

Seri touched the back of his hand with her fingertips. Warmth shot up his arm and down to his groin. Surprised by his visceral reaction, he jerked his hand back. Suddenly three years of self-imposed celibacy felt like three centuries.

Since his break with Wanda, there hadn't been any other woman in his life. Even when they'd been together, he hadn't been all that interested. That was part of the reason they'd split: Wanda wanted more than he was willing to give. Brandon could understand why she'd hated and mocked his writing. She claimed—rightly so—that he saved his passion for it, that there was nothing left for her. Even if their reasons were different, in this he and Donoval were alike. They were both emotionally unavailable.

At an early age, his mother's histrionics had taught him to keep his emotions hidden. A hypochondriac whose husband died, leaving her alone to raise Brandon, she'd projected all her fears onto him. Alternately, she'd cosseted him and demanded he take care of her. When he was twelve, she'd accidentally overdosed on her numerous medications.

Too bad knowing the source of his neuroses didn't make them any easier to live with. He still felt the effects of her bizarre child-rearing techniques. He wondered how truly weird he'd have turned out if it hadn't been for the stable influence of his paternal grandmother, who'd taken him in and finished raising him.

"I beg pardon for my boldness. I know it is forbidden to touch a wizard." Seri pulled her hand back.

Missing her warmth, Brandon looked up. "For the last time, I'm not a wizard."

She tucked her hands between her knees and held his gaze. "Even if you don't send me back to my world, would you grant me one favor?"

He sighed. "What?"

"Let me know my friends' fates before I cease to exist."

The fear in her voice made him reach out and grasp her hands in his own. He ignored the jolt of heat. "You're not going to cease to exist. You're a real person. I can touch you." Wanting to comfort her, he rubbed his thumbs over the back of her hands. Though she was strong and unquestionably capable of wielding the sword she carried, her skin felt soft and smooth. "Believe me, fictional characters don't suddenly become flesh and bone."

He once again refused to consider the possibility his grandmother's tales might be true.

"If I'm not Serilda d'Lar of the kingdom of Barue, who am I?"

The despair in her voice and eyes strengthened Brandon's resolve to help her find a way out of her delusion. He squeezed her hands. "That's what we need to figure out."

The warmth of the sorcerer's hands made my heart race. I wanted to move closer, to curl against his chest, to feel his arms hold me tight. How many years had it been since I'd been able to let go, to allow someone else to shoulder my burdens?

Never.

For some reason, my mother and father, though not unkind, hadn't shown me the same warmth they gave my younger siblings. As the oldest child, I'd been in charge of my siblings' care until Roark claimed their lives. The monks had sheltered me, educated me, and given me distant affection, but in the end they too fell to Roark's evil; their books and learning provided little protection against Roark's sword. Though Donoval had been my lover and wanted me as his bondmate, his demanded cost— my independence—had been too high. Loving him had frayed my heart, because his heart and soul belonged to Shallon and its people. What he could give me would never be enough.

My longing to be first in someone's heart startled me. I had never thought of it in those terms before.

"Will you let me help you?" he asked.

The wizard's offer touched me, and for a moment his disbelief in who I was made me doubt myself.

Part of me wanted to cling to my identity, fictional though it might be; another part wanted to give it up, to become a real woman in this man's strange and alien world. But, no.

I shook my head. It was my bad luck to have been created by a powerful yet inept wizard. "I can't lie to myself. For you to help me—if that's what you intend—you have to believe."

Brandon rubbed the throbbing spot between his eyes and tried to force himself to sleep, but thoughts of the woman in the room down the hall kept him awake. Not knowing what else to do, he'd shown her to the spare bedroom and retreated to his own. Retreated? Hell, he'd run away.

He shut his eyes and prayed he'd wake up in the morning to discover this was nothing but a dream.

Nope. His eyes popped open. He didn't want Seri to be a dream. For the first time in years, maybe in his entire thirty-five years, he felt alive. Only when he lost himself in his writing did he feel anything close to this.

It figured that the first woman to attract him in years would be a nutcase who thought she was a fictional character. But damn it, she felt real! Her scent of leather and musk still filled his nostrils. Memory of the soft swell of her breasts over the skimpy leather bra she wore—embarrassingly, he'd really never realized how impractical the costume he'd given her was—made moisture pool in his mouth and his cock come to sudden attention.

He groaned. Since his unsuccessful attempt at a normal life with Wanda, he'd avoided real people. They were difficult, messy creatures that demanded time and attention, energy he could be spending on his writing. Fictional characters were easier. He directed them. They did what he wanted, how and when he wanted. It pained him to realize that he'd tried to get the same from Wanda, which was another reason she'd walked out. Guess the lessons of childhood were harder to dismiss than he thought.

Unable to sleep, he got up and plucked a random book off the bookshelf. When he recognized the title, he almost dropped it: *Warrior Woman: Serilda's Quest.* Book one. Instead, he went back to bed and started to read:

Standing in front of the burned-out shell of what used to be a monastery, at the tender age of ten and six, Serilda d'Lar of the kingdom of Barue revowed her vengeance against Andre Roark. With calm purpose and dry eyes, she found and buried the charred remains of the gentle monks who'd sheltered and raised her for the last six years. After that, she gathered what supplies she could find, turned, and never looked back.

Hours passed as Brandon lost himself in the story. Though he'd written the words, while writing, he'd often felt as if the story came from somewhere beyond. Again, an echo of his grandmother's warnings sent a shiver down his spine. He read on, amazed at how different the story felt from what he remembered.

Two-thirds of the way through the book, the love scene began. His grip tightened, and his heart began to pound.

Serilda knelt on the bed facing Donoval and let the fur slip through her fingers. His blue-green eyes darkened, and his fists clenched. Afraid she might change her mind, she couldn't bring herself to lower her gaze. He was an impressive specimen.

"Cover yourself," he said, but didn't look away from her breasts.

When he swallowed heavily, she let her lips curl into a satisfied smile. "Don't deny me this, Donoval. Tomorrow we go into battle. Let me have this memory."

"Tomorrow I go into battle." To emphasize his words, he stepped closer to the bed. His warm masculine scent teased her nostrils. "You will remain safely behind the lines."

"Mmmm," she responded. They'd had this fight already. Donoval believed he'd won, but Serilda refused to concede. "Then don't deny me this. I would know what it is to be a woman."

"This is not right. You're but a child!"

At times his sense of honor was downright inconvenient. She reached out and curled her arms around his broad shoulders. "I'm twenty and two, old enough to know my mind."

She pressed her aching breasts against his smooth, hard chest. Beneath his heated skin, she felt the rapid thud of his heart. As if to push her away, his hands settled on the swell of her hips. Instead, his fingers tightened and he pulled her closer.

"Be sure this is what you want. Once we

start, I'll not be able to stop." His warm breath brushed over her cheeks.

She looked up into his eyes. The raw passion there made her shiver in fear and anticipation. He wanted her.

Hard and large, his erection pressed against her belly, reminding her of what would come. It made her pause. Perhaps her first encounter shouldn't be so much of a man. Any of Donoval's soldiers would easily grant her a tumble, no strings attached. And she could control them.

No. Sex without caring was empty of meaning. Donoval was the only man she cared about, the only man she trusted; she would have him and no other. Despite his harsh manner and size, he'd never hurt her.

She twined her fingers in his shoulder-length hair and tugged his face closer. "Surrender, my love. This is a battle you cannot win."

"In this battle, there are no losers." And with a throaty growl, he took control and laid her back on the bed.

Warm and hard, his large body covered hers. His erection dug into her belly. Apprehensive of the initial pain of his possession, yet curious to continue the experience, she spread her thighs. He didn't plunge immediately into her, so she clasped his hips with her hands and urged him forward.

"Relax. There's no rush," he murmured against her cheek. He kissed her throat, then moved his lips down her chest. Her body arched upward as he suckled first one swollen nipple, then the other. Frissons of heat sizzled through her. Moisture gathered between her thighs. He continued his leisurely assault on her untried body, kissing, stroking, and sucking until she moaned in wanton need.

She gasped as his fingers combed through her nether curls and found her center. Sensation uncoiled inside her. Each caress promised something beyond her knowledge.

Deliberately he tormented her, bringing her to the edge of understanding, then slowing until she nearly cried in frustration. Her hips bucked wildly against his hand as she sought the mysterious goal he withheld. He slid a finger inside her. Her body clenched around it, and she caught her breath in anticipation, but before she could reach that final destination, he pulled his hand away.

So close to satisfaction, she whimpered in distress.

"Look at me."

At his command, she opened her eyes to meet his gaze. Tears spiked her lashes and blurred her vision. She trembled with unfulfilled passion.

He positioned himself between her thighs. Hot and hard, the blunt tip of him pressed into her. She clutched his shoulders as he plunged deep.

Unable to read more, Brandon slammed the book shut and tossed it aside. He turned off the light and flopped down on the bed. Damn it, he refused to be jealous of a fictional character. Donoval was as much a creation as Serilda!

Sleep was a long time in coming, but when it did, dreams of the woman in the other room left Brandon both weak with fulfillment and aching with frustration.

After I refused to deny who I am, the wizard fell silent and led me to a bedchamber. Fearful of pushing him farther, I too remained quiet. If he decided to write me out of existence now, I couldn't stop him. Perhaps I should have killed him when I had the chance. But if I did, what would happen to the people who lived in the world he'd created? What would happen to me?

By flicking a small toggle switch set in the wall, he lit the room with a yellowish glow from a bedside lamp. It was like magic, how this world created light with no fire. Again, the wizard seemed to think it was nothing.

He left, and I wandered around the comfortable room. A large bed dominated. A soft beige paint covered the smooth, straight walls, and a shaggy brown rug hid parts of the polished wood floor. The lamp sat on a table next to the bed, along with a square box made of a shiny material decorated with odd glowing lights and strange buttons. I touched one and jumped as a voice emanated forth. Before I could make out the meaning of the words, I hastened to punch the button again, and the noise stopped.

Had my wizard created this contraption? And what creature had angered him enough that he'd imprisoned it inside this box? Also, if capable of

such magic, why did he grant me such leeway? I
shuddered and looked away.

A shelf full of books caught my attention, though
they were of a different construction than I remembered. I hadn't seen a book since Roark burned the
library at the monastery. Reading was a pleasure I'd
long missed.

As I started to reach for one, I noticed some of
the titles: *The Barbarian King: Donoval's Revenge*
and *Warrior Woman: Serilda's Quest*. I snatched
back my hand. Part of me wanted to read what was
written in those tomes, another part sensed something terrible would happen if I did.

Prudence ofttimes serves better than boldness,
Brother Eldrin's voice echoed in my memory.

Clutching my trembling hands together, I sat on
the edge of the bed and eyed the lamp again warily.
Was one of those beings my wizard had spoken of,
ComEd or Nicor, responsible for its glow? How
much control did he hold over those creatures? If I
sought to extinguish the light, would they object?
Questions without answers made my head ache.

Weary to my core, I lay down. Much in this world
was beyond my comprehension, but the mattress
brought bliss as it cradled my body. I ran my palms
over the silky throw covering the bed. Whatever
else this wizard might be, he was wealthy and
powerful—if inept, I reminded myself. And my fate
now rested in his hands.

Long ago, I'd learned to fight the battles I knew I
could win, retreat from those I could not, and recognize the difference between them. This battle fell
into neither category.

What cannot be solved must be endured. In sleep

you release your burdens to the universe. As always, Brother Eldrin's wise words showed me the path; I closed my eyes, cleared my mind, and let sleep claim me.

Warm lips trailed down my throat. Passion welled up inside me as those lips moved lower and closed over the hardened tip of one breast. A surge of heat shot to my groin. I opened my eyes and looked at the top of a golden head. Donoval?

No, this man's hair was short, and the strong hands that stroked my belly felt softer than Donnie's.

The wizard?

I put my hands on the man's head to lift it, then froze in anticipation as he moved his hand lower. His fingers slid through the damp curls between my thighs and stroked the sensitive nub there. Rational thought splintered. My eyelids fell shut.

From that small point of contact, heat radiated through my body. Years had passed since I last lay with Donnie, long, lonely, frustrating years without intimate physical contact with another human being.

Good sense demanded I catch my breath, regain my equilibrium, and discover who invaded my bed. Instead, as he used his hands and mouth to drag me deeper into a sexual haze, I surrendered without protest. Like a person dying of thirst, I drank in the sweet, warm flood of sensations his touch engendered. Questions faded from my consciousness as he wrung gasps of pleasure from my lips. Hungry for the satisfaction he promised, I didn't care who he was.

With little warning, my release came, sudden and explosive. It wasn't enough. I wanted more. I needed him to fill the emptiness inside me. I reached out and found empty air. I opened my eyes to . . . find myself alone. Cool air blew across my sweat-slicked body, but it was disappointment that made me shiver.

Tugging the bedcovers around me, I curled into a ball and cried for all that I'd lost and all that I'd never have.

The sun's warmth touched my face. Memory of my dream left me feeling both sated and frustrated. I stretched, and my muscles groaned in protest, but the ache was a sweet one that I remembered fondly. After Donnie, I hadn't had the time or the inclination to bother with another man. If he couldn't accept me as I was, a warrior, I doubted any man would.

I opened my eyes and blinked at the glare coming in through the window. A large expanse of clear glass covered the opening. Through the window I could see down over a small rise to a river. Sunlight glistened on the water's surface. Waterfowl drifted in the current. Trees lined the bank, their branches dipping gracefully downward. The peaceful, summery scene reminded me once more that I was no longer in my world. Last night the window had been covered by cloth.

Alarmed, I bolted from the bed. How could I have slept so soundly that I hadn't heard the wizard come into the room? Had he stood and watched me sleep? Had he entered my dream? The thought gave me a strange chill, not unpleasant but disconcerting.

As within the acorn sleeps the mighty oak, the

future lies within the dream. Brother Eldrin's remembered wisdom added to my unease.

A sharp tap at the door made me jump. I grabbed my sword and drew it from its sheath as the door opened and the wizard stepped in carrying a tray. At the sight of my blade, he stopped.

"I thought we'd passed that stage."

"What?"

He shot a pointed glance at my weapon, though he didn't appear frightened.

"It's not wise to startle me, wizard." I sheathed the sword with a less than graceful motion. Being caught off guard got a person killed.

He placed the tray on a chest of drawers and turned toward me. "My name is Brandon, not wizard. Think you can remember that?"

I nodded but didn't agree to call him anything else.

"I made you some breakfast."

My mouth watered at the sight and smell of the food: two perfectly cooked eggs, some thin, crisp strips of meat, a slice of toasted bread slathered with a shiny purple paste, and a glass of citrus drink.

"Men in my world don't cook, except maybe to roast a chunk of meat over an open campfire, and then they usually char it on the outside while inside it remains bloody." I sat on the edge of the bed nearest the chest and reached for the food. I didn't mention that my own skill with food preparation was more masculine than feminine. "The monks didn't consider food a priority. They fed the soul first and gave the body just enough nourishment to maintain life. Food was a necessity, not a pleasure.

And though Mauri's cooking might be bad, it's edible and keeps us from starving."

"Yes, I know. I'm afraid that bit of writing resulted from my rebellion against the fact that my wife refused to cook."

My hand froze on the way to my mouth. Egg yolk dripped onto my thigh as I stared at him. "You're married?" Why the thought bothered me I wasn't sure.

"*Was* married. Past tense."

I put down the eating utensil. "She died?"

"Hell, no. We're divorced."

"Divorced? What is this?"

"That's right, in Barue there is no such thing." His raised eyebrow and mocking tone told me he still didn't believe I was Serilda. "Marriages are for life. Only death ends one. Here, divorce is a legal means of ending a marriage."

"It strikes me odd that you could forget such a thing about a world you created. Having my fate tied to some man's forever is the main reason I refuse to marry."

He shrugged. "Since few if any of my characters ever marry, it hasn't been a problem. Marriage implies a happily-ever-after ending, and I don't write romance, I write sword-and-sorcery adventure stories. Eat before the food gets cold."

Hunger won out over bemusement. I wolfed down the food but no longer took any pleasure in its taste. When I finished, I found him watching me. "Now what?"

My skin heated as his gaze moved from my head down to my toes, then back again to rest for a moment on my breasts. I fought the urge to cover the exposed flesh. I'd never felt uncomfortable about my body before; leading men into battle left little opportunity or time for modesty.

"I think we need to get you some more appropriate clothing."

"What's wrong with what I'm wearing? You fashioned it for me."

His cheeks reddened. "Yeah, well, it seemed like a good idea at the time."

I'd never seen a man blush. The sight eased my growing annoyance. Though he'd apparently created me with his magic, I sensed his intentions weren't evil. He seemed as confused by my emergence in his world as I.

I stood. "A change of attire is fine. To speak the truth, I've never cared for wearing leather, and this outfit leaves far too much skin exposed to be comfortable or practical in battle or anywhere else." So, why hadn't I changed? Just one more indication of the power this man had wielded over me until I gained awareness. I'd no longer allow him to dictate my life or my choices.

*"Wisdom decrees, when in a foreign place
it is healthy to follow local customs."*
—Brother Eldrin, Order of Light

Chapter Four

"Wait here a minute. I'll get you something to wear until we get to the store." Brandon grabbed the tray and hurried out of the room. The sight of Serilda in her skimpy leather bra and skirt that exposed far too much of her smooth golden skin affected him more than he wanted to admit. The sooner he got her into something less revealing, the happier he'd be.

Who was he kidding? He liked her meager outfit. The only outfit he'd like her in more would involve even less. An image of her stretched out naked on the bed's satiny comforter flashed in his mind. He shifted in discomfort as his body responded inside his tight jeans.

Irritated with the direction of his thoughts and determined to keep his relationship with Seri simple, he dumped the tray in the kitchen and stomped back up to his bedroom. Cursing himself and his suddenly overactive libido under his breath, he rummaged in the back of his closet and found a pair of bike shorts, a T-shirt, and a pair of sandals that were too small for him but might fit her.

When he returned to her room, she was gone. He clutched the clothing in his hand and searched. No evidence remained. The once-rumpled comforter was smooth. There was no clue as to her whereabouts.

Had he dreamt the whole encounter? If so, he should feel relieved. Instead, disappointment washed over him. He sank down on the bed and examined his feelings. Though he couldn't quite believe the woman was Serilda, he found he didn't want her to disappear. Bizarre or not, something about her had been intensely appealing.

The sound of water running caught his attention. He heard a splash, then a female sigh. He smiled as understanding dawned: Though primitive in many ways, the people in Serilda's world favored bathing, and Brandon had provided them with the luxury of simple plumbing. She'd discovered his bathroom and the joys of more modern design.

He smacked his forehead. What was he thinking? Of course she'd found the bathroom. She wasn't Serilda, and she would have no real reason to be surprised by contemporary lavatories. Heaven help him, he was being sucked into her delusion. He did a mental about-face. She had to go. *Now.*

Without stopping to consider his actions, he stomped down the hall and through the door to the bathroom. A cloud of steam billowed over him.

Aside from its scenic, isolated location, one of the selling points of this house had been the large, luxurious bathroom. The previous owner had spared no expense. It had an oversized heated whirlpool tub and a 10' by 10' marble-lined walk-in shower, as well as two sinks and radiant heat in the marble floor. Brandon's gaze traveled from the two scraps of leather, the pair of boots discarded on the tile floor, and the sheathed sword placed within careful reach of the tub to the naked woman about to step into the water. Heat rushed to his groin. Then the thin tracing of white scars marring the otherwise smooth skin of the woman's back sent a sudden chill through him.

In book two, *Serilda's Revenge*, Roark, determined to learn Serilda's enchanted name and gain control over her, had ordered his master torturer to apply bloodworms to her back. In the process of feeding, bloodworms excreted a toxin that burned the skin and ran through the victim's nervous system like liquid fire. The pain they caused was excruciating and unremitting. Brandon remembered his sense of horror and pity as he'd written the scene. Though halfway through he'd wanted to eliminate it, the episode had been too important to Serilda's character development, her motivation, and the plotline, so he'd gritted his teeth and finished. Afterward, critics had raved about the realistic feel of the scene, but he'd never reread it, nor had he allowed Serilda to think about that time again. He'd had her bury it deep inside—though the scars, mental as well as physical, remained with his guilt.

Apprehension slid down his spine. If this woman was crazy enough to re-create scars on her back in her attempt to become Serilda, what else might she be capable of? Then another even more frightening thought occurred. What if she was telling the truth? What if she really was Serilda? He shook the idea away, as he had before. He couldn't let himself be convinced of the impossible by these tricky details.

And he'd rather be dealing with a wacko fan than consider the state of his own sanity.

She didn't blush or try to cover herself as she turned her face to him. She simply said, "I prefer to bathe alone."

Without waiting for his response, she stepped into the tub and sank down in the water. The sight of her full breasts with their dusky pink nipples just breaking the surface made his mouth go dry. Fear evaporated, along with coherent thinking. He stood frozen as his gaze moved down over her belly to the tangle of reddish brown curls at the juncture of her thighs. Memories of Serilda's intimate encounters with Donoval raced through his mind.

Serilda was aggressive and passionate in her love-making, as she was in all other aspects of her life. Readers wrote often to tell him how much they enjoyed her love scenes with Donoval. Before a battle in book one, she and Donoval had come together in a blaze of adrenaline-fueled heat . . . that burned the relationship out by the end of book two. Though affection and friendship remained between them, Serilda had put an end to the love affair. She'd refused—or rather, he reminded himself, he'd chosen to have her refuse—to give up her crusade against Roark for a life of peace as Donoval's bondmate and queen.

Memories of the scenes he'd written, mental images of her skin glowing in candlelight, her lips moist and full as they traveled over Donoval's muscular body, made him shudder with desire. Though he'd told himself he'd chosen to end the characters' sexual relationship because of the needs of the series, honesty forced him to admit he'd done so in self-defense. Serilda's sexual relationship with Donoval stopped the same time as his marriage and his sex life came to an end. The only time in the last three years that he'd regretted his celibacy was while reading that scene.

"I assure you I haven't changed since you wrote me into existence," she said. Her sarcastic drawl broke through his trance.

He blinked and averted his gaze. "I-I'm sorry. If you twist that dial on your right the water will bubble. The sensation is pleasant and relaxing," he found himself babbling. "When you're done, here are some clothes." He placed them on the counter and backed out of the room.

As he closed the door, he banged his forehead against it. He headed away, but the sound of her laughter followed him down the hall.

Instead of my leather bra, this soft fabric felt lovely against my skin and teased my nipples to points. I gratefully donned the short, stretchy trousers the wizard provided and left my leather skirt lying on the floor. The sandals were a bit large but more comfortable than my tight boots.

Why had the wizard brought me these odd garments rather than conjuring something more appropriate? Of course, how could I know what was appropriate in his world? Reluctantly I turned and surveyed the stranger in the mirror on the back of the bathing room door.

I tried to puzzle out the meaning of the words inscribed in bright blue on the yellow shirt that reached halfway down my thighs to cover most of my short trousers: *Been there, done that, bought the T-shirt.* No matter how I tried, the phrase made little sense. Was a T some form of magic attached to the shirt? Perhaps it was a wizardly incantation. I could only hope that whatever it meant would prove harmless.

Unable to change anything, I dismissed it from my mind. Since arriving in the wizard's world, I recognized most of my life was out of my control.

The short trousers had no belt or loops to hold my sword, so I gathered the shirt on one side, tied it in a knot and stuck the sword through. Though not a great solution, it worked. I looked and felt strange, however.

Taking a deep breath to settle my jangling nerves, I headed out to find the wizard. He'd said something about shopping for more appropriate attire. Memories made me smile. Mauri loved to shop; I did not. Whenever possible, she tricked me into taking her to the local market. There she spent hours oohing and ahhing over clothing and trinkets until I bought them just to get her to leave.

The thought of Mauri left alone, without me to look after her, made my heart ache. I'd promised her my protection: though invariably cheerful, she'd already suffered too much in her young life. Sudden anger made me pause on the stairs. All of Mauri's pain, Jole's distress, my people's suffering, and my torment stemmed from one person. That person wasn't the one I'd blamed since I was ten years old: Andre Roark. No, the guilt lay at this wizard's feet. The fact that he believed his creations to be without true feeling didn't excuse him. Those with power, even those who were inept with it, had to be held accountable.

But how to fix this? My shoulders sagged.

When I'd first realized what I was, I'd thought I could force the wizard to right the wrong he'd committed and return me to my world, but I hadn't worked out how he might do so. Once I met him, I found him both more and less than what I'd expected. Now I wondered if there was any hope that he knew how to set things right. Or even what right might be.

I also realized that in order for me to return and live again in my world I'd have to forget what I now knew about myself. In doing that, I'd likely lose my free will. I'd become a puppet once more.

As always, the burden of solving the problem fell on my shoulders. And until I figured out how to do so, I had to rein in my anger—and the unwanted physical attraction that had begun to grow inside me—for the wizard.

He was at the bottom of the stairs. As he caught sight of me, he smiled, and despite my resolve, my anger evaporated. I found it hard to hold on to my justified rage when looking at a man dressed in a blue, short-sleeved shirt with a picture of a strange grinning orange cat on its front and a pair of faded blue half-trousers with ragged edges. They hugged muscular legs. He looked sweet, sexy, harmless, and as bizarre as I did. Against my will, I smiled back.

"Are you ready to go . . . ?" He started to speak, then caught sight of my sword. "You'll have to leave that here."

I shook my head. "I go nowhere unarmed."

He closed his eyes and pinched the bridge of his

nose between his thumb and forefinger. "People in this world do not go around carrying weapons."

I gripped the hilt of my sword. "Then they are fools."

He considered for a moment, then gave a resigned sigh. "I'm the fool. All right, bring the sword, but you'll have to leave it in the car when we get to the mall. Come on, let's go shopping."

I grunted but didn't quite agree.

"Not fond of shopping?" he asked as I followed him out of the house.

"It's a necessary evil."

He laughed and led me to another building on the side of his dwelling. "Then you're an unusual woman in more ways than one. I don't care much for shopping, either, but I do think you need something to wear. Of course, if you'd rather not shop we can always take a run over to your place and pick up some things." He shot me a sly look.

"Or you could conjure clothing for me," I suggested.

"One thing I'll say for you, you stay in character." He shook his head, then turned his attention to a small pad of numbered keys set on the wall next to a large door.

With an angry growl, the door started to rise. The noise startled me. I jumped back and tried to yank my sword free, but it tangled in its makeshift fabric knot.

"Easy there!" The wizard clamped his hand over mine. "It's just a garage door opener, not a beast to slay!"

His words made little sense, but his amusement

reassured me there was no danger, even if it was at my expense. I went still.

The growl ended as the door stopped moving and rested overhead against the building's inner roof. I calmed my pounding heart and peered cautiously inside. As my eyes adjusted to the dark, I took a step back.

The wizard turned to look at me. "What now?"

"What is that?" I pointed to a shiny black hulk that dominated the shadows of the cavern beyond.

"What? You mean my SUV? It's a vehicle. A . . . carriage."

I edged closer behind him. It looked like no carriage I'd ever seen. Its massive, boxy frame looked too heavy to be pulled by any horse. I sniffed the air. It smelled not of straw and manure but of metal and some pungent odor I didn't recognize. "Where are the horses?"

He patted the front portion, just below another expanse of glass. "Three hundred horses under the hood of this baby."

For a moment I forgot he was a wizard. "How did you squeeze three hundred horses in there?!"

His laughter rasped across my already raw nerves. "Well, if nothing else you're good for a laugh. It doesn't really have horses under its hood. It's a machine. It has an engine. We measure the power of the engine—what propels it—by horsepower." He reached out and opened a panel on the SUV's side. "Come on and get in."

Since he went around the other side of the SUV and climbed inside, I trusted it was safe. The interior was more luxurious than any carriage I'd ever seen.

Butter-soft gray leather covered the comfortable seats and inside walls. The not unpleasant, tangy scent of metal and dyed leather teased my nose. A nappy gray rug softened the floor. In front of me under a large expanse of perfectly smooth glass was a strange array of buttons and dials.

"Close your door and put on your seat belt," he said.

Not sure I was being wise, I pulled the heavy door shut, then looked at him in confusion as I struggled to accept the existence of a machine that ran on the power of horses shrunk down and hidden in its front. "Seat belt?"

"Oh, for Pete's sake. Enough is enough." He reached across me and dragged a wide belt over my chest. The feel of his arm brushing against my unbound breasts sent a tingle of awareness through me. The memory of my dream heated my blood and made me forget my fear.

The metal end he held clicked into a receptacle anchored to the side of the seat, and I felt trapped by the band that now traversed my chest from right to left and the other across my hips. For what reason did we need to be strapped inside this vehicle? But no sooner had I quelled my urge to panic, than the machine came to life.

It gave a muffled roar and a rumble, and I jumped and tried to clutch the hilt of my sword—but it was caught beneath one of the bands around me. I let out a furious squeak, but the wizard touched my knee.

"Relax! You're safe. I promise."

The warmth of his hand and the soothing tone of his voice eased my trepidation. I let myself relax.

Whatever else he might have done, my wizard hadn't yet lied to me. Until he did, I'd give him my trust—at least in this.

The SUV had a great suspension; it flew smoothly over and down the bumpy gravel drive. Remembering Seri's response to the garage door opening and her first sight of the SUV made Brandon smile. It probably wasn't kind of him to enjoy her discomfort, but damn, he'd had his own share of surprises these last twenty-four hours. It felt good to turn the tables.

Her fictional world had only the simplest machines. Nothing powered by gas or electricity. She seemed to act in accordance with this. Either she was a great actress or completely cuckoo. He supposed that changed none of his previous conclusions.

Once on the main road, he pressed down on the accelerator. The SUV responded with a gratifying burst of speed.

As he drove, he worried. He'd decided to take her to the new shopping mall that had opened about an hour's drive away. Though he didn't spend a lot of time in town, he knew the people of Council Falls were curious about him. Bringing Seri into town would only stir their interest.

Out of the corner of his eye, he watched her reaction to riding in a car. At first Seri sat frozen, her hands clutching the armrests. After a few miles, he could see her start to calm down and enjoy the journey. When he opened the sunroof, she raised her face and let out a small gasp of amazement.

"Relax," he told her. "It'll take us about an hour to get there."

"Where are we going?"

"To a mall."

"What is this . . . mall?"

"A place to shop—a marketplace."

She let out a small groan and turned her attention to the passing countryside.

He'd always reveled in the sense of power driving this oversized SUV gave him, though he was also a bit embarrassed by that. To the side of his vision he watched myriad expressions flash across Seri's face: fear, excitement, acceptance, amusement, incredulity. Usually with people he felt the need to talk, to fill the void, but with Seri the silence in the car was comfortable. He allowed himself to quietly enjoy it. Few other cars shared the two-lane country highway stretched out ahead and behind them. Seri studied each as it passed by.

After a while, she turned to look at him. "This carriage appears much larger and more powerful than the others."

Just then, an eighteen-wheeler came roaring around a bend and toward them. Seri's eyes widened, and she grabbed an armrest. Despite Brandon's SUV's size, it rocked as the semi whooshed by.

He tried to hide his grin. "There are bigger things on the road."

She released her grip on the armrest and twisted toward him. "You find my rational alarm amusing, wizard?"

"You've got to admit, this whole situation has its funny side."

"I admit nothing," she said, but he could hear laughter lurking in her husky voice.

He couldn't stop giving a chuckle. When she

herself let out a laugh, the tension he'd been holding inside since her appearance eased out of him. His sense of the absurd had been one of Wanda's major complaints: she hadn't understood his need to see the funny side of the world and himself. But without humor, he couldn't cope. Laughing kept everything manageable.

He wondered why humor had rarely found its way into his writing. Perhaps because Serilda's world was grim and dark, a place where emotions were a luxury. Was this a reflection of his own barren inner life? Had it been a place to release and slay his mental demons?

He'd always loved the world and the characters he'd created, but lately he'd found himself wanting and needing more, in both his writing and in his life. At times his fictional world seemed so real he feared he'd end up like his mother, totally neurotic, or like his grandmother, disconnected from reality. Or maybe, like his father, he'd just disappear. He wondered if the conflict between what he loved and what he had yet to obtain might account for his writer's block.

"Is this carriage difficult to drive?" Seri asked. "Could I do so?"

Her question distracted him from his musings and brought him back to reality. "Not too difficult, but you need a license. I don't suppose you happen to have one on you?"

She ignored his challenge. "Tell me about your world. It's so different from mine. This carriage, the way you command light, heat, and cold are marvels. Why didn't you include them in the world you created for my people and me? Why force us to use four-legged beasts to travel? To heat and light our homes with wood and smelly oils? What other things that would ease our lives have you denied us?" Her antagonistic questions shattered the companionable atmosphere that had begun to grow between them.

"Since I don't believe you're truly my fictional character Serilda come to life, your questions are meaningless. Serilda, her people, and her world are nothing but figments of my imagination. They aren't real. You are."

The fight seemed to drain out of her as she sagged back in her seat. The defeated look on her face made him feel like a bully. Deluded she might be, but that didn't give him leave to verbally beat up on her.

They spent the rest of the trip in silence. As they approached a more populated area, she sat forward and stared intently out the window. Her eyes widened as she caught her first glimpse of the mall.

"This building is larger than the entire city of Marisol!" She spoke of Barue's capital city as she watched the people going in and out of the structure's large glass entrance. "Where are the guards?"

If he weren't positive she couldn't possibly be Serilda, he would have sworn she was seeing everything for the very first time. "There aren't any guards. The mall is open to anyone." He felt silly explaining the world, but he couldn't just ignore her pretense of awestruck curiosity.

He turned into the parking lot of the mall and found a spot in the crowded lot. With a groan he realized it was Saturday. Living alone and working from home, it was easy to lose track of the day.

"You'll have to leave your sword in the car," he

said. When she hesitated, he swore, "There's no need for it here. I promise."

He couldn't control his sense of satisfaction when, albeit with evident reluctance, she placed the sheathed sword on the SUV's seat: she trusted him!

Inside the mall, he groaned again. Different booths than usual filled the large walkways, and people milled everywhere.

"Are these the merchants?" Seri approached a booth filled with crystals, diaphanous garments, and other New Age items.

"Sort of," he said. "The mall is hosting a science fiction/fantasy fair this weekend." At least he kept a low profile with the public, so he didn't think he'd be recognized.

She gave him a puzzled look but didn't ask for further explanation.

With everything that had happened, not even with Hillary's reminder had it registered that this was the weekend of Sci-con. Several months ago he'd been asked to participate in the book-signing portion of the fair, but as usual he'd declined. Over the years, he'd worked hard to overcome his irrational fear of crowds, but he knew better than to push his luck. Shopping was doable, but sitting at a table with a horde of fans pressing around him would strain his limits.

Judging the look-alike contest had never been an option. The idea of looking at other people's interpretation of Serilda made him queasier than actually interacting with them. He'd created her for himself. Oddly, Seri's resemblance to Serilda didn't bother him. She had a depth he knew his character lacked.

Because she's a real person, not some character out of a book, he reminded himself.

Keeping Seri close to his side, he made his way deeper into the mall. Sounds and smells swirled around him. New-age music and the chatter of a hundred voices all talking at once blurred together. Cinnamon from the Cinnabon store mingled with the aroma of baking pretzels. His muscles twitched, and his heart rate sped up. He knew he should grab Seri's arm and hustle her out, but whether for her sake or his he wasn't sure. Instead he took a deep, calming breath.

"Let's get this over with."

I twisted my head to and fro, trying to see everything at once as the wizard pulled me along at a rapid pace. Sounds, colors, smells, and motion rose up from everywhere. High above, glass panes in the ceiling gave a view of blue sky. Along both sides of the wide corridor filled with colorful booths, large windows displayed innumerable items, from clothing to housewares to things for which I had no name. My head swam at the quantity of items and the variety of choices available in this world.

No one guarded the treasures so casually on view, either. People moved freely among the booths and in and out of the shops. Their voices and the laughter of the children skipping alongside nearly drowned out the sound of music playing. How different this marketplace was from those at home. Merchants there guarded their scant precious wares diligently against the beggars and thieves that abounded because of Roark's lackluster system of justice in the areas he controlled.

I wanted to stop and absorb everything, but the wizard hurried me into what appeared to be a clothing shop. Once inside, the level of commotion decreased. Different music played here, a soft, soothing tune. Though bright enough to reveal rack after rack of beautiful clothing, the lighting was muted and easier on my aching eyes.

"May I help you?" an elegant if strangely clad woman asked. Though how could I tell? Everyone I'd seen so far was dressed oddly. She gazed at the wizard with feminine interest.

"Yes, my friend needs some clothing," the wizard answered. He seemed unaware of her perusal, unaware of his masculine appeal. How unlike Donnie, who, though he'd never acted upon it during our time together, was well aware of his effect on women.

"Of course." The woman nodded and turned her gaze from the wizard to me with obvious reluctance.

I didn't understand the surge of possessiveness that made me lean in toward him. With a disappointed sigh, the woman said, "What type of attire is your friend interested in?"

Since she addressed the question to the wizard rather than me, and unsure of how to answer anyway, I shrugged.

"Casual stuff," the wizard answered. "Slacks, shorts, shirts, and shoes. Also, she'll need . . . underwear."

I grinned, recognizing his discomfiture.

"Almost a complete wardrobe," he continued. "Airlines lost her luggage."

"Airlines?" I asked, then grunted as he poked me in the ribs with his elbow.

The woman raised an eyebrow and asked me, "What size do you wear?"

"My friend doesn't speak much English," the wizard interrupted. "I don't think she knows her American size. She's been out of touch for a long time, so she's not up to date with styles and such, either. Maybe you can help her pick out something flattering."

He smiled at her, and the way the woman fell all over herself to help him made my gut churn. "I'll just wait here while you ladies shop." He plopped himself down on a chair in an open area of the large store.

The woman quickly turned professional. She stuffed me into a small stall lined with mirrors and handed me item after item of clothing to try on. Usually clothes held little interest for me; they were merely something to cover and protect me from the elements—and looking back, the ones I'd worn had done exceedingly well considering their design. But these articles of clothing were different. Made of soft, colorful cloth, they felt good against my skin. When I looked in the mirror, I barely recognized the tall, shapely woman looking back at me. I was like a courtier!

I studied several small tags attached to the clothing. Some of the words about the care of the fabric I could read, but being unfamiliar with this world's monetary system, I couldn't decipher the costs. How much was $100 in gold or silver coin?

Again I wondered why the wizard hadn't conjured me some clothing instead of bringing me to this amazing bazaar and spending his coin. Did he mean to intimidate me with its size and splendor, cow me into acquiescence with this show of wealth, if indeed that was what this was? I had to assume it was, what with all the glass walls and sumptuous fabrics. But why do this when he had merely to speak a spell to put me back under his control?

None of the solutions I considered fit the man I was coming to know. The wizard was kind and considerate. Funny and intense. Stubborn and frustrating. With him, I felt like more than a simple commander of troops, more than Barue's last and best hope to defeat Roark. More than his creation. He made me feel like my life, my wants, my needs mattered. He fed and clothed me. He spoke of me and to me as a real person.

Another more disturbing idea occurred to me. Perhaps he wasn't the powerful but inept wizard I believed him to be. If he was indeed only what he claimed—a scribe or troubadour—how and why had I come to be here? What power had summoned or created me?

And . . . what chance did I have of ever returning to my home?

*"With age a leopard's spots may fade,
but do not forget he remains a leopard."*
—Brother Eldrin, Order of Light

Chapter Five

Brandon watched as Seri tried on outfit after outfit, shorts, slacks, skirts, blouses, and shoes in a dozen different combinations, each more attractive than the last. Considering how much he'd hated shopping with Wanda, he was surprised to find himself enjoying the impromptu fashion show. And maybe it was because of Seri's reluctance to accept more than the bare minimum from him, but he insisted on buying almost everything she tried on. Her restrained pleasure and excitement was infectious.

She came out of the dressing room in an ankle-length wispy dress that molded to her upper body like a second skin and floated around her hips and legs like a cloud, and his heart rate accelerated. The soft cream color with its pale rose pattern turned her complexion a honey gold and her hair to bronze. Thin straps left her shoulders and arms bare, while its scooped neckline emphasized her breasts. Though this dress covered more of her body than the skimpy outfit of earlier, it stirred his imagination and libido to new heights.

A touch of insecurity entered her eyes as he stared.

"We'll take it," he said, and handed the saleswoman his credit card. "Wrap up the rest. She'll wear this home."

Smiling, the saleswoman gathered up the clothing and hurried off to ring up the sale before he changed his mind. Brandon could almost see her mentally calculating her commission, and he was glad he'd made both women happy.

"It's not practical!" Seri stroked the material covering her hip with a loving hand. "You've already purchased far more than I need."

Whatever this woman was after, he didn't think it had anything to do with money. He shrugged. "Consider it payment."

"Payment for what?" Her gaze was wary.

"I don't know. For helping me overcome writer's block?"

"And how do I perform this task?"

He ran his hand over the base of his neck. "I'm not sure, but we'll work something out. For now, just enjoy the clothing."

"I—" She started to speak but was interrupted by the saleswoman's return.

Brandon signed the credit card receipt, made arrangements to have the clothing delivered (he didn't care to have to cart the numerous bags and boxes), and then turned to Seri. "Come on, let's get out of here." He glanced at his watch. "It's nearly one. Are you hungry?"

She grinned. "Starving."

Back out in the mall, the reality of the sci-fi/fantasy fair hit him. The noise and the people swarming everywhere made him feel claustrophobic. His heart started to pound, and his palms grew damp.

Seri, on the other hand, seemed to revel in the excitement. Her hunger apparently forgotten, she dragged him along as she moved from booth to booth to see the fair merchandise. A booth selling swords and knives caught her attention. To keep pace with her, Brandon pushed away his impending panic.

Before he could stop her, she picked up a sword. Without putting any of the people around her at risk, she tested its weight and balance with a series of balletic movements. Her dress swirled around her legs as she moved. Several people applauded.

"Wow!" the young man in the booth said. "You're good. A complete natural with that. Are you interested in buying it?"

"Thank you, but no. The balance on this sword is off." She carefully replaced the weapon. "In battle that could mean the difference between life and death."

The young man's smile wavered. "Yeah, well, most people just hang them on their walls." He stared at her for a moment. "You look familiar. I . . . I know!" He grabbed a well-read paperback from behind the counter.

Brandon cringed. He tried to tug Seri away, but she was busy examining the display of knives.

"You look like her." The young man shoved a copy of *Warrior Woman: Serilda's Valor* under her nose.

Memory of what he'd read the night before increased Brandon's growing panic.

She grimaced at the scantily clad woman holding a

sword aloft in two hands as she stood over the body of a fallen opponent. "I don't believe so," she replied.

"Yes, you do. Though you're prettier."

"Thank you." Seri smiled at the young man.

He blushed and turned his gaze on Brandon. An expression of amusement crossed his face. "Hey, man, if your hair was longer you could almost pass for Donoval. Are you two here for the contest?"

He groaned. As promotion for his next Warrior Woman book, *Serilda's Judgment*, and the pending movie deal, his publisher was running this contest. Insane. Ridiculous. As if any real woman could compare to the image in his mind.

The woman next to you far surpasses it.

He ignored the annoying voice in his head.

"No," he snapped at the young man. Before Seri could ask, Brandon grabbed her arm and pulled her away. Unfortunately he headed the wrong direction and ran smack into the middle of the festivities. Everywhere he looked, men and women were dressed in costumes straight out of the pages of his books. He and Seri were surrounded.

Seri froze in her tracks, pulling him to a stop. "What *is* this?" she demanded.

"You don't want to know," he muttered, and reached again for her arm. "Come on, let's get out of here."

"Mauri?" She evaded his grasp and took a step in the direction of a young girl dressed in costume.

The child looked up and smiled, but then an older woman in a Serilda costume and a red wig took her hand and led her toward a low stage in the middle of the mall's main court.

"Here we have Megan O'Connor as Mauri," a

man's voice said over the loudspeaker. The stage where the girl was being presented was set to resemble the great hall in the castle Andre Roark had commandeered.

Seri flinched and looked at Brandon in growing confusion. He had to get her out of here.

"Lovely costume, Megan. Judges, what do you think?" the announcer continued.

Before Brandon could snag her arm, Seri moved toward the stage as if in a trance.

"Wow! You're Brandon Davis. *The* Brandon Davis." A young man stepped between him and Seri. "They said you wouldn't be here. Would you sign my books?" He shoved a stack of novels and a pen into Brandon's hands.

Not wanting to call any more attention to himself, he murmured an assent and dashed off his signature inside the books. By the time he finished and managed to slip away, the announcer was speaking again.

"Thank you, Megan. We'll take a short break while the judges tally the vote for the Mauri lookalike and then we'll come back for the main event . . ." The announcer paused for effect. "The Serilda contestants! So stick around, folks. The best is yet to come."

Brandon looked around. He'd lost Seri.

In a fog, I watched the little girl move across the dais and disappear into the crowd. Everywhere I looked I saw people I knew: Jole, Hausic, and several girls of ten and three who bore more than a passing resemblance to Mauri. They hovered around the dais. And yet, none of them were who they appeared.

I grabbed one girl by the arm and turned her to face me. She squeaked in alarm and tried to twist free. I held tight and peered into her face. Pale blue eyes, not dark brown, met my own.

"Lady, let me go or I'll call my mom," the girl said.

I released her and stumbled back. Was this some trick of the wizard's? Had he summoned alternate versions of his creations as a frightening display of his power? Yet none of these people seemed aware of not being real. They appeared entirely comfortable in this world.

I battled the panic churning inside me. An ache formed behind my eyes.

"Lady, you'd better get into costume," the youth from the sword merchant's booth said at my side. "You look like Serilda, but you'll never win in that getup."

I turned to him in confusion. "Costume? I don't have a costume."

"That's too bad. I've seen some of the other contestants, and you'd win hands down. Hey, I know what. I've got a friend over at another booth who might be willing to help you out if you'd agree to mention his shop if you win. Come with me."

I hesitated for a moment and scanned the area for the wizard. He was nowhere in sight. Where had he gone? Did I dare leave his side? Had he abandoned me?

"I'm Matt. Come on. First prize is a hundred bucks." The lad reminded me of Jole in manner if not in looks.

"Bucks?"

He grinned at my lack of understanding. "Bread. Cash. Money. You know, coin of the realm."

I had no idea what things cost in this world, but a hundred sounded like a substantial amount, the same as the cost of the one item of clothing the wizard purchased for me. Perhaps I could repay him for some of what he'd spent.

Matt grabbed my arm and tugged me deeper into the crowd. Curious to see what would happen, I followed.

The next few minutes passed in a blur. Matt hurried me to a booth filled with garments similar to those I was familiar wearing. The proprietor, an older man named Rick, smiled when he saw me. After a brief discussion he agreed to provide me with attire for this contest to see who most resembled the people from my world. I'm not sure why I agreed to participate in such an odd endeavor, but Matt and Rick's friendliness, and their enthusiasm for the competition, eased my apprehensions.

Soon I found myself clothed in leather sandals, soft leather trousers, and a cloth tunic. Matt handed me the sword I had tested earlier, and I strapped a wide belt around my waist. Not giving myself time to consider the wisdom of what was happening, I let him rush me back over to the dais.

"Good luck," he said. "We were just in time."

"And now, ladies and gentlemen, what we've all been waiting for: the contestants for Serilda!"

Four women dressed in versions of my leather bra and skirt outfit went to stand on the dais, and I followed suit. I now wore a much more practical outfit than usual. The sight reminded me of how the wizard had manipulated me for so long. Amusement soothed my resentment, however. None of these women bore even a passing resemblance to me. Though all had short reddish hair, one was tall and flat-chested, the other short and plump, another too old, and the last too young.

I stood between them and listened to the murmur of the crowd.

"The judges have made their call," a voice overhead said. "Contestant Number Three—I don't seem to have your name here—could you step forward?"

The short, plump woman next to me gave me a poke in the side. When I glared at her, she said in a sulky voice, "He means you. You won."

A man came toward me holding a small silver chalice and an envelope, and the other women filed off the dais.

"Congratulations on winning the Serilda lookalike contest! Here's your prize," the man said, and handed me the chalice and envelope. He next spoke to the crowd: "And now let's bring all the winners on stage so the audience can get some pictures. Afterward, you're welcome to come up for autographs and have pictures taken with your favorite character."

Though I wanted to bolt off the dais, I stood frozen as the man continued, "Come on up . . . Mauri, Hausic, Jole, and Donoval!"

Stunned, I watched as the pretend Mauri, Jole, and Hausic climbed the stairs and came to stand alongside me. Their similarities to the people I knew and loved made me feel dizzy and disoriented. When the fake Donoval bounded to my side and bent me over his muscled arm, at first I didn't react.

The envelope and chalice slipped from my grasp and clattered to the floor. But as his wet lips slobbered over mine, my first instinct was to shove the sword I clutched in my damp palm through the imposter's belly.

I resisted and jerked my lips free of his. He smiled and straightened but didn't remove his arm from my waist. When I twisted out of his grasp, his smile faded.

"And where would Serilda be, if not for her archenemy?" the announcer paused for a moment. "Andre Roark!"

At the sound of Roark's name, I went still. A cold sweat prickled down my spine. I forgot that this was all make-believe, that Mauri, Jole, and the others didn't exist in this world. Other than myself, none of the people around me were who they pretended. They were all chimeras.

Over the roar of rage in my head, I heard people clapping, whistling, and yelling. I turned my gaze toward the man who'd haunted my nightmares for the last ten and five years, the man who'd destroyed my world and killed nearly everyone I loved.

Dressed in typical dark, skintight leggings and a loose silver tunic over a white full-sleeved shirt, at forty and nine Roark wore his years well. Only a few strands of gray at his temples marred the midnight black of his shoulder-length hair. Tall and thin with almost feminine features, he had the look of an artist rather than a warrior, but I knew well the strength of his sword arm and the evil that lurked in his heart.

A smile on his deceptively handsome face, his hand outstretched in an unfamiliar gesture, he moved across the dais toward me. Unease slithered down my spine.

Where were Roark's weapons? His guards? He never ventured out of his stronghold unattended, weaponless. What manner of trap had he set?

No matter. I tightened my grip on the hilt of my sword. Physically and mentally, I prepared myself to strike. A few more feet, one quick thrust, and my nightmares would end.

Brandon saw the telltale signs of a warrior about to attack in Seri's wide-legged stance. Her sword was held in a firm but careful grip, and her eyes tracked her target. How could the rest of the cheering crowd be oblivious to the tragedy about to unfold? He'd never get to her in time.

"Seri! No!" he screamed above the noise. It did no good; she attacked.

At the last moment, she pushed her thrust up and to the side. Color drained from the fake Roark's face as her blade sliced through the air over his shoulder. A lock of black hair floated to the floor. He stopped in his tracks. "What the hell?"

A shout of excitement rolled through the crowd. In relief, Brandon released the breath he'd been holding, then pushed his way up on stage.

As he reached Seri's side, confusion and horror darkened her gaze. She leaned into him. He took the sword from her trembling hand and tossed it to the young man from the weapons booth who stood waiting.

"I think we'd better get out of here before anyone realizes what almost happened," he said.

Seri nodded.

Over the noise of the crowd, Brandon heard the Roark contestant yelling at the contest coordinator, but everyone else seemed sanguine. Cameras flashed. People surged forward. Seri huddled against Brandon's side as they moved off the stage and away through the crowd.

"Hey, wait!" the young man from the weapons booth followed them. "You forgot your prize! And you need to return the costume to Rick. I really liked that last bit with the sword, though. Very dramatic."

Brandon took the chalice and envelope and thanked him. "How much for the costume?"

The young man named a price. Brandon dug the money out of his wallet and shoved it at him. "Keep the change."

"But what about the lady's dress?" The youngster held out a plastic bag.

"Thanks." Brandon snatched it and hurried Seri toward the mall entrance.

He ignored the contest coordinator who called after them, "Wait! I need your name!"

By the time he tucked Seri into the passenger seat of the SUV, she was pale and shivering. Despite the warm outside air, he turned up the heat, pulled the SUV out of the parking lot, and headed toward home.

For a long while Seri said nothing. With her head back and her eyes closed, he'd almost believe she was asleep. Except for the tense look on her face.

About twenty minutes into the trip she spoke. "I almost killed that man," she said in a strained whisper.

"But you didn't."

He looked over at her. Tears ran down her cheeks.

The Serilda he'd created never cried. Never showed fear. Never had a moment of doubt. Common sense had told him to turn this woman over to the authorities, and his hesitation in doing so had nearly cost a man his life. What the hell was he doing?

"He wasn't Roark, was he?"

"No, he was just some guy in a stupid costume." Brandon fought annoyance with both himself and this woman's charade.

"What manner of world is this?" She dashed the tears from her cheeks and twisted to face him. Her tone grew stronger. "To what purpose did you bring me here?"

He rubbed his hand over his jaw. "For the last time, I didn't bring you here. I'm not a wizard. I'm just a writer. Serilda's world and the people in it are pure invention. They don't really exist. *And you're not Serilda.*"

"If I'm not her, who am I?"

"I don't know." As he looked at her, another wave of compassion swept through him, the same emotions that had attracted him to her all along. He reached over and put a hand over hers. Her flesh felt dry and insubstantial. He had the oddest notion that if he squeezed too hard she would crumble to dust. "I know you're a flesh-and-blood person, though, not some fictional character out of the pages of a book. *My* book. Somewhere out there you have a life and people who care about you. Let me help you find that life."

She shook her head. "You make me want to believe, but my memories, my feelings, and everything inside me says I'm Serilda. My life and the people I care about are in Barue."

Brandon fought despair. "Well, if you can't consider the possibility that you're suffering from some kind of mental delusion, I really have no choice but to turn you over to the authorities."

Of course, even if she didn't realize it, his words were an empty threat. He couldn't abandon her. All his life he'd run away from his problems, taken the simplest path rather than facing his life's challenges, compromised what he really wanted and took what required the least risk on his part. As a child he'd been trapped by his mother's disconnect with reality. He'd learned early on to go along to get along. After she died and he went to live with his grandmother, his life got better, less psychotic, but the damage was done. He'd even created his fictional world as a place to hide. Turning Seri over to the police would be another concession. In a way, he was responsible for her delusion, her situation. This time, he found he couldn't—didn't want to—run away.

"If I agree to consider your truth, you'll allow me to remain with you?" she asked.

He knew he should refuse, that he should head toward the nearest hospital and have her committed. His need to help her himself was a bit selfish. Yet in the short time she'd been in his life, something inside him had changed. Whether for good or ill he didn't know yet, but he was determined to see things through to the end. "You have to promise no more swords or weapons of any kind, no matter the provocation."

She hesitated for a moment, then said, "By the light of Algidar, I do so swear."

Brandon groaned. She'd used the most sacred oath

of his fictional world's deity. "Okay, but one slip and you're gone."

"I understand. Earlier you mentioned midmeal. Is that still possible?"

"Yeah, sure. There's a drive-in just ahead. We'll stop there." He glanced over at her. She seemed relaxed again as she gazed out the window at the fields of corn and soybeans, and at the small farms they passed. How quickly she seemed to recover from her confusion and fear. He wished he could do the same. But thoughts of what might have happened kept running through his head. He shivered.

On the outskirts of town, about twenty minutes from home, he turned in to the drive-in restaurant lot. Along with the scent of moist earth and newly mown hay from a nearby farmer's field, the smell of hamburgers and fries wafted on the summer air. To the west dark clouds gathered, heralding a coming storm, but for now the sun still shone bright and warm. The sound of a distant tractor provided a background to the hum of cicadas and the chirp of the sparrows hopping around looking for forgotten crumbs.

This late in the afternoon, the lunch crowd was gone and the dinner crowd had yet to arrive, so other than a few people inside the drive-in's small dining area, they had the place to themselves. After a quick look around, he led Seri to one of the concrete tables outside. "Don't go anywhere," he warned her; then, with a feeling of misgiving about leaving her alone even for a minute, he headed around the other side of the building to get their food.

* * *

The sun warmed the chill in my soul as I sat on the hard stone bench and watched the wizard disappear around the corner of the building. He believed I'd put aside my reaction to almost slaying the Roark imposter, but the truth was my insides still churned. While often necessary, killing did not come easy to me. I certainly did not want to slay an innocent.

This world differed in many ways from the one I knew. Here, well-dressed and well-fed, the people moved about without fear or constraint by those in power. Shops overflowed with merchandise, fields grew an abundance of food. Even the weather seemed less harsh. The sun shone mild in a cloudless sky; breezes blew fresh with the scents of rich soil and growing things. Was it as idyllic as it appeared? Experience warned me to be wary. The shiniest apple ofttimes hid the biggest worm. What lurked beneath the surface of this perfect world?

And could I do as the wizard demanded? Forget who I was? Abandon my life? Become a person of his world? Is that why he'd summoned me here, to grant me a real existence? Then why did he not just say so? Why deny that he'd created me? Perhaps I had to prove myself worthy, pass his tests, before I could lay claim to reality and true independence. But how to do so? Did I accept his views as stated? Or was this a different test?

My head ached from the dilemma. Did I even wish to become part of this world? And, if I did, what would become of the others I left behind, my friends and allies? I wanted to question the wizard about this, but his threat to turn me in to the authorities tied my tongue. In Barue, many of the authorities were corrupt or answered to Roark. I already had knowledge of Roark's hospitality. I had no desire to learn how this world treated unwanted guests.

Until I discovered more, I'd acquiesce to the wizard's dictates; I'd pretend to reject my true identity. I'd follow Brother Eldrin's wise counsel: *When the wolf wishes to catch many sheep, he doesn't snarl and bare his teeth and charge blindly forward, he hides his true nature and moves quietly among them. The time to attack presents itself.*

My decision made, I let all tension drain away. The scent of frying meat made my stomach growl with hunger.

"Hi, do you want a kitten?"

At the sound of a voice behind me, I jumped up and whirled around. The near-tragedy, confusion, and hunger made me lax. Despite my promise to the wizard, I instinctively reached for my sword—which fortunately was in the vehicle.

Wide-eyed, a boy of perhaps ten and one stared up at me. In his hands he held a box made of a hardened brownish paper.

"I didn't mean to scare you. Just wanted to know if you'd like a kitten." He plunked the box down on the stone table in front of me. "They're free. Dad said we have enough cats in the barn. We keep our girl cats spayed, but some city person dumped a pregnant one on us. She had a litter of eight. I found homes for five of them so far. Got these three left. Take a look."

I stood frozen as the boy babbled on. Most of what he said washed over me unheard. My eyes focused on the small mewing bundles of fur that he was carrying.

Phelines. Though I'd never seen one, I'd heard tales of these amazing creatures. Because of the constant strife and fighting and resulting lack of food, animal companions were rare in Barue. Despite the legends surrounding them, the few canids and phelines left usually ended up in someone's cook pot. As a result, rats and the diseases they carried abounded in Barue. To see these creatures of myth and legend rendered me speechless.

"Hey, lady. Are you all right?" When I looked at him, the boy took a step backward. "Well, do you want one? I've gotta get home."

"You wish to give me a pheline?" I couldn't believe my good fortune. Legend held that phelines bestowed wisdom, wealth, and power upon their companions. Legend also said that those who misused those gifts would suffer. Of course, Roark was said to have many phelines in his palace, and as far as I could tell, he had yet to pay for his crimes.

The boy saw the enthusiasm I displayed. "You can have them all if you want. Animal control won't take 'em. They're full up, and if I bring them home Dad will probably drown them."

This was an answer to my prayers! Not only would I be able to present the wizard with a gift beyond value, I could retain a pheline for myself. I gripped the edge of the box. "Thank you, yes, I'll take them all." I pushed aside the tiny part of me that wondered why the boy would be willing to part with creatures so precious.

"That's great! Here." He shoved a clear bag filled with tiny hard brown nuggets into my hands. "Some kitten food." And without another word he scampered off.

Something wet and rough scraped across my knuckles, then something sharp bit into the flesh on the back of my hand. I jerked my hand away and looked down to see one of the tiny phelines attempting to climb out of the box. The other two had curled together and fallen asleep, but this one looked boldly up at me and uttered a plaintive meow.

I curled my hand around its middle and lifted it up to my face. Pure white, silky fur tickled my palm. Wide blue eyes met mine without flinching as its body draped over my fingers. When it started to vibrate with a deep rumble that seemed too loud for its little form, I nearly dropped it.

The noise of a vehicle pulling into the paved area in front of the eating establishment brought me back to myself, and I glanced around dazedly. The wizard would return soon. This was not the place or the time to present his gift.

I returned the white pheline to the box with the other two, one black and one gray. I put in the bag of food and used the flaps to shut the box. I hurried over to the wizard's conveyance and placed the box on the floor behind his seat. I'd only just returned to the table when he arrived with the food.

"A wise man fights with neither fools nor women."
—Brother Eldrin, Order of Light

Chapter Six

Brandon put the food-laden tray down on the table and sat down across from Seri. She looked different from when he'd left her a few minutes earlier: less stressed, more relaxed. A knowing smile hovered around her lips and lit up her face.

She eyed the food with appreciation. "There's enough here to feed an army."

"I didn't ask what you wanted, so I got a bit of everything. Hamburgers, hot dogs, fries, onion rings, and some ice cream. What would you like?"

"I don't know. Everything smells wonderful. I'm hungry enough to eat a tarak." She smiled as she named the desert lizard common to Barue. With sharp teeth and claws, a thick scaly hide and a bad attitude, the creatures were difficult to catch, harder to kill, and unpleasant in taste—but they bred like rabbits, providing a meager source of nourishment for desert tribes and travelers.

"You'll enjoy this more." He handed her a hot dog smothered with all the fixings.

She took the offering and sniffed it. The aroma

of grilled meat, onions, mustard, and ketchup must have pleased her, because she took a bite. A look of delight spread over her face. In seconds she had devoured the hot dog and reached for a hamburger.

Fascinated by her appetite, he almost forgot to eat. Most women he'd known—his mother, Wanda, and Hillary—merely nibbled at their food. They always claimed to be on diets yet never seemed to lose any weight. His grandmother had been the exception. Until her death, she'd eaten anything and everything and never gained an ounce. She'd claimed magic kept her thin.

Seri ate with gusto and didn't seem interested in counting calories or carbohydrates. Whatever she did in life, she kept her body trim and fit. The pile of food diminished. She glanced at him. Her hand paused as she reached for the now-melting ice cream.

"Why aren't you eating?"

The sudden suspicion in her tone reminded him to tread carefully. He grabbed a handful of fries.

She relaxed and picked up the dish of ice cream. "What is this?"

"Chocolate ice cream. You'll like it."

"Mmmm," she groaned around a mouthful. "This is astonishing. I think I could easily live on this alone."

"It's full of fat and sugar, and loaded with calories."

"I know fat and sugar. But what are calories? Are they dangerous?" She gave the now empty container a wary glance.

"Only to your waistline."

Understanding spread over her face. She grinned. "Ah, I see. You fear I'll grow obese and lazy."

"No, I didn't mean that . . . I only meant . . . well, I . . ." He stumbled.

She leaned forward and placed her fingers over his lips. "I but tease. Only the very rich and powerful can afford to grow stout and indolent. And those that do so soon lose their wealth and their power to those who are hungry."

Slick from the fries and cool from the ice cream, the feel of her fingers against his lips sent a jolt of awareness straight to his groin. Without thinking, he sucked one finger into his mouth. The taste of salt and Seri exploded on his tongue.

Her voice trailed away. He pushed aside the tray with the remains of their lunch and leaned across the concrete table. She pulled her hand from his mouth and replaced it with her lips.

She tasted of chocolate, cool chocolate ice cream. The smell of grilled hot dogs and onion rings filled his nostrils. But the hunger inside Brandon wasn't for food. Eager for the taste of the woman he kissed, he ran his tongue over her lips. They parted on a sigh, and he delved within.

Hot and tangy, her flavor sucked him in. Heat burned away rational thought as he lost himself in the kiss. Their tongues thrust and parried, the tempo increasing with every breath. Not satisfied with the limited contact of their mouths, he put his hand around the back of her head. Soft red curls twined around his fingers.

Honk! Honk!

"Hey, man! Get a room!" a loud voice rang out.

Laughter followed, as a car filled with teenagers pulled into the lot.

Brandon jerked away. His elbow cracked against the stone table. Pain ran up his arm. He welcomed the distraction. Seri looked dazed as she settled back on her bench.

Embarrassed, Brandon loaded the garbage from the meal on the tray and used it to hide the erection pressing painfully against his zipper. "Time to head home," he said. What had he been thinking?

That was the problem: when he was around her, he didn't think, he reacted. The depth of his desire for her amazed and alarmed him. She'd come into his life little more than a day ago, and she stirred his blood more than any woman he'd ever known. Common sense and decency dictated he keep his hands off her. She was alone and lost. But his primitive male side urged him to take what he wanted, what he needed from her, the risks be damned. He bit his lip, hoping the small pain would still the unfulfilled passion throbbing inside him. The flavor lingering on his mouth defeated his purpose.

He tossed the garbage in the can and stomped over to the SUV. Seri followed without saying a word.

Roiling dark clouds now hid the sun. The air outside felt thick and muggy with a coming storm.

Once on the road, he closed the windows and turned on the air-conditioning. The blast of frigid air did little to ease his internal heat.

"When we get home, I'm calling an old friend of mine to see if we can't figure out who you are and where you're from."

She didn't respond to his harsh declaration.

Calling Sam Picket a friend might be stretching things a little. They'd gone to college together and for a time been close, but despite Sam's efforts to keep in touch, Brandon hadn't seen the man in nearly ten years. Maybe it was the birth announcement for Sam's first son that Brandon had received several months ago that had triggered his current reassessment of his life.

Sam was an ex-Chicago cop turned private investigator. Brandon hoped he was available for hire. The sooner he found out where Seri belonged and got her out of his life the better.

I sat silent as the wizard drove. Though he said nothing more, I could almost hear his thoughts. They echoed mine. Without warning passion had flared between us. His taste, rich and smooth like the frozen confection, only hot as flowing lava, remained from his kiss. From the simple touch of our lips, my breasts ached and moisture dampened my thighs.

I'd gone to Donoval full of youthful curiosity, and I'd received pleasure, but with him I'd never experienced the rush of need and want I felt when the wizard touched me. Until now, sex had been an agreeable diversion, much the same as a good meal or a warm bath, enjoyable but not necessary. My desire for the wizard confused and angered me.

"Have you bespelled me?" Unable to restrain myself, I blurted the question.

"What? Bespelled you? With what?" He looked annoyed.

"Desire."

He slammed his fist against the wheel rising up

from the console in front of him. "Hell no! I keep telling you, I'm no wizard."

"Then why do I respond to you so? This is not usual for me. Is this a test I must pass?"

"You're talking nonsense. A test of what?"

"To prove my worthiness to become a real person."

"How many times do I have to tell you? You are a real person."

The confusion and frustration on his face reflected my own bewildered state. I shook my head. "At least once more."

He chuckled, and I felt his anger drain away. Like a warm breeze, his amusement caressed me.

"I know I promised to consider what you've told me, and I have no wish to anger you, but despite your insistence I'm not a creature of your creation, I remember no other identity. If I relinquish my belief in your wizardry, where does that leave me? If you didn't bring me out of my world into yours, how did I come to be here? And what will be my fate?"

His tone softened. "You're safe. We're going to figure things out. Relax." He reached over and covered my hand with his. "Trust me."

At that moment I did. The warmth of his skin against mine eased the chill inside me and stirred an answering heat. Before the embers burst into flame, I snatched my hand to my lap. His hand lay alone on the seat between us.

"Ouch!" he cried, and grabbed for something on his shoulder.

I looked up to see a small white bundle of fur flying at me. Instinctively, I caught the pheline. Needle-sharp claws dug into my hands as the creature hissed at being so roughly handled. Our conveyance swerved and rocked as the wizard struggled to maintain control. We hit the edge of the road. Gravel spewed. The wheel spun out of his hand. We bounced down a grassy embankment. A massive boulder loomed before us. I closed my eyes and clutched the spitting, clawing pheline to my chest.

Ca-thunk! The conveyance slammed into the rock. Something exploded into my face. I jerked forward and back but was held in place by the belt. I appreciated that the wizard had made me wear it.

The machine's engine sputtered and died. The sound of the crash faded to silence in my ears. I opened my eyes. Steam hissed from under the crumpled front of the metal carriage. In my hands, the pheline wriggled for a moment to get free, then settled against my chest with a soft rumble. From the backseat I heard the plaintive mews of the other two phelines trapped in the overturned box.

"Are you hurt?" the wizard asked. The concern in his tone touched me.

"I'm uninjured. That white cloud protected me." I pointed at the now limp bag draped across my knees.

He unhooked his belt and turned toward me. "What in the hell is that?" He glared at the pheline curled in my lap.

"A pheline." I held out the small creature, but somehow I doubted he was in any mood to appreciate my gift.

Brandon stared in angry disbelief at the tiny bundle of ruffled fur in Seri's hands. "Where in the hell did it come from?"

"Don't yell. You'll frighten her." She cuddled the kitten close and glared at him.

"I'll yell if I damned well feel like it! That damned cat just caused me to crash my car!" He rubbed at the small pinpricks on his shoulder from the cat's claws.

"Don't blame your inability to control your machine on this innocent creature." She bristled like he'd always imagined an angry tarak would. The kitten blinked its large blue eyes at him and daintily licked its paw.

He let out a gust of breath, flopped back in his seat, and squeezed his eyes shut. "What more can go wrong?"

"Are you injured?" Seri asked in a softer tone.

He did a mental inventory of his parts. Everything seemed to be in working order. Aside from an accelerated heartbeat and the aches he knew they'd both be feeling later on, they'd gotten off lightly. He opened his eyes and looked at the still steaming, crumpled hood. His brand-new SUV hadn't been so lucky.

"I'm just dandy."

"I'm unfamiliar with this word. Does it imply you are intact?"

He jumped as she plopped the kitten in his lap and tiny claws latched onto the skin of his thigh. With one hand he snatched the kitten away from that more sensitive flesh, then turned to see Seri kneeling on the seat, about to tumble headfirst into the backseat. With his free hand, he grabbed the back of her tunic. "What are you doing?"

She pulled against his hold. Her fanny wagged in his face. "Ah, I have them."

"Have who?" he asked with some trepidation.

She twisted and landed back in her seat with two more kittens in tow. Like mismatched mittens, one black and one gray, they hung in her hands.

"Why me, God?" He raised his eyes, then asked her, "Where did they come from?"

"A young lad at the eatery gave them to me." At his dazed look she paused. "I too was astonished that anyone would wish to give away such magnificent creatures. Are we not blessed to be their caretakers?" She brushed her cheek against one of the kittens. He could hear it purring.

Brandon remembered a vague reference he'd put in one of his books about a rare catlike creature. "Is everything I've ever written going to come back to haunt me?" he asked.

Seri didn't answer.

The kitten he held licked his hand. Its soft rumbling purr vibrated up his arm. Despite his usual aversion to creatures with fur and claws, he settled the kitten gently on the seat.

As he got out of the SUV to check the damage, he said, "Stay here." He wasn't sure whether he spoke to Seri or the kittens. Neither did he have any certainty they'd listen.

A thin curl of steam hissed from under the seam of the hood. From this angle the damage wasn't as bad as he'd feared, but the SUV would be in the shop for more than a few days.

"Don't worry, you'll soon be all better." He patted the fender.

"I thought you said it wasn't alive."

He jumped at the sound of Seri's voice in his ear. "Don't sneak up on me like that. And it's not."

"Then why do you stroke and speak to it?" She peered around him at the bent and twisted metal.

"I'm not sure," he admitted. "Probably a throwback to man's relationship with four-legged transportation. Speaking of four legs, where are the kittens?" He told himself his concern was for the leather seats, not that the kittens might get loose and lost.

"I secured them within their box. They're asleep."

"Good. Now we have to figure out how to get home before it starts to rain."

She followed his gaze first to the dark clouds now obscuring the sun, then to the empty two-lane road. "How far are we?"

"About five miles."

"We can walk."

The sound of an approaching vehicle stopped him from agreeing. They waited at the side of the road as a dusty old pickup rumbled to a halt. A middle-aged man dressed in denim overalls and a flannel shirt leaned across the seat and pushed aside the large, shaggy brown dog hanging half out the passenger side window. "You folks okay?"

Brandon kept back from the dog as he answered. "We're fine, but as you can see my car isn't."

The man looked around. "Deer run you off the road?"

"Kittens."

"Kittens? Haven't heard that one before." The man scratched his head and laughed.

"It's a long story." The local gossip mill was going to have blast with this one. "Can you give us a ride into town?"

"Sure, but Rich's is closed." He referred to the one mechanic/body shop in town. "Hey, you're that writer guy who bought the Lawrence place, aren't you? Brandon Davis? I haven't had time to read your books yet, but my wife and kids love 'em. They're down at the new mall today for some fantasy hoopla. Hop in. My farm is just up the road from you. I'll run you home." He pushed open the door. "Beau, you get on in back," he told the dog.

The dog jumped down. Brandon froze as the animal paused to sniff his legs, then headed to check out Seri.

"Beau!" the man called. With a disappointed look, the dog turned and trotted to the back of the pickup.

"Get in," the man said to Brandon and Seri. "Ain't got all day. Rain's a-coming." A smile softened his words as he glanced at the darkening sky.

"Wait," Seri said, and she hurried down the incline to the SUV. A few seconds later she came back carrying the box of kittens and her sword.

The man frowned at the sight of the weapon but didn't say anything as she climbed into the cab of the pickup. Brandon followed and shut the door. Crowded together on the bench seat as they were, the soft swell of Seri's breast on his arm and the curve of her hip against his made him shift in discomfort, but there was no escape. Even her legs tangled with his on their side of the floor divide.

With effort, Brandon dragged his thoughts away from her. "What about my car?"

"Should be okay here for a bit," the stranger said. "Did you lock it?"

Brandon pushed the remote lock, then nodded.

"Name's Dan, Dan Parson." The stranger reached his arm across Seri.

"Brandon Davis." Brandon shook the man's rough hand. "And this is Seri."

"Pleased to meet you, Seri." Dan gave her costume, her sword, and the box she clutched protectively in her lap a curious glance but didn't comment. He simply asked, "You from around here?"

"No, I'm from—"

"She's staying with me," Brandon interrupted before Seri could blurt something inappropriate. He told himself he was protecting himself from even more gossip if the story got out that his houseguest thought she was one of his fictional characters. "She's an actress they're considering for the part of Serilda in the movie."

"Thought you looked familiar. Guess you were at the mall for the fantasy fair. D.J.—that's my older boy, Daniel Junior—he's got Warrior Woman posters all over his room." Dan's weathered face turned red beneath his tan. "You know how it is with teenage boys. But you're much prettier in person. He'll be crushed that he didn't get to meet you—either of you."

"Give me your address, and I'll send him some autographed copies of my books," Brandon said to distract the man's attention from Seri.

"That's mighty nice of you. Thanks." Dan continued to chat as they drove. He didn't seem to notice or care that neither Brandon nor Seri had much to say.

The short ride seemed to take forever. With every jounce of the pickup, Seri's body rubbed enticingly against Brandon's. The sweet scent rising off her body tantalized him. To keep from reaching for her, Brandon gritted his teeth. She appeared oblivious to the contact, until he noticed her white-knuckled grip on the box.

Finally, and yet too soon, they pulled up the gravel drive in front of Brandon's house.

"Thanks for the lift, Mr. Parson." Brandon got out of the pickup. Clutching the box to her chest, Seri hopped down next to him.

"Dan," the man insisted as he dug a crumpled business card out of his overflowing glove compartment. "Here's my wife's card. She sells real estate. You can send the books to this address. Thanks in advance. D.J. will be thrilled." He waved as he drove off.

"Damn!" Brandon realized he hadn't asked the man to call the towing service.

Seri raised her gaze from peeking inside the box. "What's wrong?"

"We'll have to walk after all."

"Why?" she asked. She didn't look a bit guilty as he glared at her.

Sudden anger made his tone harsh. "Because you smashed my phone."

"Knowing when to run away shows true wisdom."
—Brother Eldrin, Order of Light

Chapter Seven

After giving Seri terse instructions to stay in the house and out of trouble, Brandon set off for town. He ignored the growing wind, churning clouds, and dropping temperature. The fresh breeze felt good against his heated skin.

When he'd first moved into the house a few years earlier, he'd been pleasantly surprised with how much he enjoyed hiking and jogging through the woods surrounding his isolated home. Seeing life in the wild eased his discomfort around the creatures, too. Somehow a squirrel chattering at him from a tree branch above his head was less threatening than a neighbor's dog barking from behind a fence. A spiderweb strung between two bushes glistening with early morning dew inspired awe rather than apprehension.

As he walked his anger faded, and he remembered the hurt look on Seri's face when he told her to stay home. Guilt niggled at him. In no mood to deal with it, he pushed it aside; the walk into town would give him the time he needed to think about what to do.

Even without her bizarre claim of being Serilda, her presence had turned his life upside down and inside out. When they were apart, logic told him to call the authorities, to get her out of his life. But the moment he saw her again he knew he couldn't do it. Her strength and vulnerability stirred things to life inside him that he'd thought long dead: laughter, hope, desire . . . love.

Love? His step faltered. Where had that thought come from? He shook his head. What he felt for Seri couldn't be love. Compassion. Concern. Respect. And lust, he admitted honestly. But not love. He wasn't even sure he knew what love was. His track record with the women in his life was dismal.

Rather than care for him, his mother had succumbed to demons in her mind. His grandmother, though she'd loved him and done her best, had been old when she took him in; her child-rearing style had been a strange mix of New Age philosophy and old world rules. And after he'd screwed up his marriage, he'd pretty much given up on the idea of having any kind of normal relationship.

Halfway to town, the rain started.

"Great, just great," he muttered through the water dripping down his face. An hour later he arrived.

A bell jingled as he entered the town's one diner. On the few occasions Brandon had come into town, he'd eaten here, at Maxine's. The fare was simple, plentiful, and delicious. Several people glanced up at him. Warm air, fragrant with the smell of fry grease, apple pie, and fresh brewed coffee, filled his nostrils.

"Hell of a storm, ain't it, boy? I think we're in for a spell of bad weather. Yar dripping all over Max's floor there." A grizzled old man in denim overalls grinned at him over a dinner of roast beef and mashed potatoes.

Max, the owner/cook, looked up from behind the counter. "Mr. Davis, what *are* you doing out in this weather?" The tall, rawboned, yet attractive middle-aged woman gripped his arm and propelled him to a booth. "Come in and dry off. I'll get you some coffee."

He hesitated to sit down. "I'll get your seat wet. I just need to use your phone."

"It's vinyl." She pushed him into the booth and handed him a towel. "Storm knocked the phones out."

In seconds she'd placed a steaming cup of coffee in front of him. The first sip made him aware of how chilled he was, inside and out.

"Who do you need to call?"

"A tow truck."

She lifted an eyebrow but didn't ask. Instead, she turned toward a man sitting in the booth behind him playing checkers with the Council Falls sheriff. "Hey, Rich, Mr. Davis needs his car towed. Can you spare the time?"

"Sure."

Brandon sat back in befuddled amusement as, with only minimal information from him, Max and Rich coordinated plans to collect his SUV and tow it to Rich's service station for repair. After Rich left, Max smiled at Brandon. "Small-town life has its advantages."

Cradling the coffee cup in his hands, he wondered

why he'd avoided contact with the people in town. While he now sat comfortably inside, a man he'd barely met went out in a storm to tow his car.

"Thank you for your help," he told the diner owner.

"No problem. That's what neighbors are for. Did you want something to eat?"

"No, the coffee is fine."

"Relax then. When you're ready, the sheriff will run you home. Won't you, Ken?" she asked.

The sheriff gave Brandon a searching look, then nodded. Maxine went back behind the counter.

Brandon bent his head to avoid the sheriff's sharp gaze. Though not much older, the lawman had eyes holding a wealth of experience. For a brief minute, Brandon considered telling him about Seri and letting him handle the problem. The urge passed quickly. Seri was his.

He looked up as the bell jingled and almost dropped his cup. "Hillary?"

"In the flesh." She didn't sound happy.

Lessons of polite behavior learned from his grandmother had him standing as his agent approached. Red stiletto heels clicked out an angry rhythm on the diner's wooden floor. All eyes in the restaurant followed her. He didn't blame them.

Tall and model thin, with blue-black hair cropped close to her scalp, even on the far side of forty Hillary commanded attention. Here in middle America, her looks and dramatic style stood out like a Picasso at a country art fair. Her olive complexion hinted at a European ancestry, but her dark slanting eyes and high cheekbones gave her an exotic Asian look. A sleeveless red leather catsuit with a dramatic plunging neckline clung to her small breasts and lean hips, while a floor-length black silk coat billowed around her like a cape.

Peeking up over the edge of the oversized bag she carried was Muffin. Brandon groaned. Hillary went nowhere without her obnoxious black teacup poodle. Last time he'd seen the animal it had tried to bite him.

He banked his irritation at her arrival. Despite, or maybe because of her flamboyant appearance and eccentric nature, she was an excellent agent, and a good friend.

"What are you doing here?" he asked as they sat.

"Getting lost." She waved one hand with long, bloodred nails and used the other to dab at the moisture on her face with some paper napkins. "I've been driving around in this storm for hours trying to find you. Muffin and I are absolutely exhausted, aren't we, babykins?" she cooed. In response, the dog whined and burrowed deeper into the bag.

Hillary glanced around the modest little diner and sniffed. "Not exactly LeSwank." She'd named the hottest new restaurant in New York. In Hillary's opinion, nothing outside of Manhattan was worth considering. She ignored the glares of several diners.

Without being summoned, Max came over and poured a second cup of coffee. Brandon was glad the dog was out of sight; he had no desire to be tossed out into the rain on its account. Always gracious if not always tactful, Hillary murmured her thanks and turned her gaze on him.

"Lower your voice," Brandon whispered after Max moved away, then added in a louder tone, "The food here is better." He didn't know why he felt compelled to defend the diner.

"Well, I am hungry. The food on the plane was atrocious. The flight was awful. And I've been on the road forever in a horrid little rental car. I wanted a—"

"Why are you here?" he interrupted.

She looked surprised by his question. "I was planning on coming out next week, but after you told me about that woman and then your phone suddenly went dead, I got worried about you, so I pushed up my trip. I hope you appreciate all the trouble I've gone through." She leaned forward and patted his cheek. "You are, after all, my favorite client."

When Hillary mentioned Seri, Brandon caught sight of the sheriff's interested look. Concern tightened his stomach muscles.

"Would you like to order?" Max's tone held a chill as she stared at Hillary.

"Do you have fresh su—?"

"No, we're leaving." Though the locals were generally accepting of strangers, Hillary was proving a tad too strange. It was time to leave. Before the sheriff became suspicious.

His reluctance to reveal Seri's presence to the sheriff confused and angered him. He should march over to the man and tell him the whole sorry tale; instead he stood and put a ten-dollar bill on the table. "Thanks again for your help."

"You're welcome. Come back again soon, *Mr. Davis*." Max emphasized for whom she made the offer.

Outside, the rain had stopped and the sun was trying to break through the clouds. Brandon hustled the protesting Hillary into her rental car. He took the keys and drove them home.

I stood at the window and watched the wizard stride away. His changeable moods confused me. If he valued his "phone" more than his horseless conveyance, why had it taken him so long to express his anger over its destruction?

Outside, the wind blew dark clouds across the sky, bowed tree branches to the ground, and churned the river to liquid metal. A familiar sense of impending danger hung in the air.

Even before I'd felt that first jolt of lightning and been transported into a world of nothingness, I'd been on edge. At the time I'd attributed it to the coming battle with Roark, but now I understood my unease had gone far deeper. At some level I'd become aware that all was not as it seemed in my world. Things shifted, leaving me with the strange feeling I was reliving events again and again but each time with different outcomes. I felt disoriented. No one else ever seemed aware of what I sensed.

Inside, curled together in their box, a tangled pile of black, white, and gray fur, the phelines slept. So far my guardianship of them hadn't bestowed any wisdom—forget wealth or power—on me. Still, their presence satisfied a need I hadn't realized existed in me. They were mine to guard and love.

Blue-white lightning streaked across the sky. An answering rumble of thunder preceded the patter of rain against the window.

Restless, I wandered through the wizard's house,

flipping on the lights as I went. It amazed me how quickly I'd come to accept the marvels of his world: light and heat without fire, vehicles that moved under their own power, markets filled with goods without guards, people living without fear. The urge to remain in this world tempted me. But what of those left behind in Barue: Mauri, Jole, Hausic, and the others? If I remained here, what would become of them? Real or not, I'd given my word to protect and defend them.

The room at the top of the stairs where the wizard claimed to perform his word magic drew me in. The chamber was well lit by the large expanse of windows along the far wall, despite the darkness of the storm outside. A flash of lightning brightened the sky for a moment. Thunder shook the glass. Rain battered against the window and pounded the water of the rushing river. I turned my back on the tempest.

A large wooden desk and a leather chair dominated the center of the room; papers and writing sticks littered the surface. On one side of the desk sat a strange rectangular object with a dull silver face. A smaller, flatter object covered with raised square buttons sat in the middle. Thick, snakelike things of gray and black trailed off the window side of the desk, their ends connected to the wall.

Opposite the windows, someone had painted an idyllic mural. Outside a village of quaint homes and businesses, fields of ripening grain seemed to wave in the breeze. In the town, colorfully clad people strode the streets and merchants sold their wares. Farther out, farmers tended their flocks. In the distance a mountain range rose indigo against a blue sky.

If not for Roark and his quest for power, this could be my world. Grief and anger exploded inside me. Enraged, I swept my hand across the desk. The smaller rectangle crashed to the floor. Like a flurry of large snowflakes, papers flew into the air. Crumpling a sheet in my fist, I sank to my knees and screamed out in rage.

Why had I been offered this choice: go back to a mindless life of war and heartbreak, all without true consciousness, or remain here with freedom of thought and abandon all I'd once believed in? Real or not, I knew I couldn't live with myself if I did the latter. Abandoning my people to Roark was not an option; without honor, freedom meant nothing.

A new thought struck me: could I persuade the wizard to use his magic to assist my people? Of course, he kept disavowing he had any power. And, despite the wonders of his world, nothing I'd seen had convinced me otherwise. The man had machines and miracles, but I'd seen no real magic.

Since arriving in the wizard's—no, *Brandon's*—world, all evidence pointed to the fact that he was not a wizard. No, I concluded that another great power toyed with both of us. But who that someone might be, and what purpose they might have, I had yet to determine.

And no matter the sacrifice, with or without Brandon's help, I had to go back.

The sound of a melodious chime diverted my attention. I looked around but could find no source for the sound.

"Hello? Is anyone home?" a female voice called. "Brandon, are you here?"

I moved to the top of the stairs and looked down.

A woman stood just inside the front door. She didn't see me as she removed and hung up her dripping coat.

Before revealing my presence, I took a moment to study her. A pale pink sweater with a deep V neckline clung to her full bosom. White trousers hugged her legs. The high heels on her dainty sandals only emphasized her meager height. A thick fall of shoulder-length blonde hair hid her face from my view.

She looked up, and I caught my breath. With pale, cream-colored skin, high cheekbones, full pink lips, and eyes the color of a summer sky, she had the countenance of the seraphs I'd seen depicted on tapestries.

Her delicate brows drew together, and her soft lips hardened into a thin line. Her visage changed from seraphic to devilish. "Who the hell are you? Don't tell me Brandon actually found another woman." Then she laughed, and the look of displeasure on her face dissolved into satisfaction.

Unsure of how to answer—a situation I didn't care for—I said nothing.

Hands on her hips, she tapped her foot. "Well, whoever you are, come on down. I won't bite."

Wary of this stranger, I went down the stairs. Given her small stature, I had no fear of a physical confrontation, but her stance told me she had weapons that relied little on physical size. When I reached the bottom, she craned her neck up to look me in the face. Next to her petite form I felt large and awkward, in both body and thought.

"My, you are a tall one. I wouldn't have thought you were Brandon's type. Oh well, guess there's no accounting for taste. I'm Wanda." Though her words were dismissive, her friendly tone and winning smile negated the barb. She stuck out her hand. "Brandon's wife."

Though the wizard had mentioned a wife, the reality of this woman crushed something inside of me. This was the female men wanted—petite yet well rounded. Not that I aspired to be wanted by men. All I desired from a man was his loyalty and his sword in battle.

That lie soured my stomach. I knew I wanted much more, but was loath to admit it.

Suddenly I remembered. I gave Wanda a cold look. "He said you were no longer married." Why had the wizard discarded this woman, exactly? Or had she left him?

The woman let her hand and gaze drop. "Yeah, well, that's why I'm here." Some of the confidence drained out of her voice and manner. "Seems there was a mix-up with the paperwork and we're not officially divorced. Since I'm about to get married again, I need him to sign some forms. Can I come in?"

"You're already in."

"Literal, aren't you?" She glanced up at my face, then looked away. Without waiting for an answer to either question, she moved into the main room. I followed.

"Nice place . . . if you like the country. I never would have supposed Brandon would enjoy living this far from civilization. I'm definitely a city gal. Have you known Brandon long?"

I thought back to what the wizard had told me about his books and answered, "Ten years."

"What!" Shock and a bit of hurt flashed across

her face; then she regained her composure. Brows drawn together, she gave me a searching look. "Hmm. I never read them, fantasy's not my thing, but you look a little like the character on the cover of his books. That explains a lot. Living with a writer is hard, isn't it?"

She assumed I lived with the wizard.

"Even when they're home, they aren't there, are they? Always lost in another world. I swear, the characters in Brandon's books were more real to him than I was." She giggled, but the sound held no humor.

I forced myself not to jump to Brandon's defense. Though why I felt the need puzzled me.

"Bankers like my Daniel are so much easier. Nine to five every day, and the rest of his time and attention belongs to me. A woman needs to come first in her man's heart. Don't you agree?"

With that I couldn't argue.

"What's your name?"

"Seri."

"Where is he, and when will he be back?"

"Town. I don't know."

"Quite the chatterbox, aren't you? Do you mind if I wait here until he gets back?" Her tone suggested that she intended to do so whether I minded or not.

"As you please." I shrugged and started to leave.

She curled herself on the sofa and grinned at me. "Could you get me a cup of coffee?"

Though not usually at a loss for words, this small female's self-assurance stole my desire to trade veiled insults. Who was I to dispute her right to be here? But I didn't have to provide her refreshment.

"Oh, what precious kittens!"

Her exclamation stopped me. I rushed over and snatched the box from her hands. The kittens stirred in sleepy protest.

"I wasn't going to hurt them." Her lower lip pushed outward in a way I knew men would find alluring. "I'm surprised Brandon let them in the house. He abhors animals. Calls them four-legged, fur-bearing varmints. I love them. That was one of the reasons our marriage didn't work out."

Her revelation startled me. Nothing I'd seen bore out her statement. Though he didn't seem enamored of the phelines, he'd been gentle with them. From my experience, hate did not inspire kindness in men. Blinking and yawning, the kittens started to mewl and wiggle around.

"Can I hold them, please?"

Her soft appeal eased my apprehension for the kittens' safety. I put the box on the sofa and sat down next to her. "Injure them and you'll regret it."

"We're going to have to work on your conversation and social skills." She chuckled and picked up the gray kitten. "Do they have names?"

"The gray one is Ty." Their names popped into my head. "Dee is the black one, and this is Nix." I picked up the adventurous white kitten and, despite my misgivings about this woman, our shared laughter at the antics of the kittens dissolved my antagonism.

"Unless I'm mistaken, it looks like you have company." Hillary pointed to the classic, baby pink Cadillac convertible in Brandon's drive. "Or is that your visitor's?"

Brandon pulled Hillary's car to a halt and leaned his head against the wheel. "No. It's Wanda's." Could things get any worse? Wanda and Seri alone together? Which one would survive? There was only one way to find out.

"Wait here," he ordered.

"Hell, no." His agent jumped out of the car and followed him. "This I've got to see."

Brandon's mouth fell open as he stepped inside the front door, Hillary crowding in behind him. Seri and Wanda were sprawled on the floor, laughing. The three kittens crawled over them, attacking the fingers they wiggled.

The sound of Seri's easy laughter tugged at his heart. In the short time he'd known her, he'd never heard her laugh. Chuckle, but never a full laugh.

Yipping in excitement, Hillary's dog Muffin launched herself out of the bag. Not much bigger than the kittens, she landed in their midst. Chaos ensued. Hillary screamed.

Arching their backs at the intruder, the kittens spat and hissed. Muffin lunged, and they scattered. The gray kitten jumped on Wanda. Its tiny claws pricked through her sweater. She shrieked. Seri tried to grab the fleeing kittens, but they eluded her grasp.

Muffin charged the white one and got smacked in the nose. With a yelp of pain, she darted between Brandon's legs just as he started forward. In his attempt to keep from stepping on the dog, he tripped. Arms windmilling, he fell. Hillary grabbed for his shirt but missed.

Seeing a kitten directly in the path of his fall, at the last second Brandon twisted his body away from the open area. His head thudded against the edge of the hall table.

The lights went out.

At first I watched the scene unfold with humor. The sight of Brandon flailing his arms as he tried to avoid stepping on the yapping little canid, while Wanda shrieked and the other woman attempted to grab the creature, couldn't help but make me smile. Then Brandon fell. His head hit the table with a dull thud, and he lay still.

"Oh, no! Brandon! Is he bleeding?" Hands fluttering, Wanda backed away. "I can't stand the sight of blood."

The other woman pushed past and placed two fingers against his throat. "No, but he's unconscious."

"Maybe we should call 911," Wanda suggested.

The other woman looked around the room. "I don't see a phone." She pulled a small object from her purse and poked at it. "I can't get a signal on my cell, can you?"

Wanda grabbed a bag off the floor and took out a similar object. "No, but . . ."

The two women ignored me as they argued over what to do. Brandon groaned, and they both jumped back.

The sight of him lying hurt and defenseless shook me in more ways than one. Despite his obvious lack of magical ability, his words had brought me to life. He anchored me in this world. If something happened to him, what would become of me? Would his death mean mine as well, or would it prevent me from leaving this world?

Yet his helplessness struck me deeper than this selfish reaction. From my first moment of self-awareness, his voice formed the center of my universe, the shining star I reluctantly circled for light and warmth. In the few hours I'd known him, his kindness, humor, and compassion intensified my feelings for him to a level of caring I'd sworn never to allow myself again.

Since Roark destroyed my family, my sole reason for life had been to end his reign of terror. Aside from basic physical requirements such as food and shelter, I rarely thought of what I needed or wanted from life. I pledged my skills to defend those under my protection, but I refused to open my heart to them. Doing so left a person vulnerable. This sudden concern for another disturbed me, made me question my purpose.

Brandon moaned. Further introspection would have to wait.

"Go get a wet towel," I told Wanda. "You"—I pointed at the other woman—"corral your beast." The little canid still pranced around the room. "Its shrill barking makes my head ache."

While the women responded to the authority in my voice and scurried off to do my bidding, I maneuvered Brandon's limp body onto the couch. By the time I'd finished my breath came hard. He was heavier than I'd thought.

Wanda returned and handed me a dripping towel. I wrung it out over a small basket situated near the couch and placed it against his brow. He groaned again and blinked.

"Brandon, can you hear me? Wake up, please." Wanda crowded close. I didn't object as she pushed me aside. Though he claimed they were no longer married, the concept of what he called divorce troubled me.

In my world—the world he'd created—marriage was for life. Men and women deliberated long and hard before they entered into that most sacred contract. Often they lived together for years, bearing many children before they took the final vows of matrimony. No one thought less of them for it. Those who married in haste would spend a lifetime repenting. Once spoken, only death could break those vows. Occasionally a married couple might choose not to live together, but they remained married until one partner died.

"What happened?" He struggled to a sitting position. The cloth plopped into his lap.

"You fell," the second woman answered.

"Hillary? Wanda? What are you doing here?"

"You don't remember?"

"No . . . yes." He touched the lump above his left ear and flinched. "God, my head hurts."

I stood off to the side out of his sight. Now that it was clear he would live, I let the other two hover over him.

"You should probably go to the hospital and get checked out," Hillary said.

"I'm fine."

"You're not fine. You banged your head pretty hard."

"How long was I unconscious?"

"Only a minute or two, but—"

"Just get me a couple aspirin. They're in the cabinet over the sink."

Wanda scurried off to the kitchen and in a few

seconds came back with a glass of water and several small white objects.

"You're sure you're okay?" Hillary leaned over the back of the couch. Wanda hovered behind her.

Brandon grabbed the objects from her hand, tossed them into his mouth, and took a gulp of the water. "Did I land on any of those stupid cats or Muffin?"

"The kittens are fine—they're hiding under the furniture—but Muffin is nursing a scratched nose and a bruised ego."

At the sound of her name, the guilty canid gave a happy woof and jumped out of Hillary's bag. "Oof!" The air whooshed out of Brandon as the canid landed on his belly. The beast scrambled up his chest to lick his face. Brandon closed his eyes and groaned but didn't object to this latest indignity.

"This is what happens when a man lets females into his life—he ends flat on his back with dog slobber all over him. What's next? *No.*" He held up his hand as both Hillary and Wanda started to speak. "Don't tell me. Whatever it is can wait until tomorrow. I'm going to bed. You ladies can sort yourselves out."

I had to smile at his aggrieved tone. He moved the little canid to the floor, then heaved himself off the divan. Ignoring the two other women's protests, he disappeared up the stairs.

"Now what do I do?" Wanda asked. "Daniel is getting impatient to get married, and I can't do that until Brandon signs these papers."

"You'll just have to come back tomorrow," Hillary said.

"No." Wanda plopped down on the divan and crossed her arms over her ample chest. "I'm not leaving here until he signs."

Hillary sat next to her. "And I can't go until I get the rest of his latest manuscript. I came straight from the airport. Didn't even arrange a hotel for the night—"

"Neither did I," Wanda said.

Hillary sighed. "Guess we're stuck here until tomorrow." Muffin jumped into her lap.

I felt a moment's irritation that their concern over the wizard seemed to have vanished; then I recalled my first selfish reaction to his injury. Who was I to judge them? And they had legitimate places in his life here, whatever those might be. These women knew him as I did not; they had long-standing relationships with him. All I had was the belief that he created me, and an overwhelming passion.

No place existed for me in this world. My destiny lay elsewhere. No matter the cost, I had to go back, but I had one thing left to do.

Early evening sunlight still filtered through the closed drapes as Brandon showered, took two more aspirin, and fell into bed. His head and body ached, and he craved the oblivion of sleep, but it eluded him. He knew he should have stayed downstairs and sorted out what Wanda and Hillary wanted, protected them from Seri, or her from them, he wasn't sure which. Instead he remained true to form, when the going got tough, he got going . . . away.

Avoidance. It had always worked before. Or so he told himself, though inside he knew the truth. Evading a problem never solved it, just postponed and usually compounded it. Alone, each woman was capable of mass destruction. He shuddered to think what trouble the three of them together could stir up. Total annihilation, probably his.

The sound of voices, a car door slamming, and the roar of an engine—Wanda's Cadillac's V-8 if he wasn't mistaken—distracted him. Good riddance. One down and two to go before his life returned to normal.

The emptiness inside him at the thought of Seri's departure was disturbing. Normal—if that's what the empty vacuum of his life had been—no longer held the same appeal. He forced himself not to get up and check to see if she'd stayed. If she decided to go back to wherever she'd come from, wouldn't he be better off?

Like old home movies, memories of the day flickered through his mind. Seri in his car, eyes wide with fear and wonder, watching the world whip by. Her delight at the sight of the goods displayed in the mall. How she looked, that filmy dress clinging to her body. Dressed in the vendor's faux warrior attire, her body tense as she prepared to kill her nemesis. The salty sweet taste of her fingers against his lips, and then the heady explosion of flavor and texture as her mouth met his. A different ache grew inside him, one that aspirin couldn't touch. As crazy as it might make him, each passing moment with Seri chipped away at his disbelief in her wild claims and opened him to hopes and dreams that had abandoned him long ago.

He dozed.

Footsteps moving past his door woke him. Though he couldn't make out the words, he recognized

Hillary and Wanda's voices. Shit, they were still here? A door opened and shut. Typical Hillary and Wanda, they'd invited themselves to stay, and, if he wasn't mistaken, commandeered the guest room. Which left Seri the living room couch.

He sat up, then fell back with a groan. Unlike his fictional characters who got the hell beat out of them, were shot full of arrows, were skewered by swords, fell off horses, and then with little more than a cup of herbal tea in the way of medicine did it all over again the next day without seeming to feel a thing, every muscle, bone, and joint in his body ached.

Tomorrow would be soon enough to deal with things.

*"Vicious as a tarak can be,
she never eats her own kits."*
—Brother Eldrin, Order of Light

Chapter Eight

The door clicked open. Brandon looked at the woman silhouetted in the doorway. Seri.

"May I enter?"

He scooted into a sitting position and managed to croak out, "Y-yes," from a throat gone suddenly dry.

She stepped into the room and closed the door behind her. The dim light heightened his other senses. He heard the swish of the cotton T-shirt she wore as she moved closer. Rich and warm, her scent teased his nose. His heart rate doubled.

Realizing that he clutched the sheet to his bare chest like some virginal historical romance heroine, he let it drop to his waist and said, "I'm sorry about Hillary and Wanda taking the guest room. Did you need something? There's extra linen in the hall closet. If you want, you can have my bed, and I'll take the couch for tonight." He found himself babbling.

As his eyes adjusted, he watched her walk over and stand next to him. He tried to swallow the lump in his throat.

"The bed will be fine." She lifted one knee onto

it and leaned forward. Her warm breath on his cheek sent a tremor through him. "But there is no reason for you to leave."

She trailed her fingertips across his chest as her lips teased the corner of his mouth. Heat surged into his groin. The boxers he wore tented.

"W-what are y-you doing?" He knew exactly what she had in mind, he just didn't know why.

Part of him wanted to reach out and grab her, wanted to take what she offered, wanted to lose himself in her, but it would be wrong. He might not be as strong, heroic, or honorable as his fictional hero, Donoval, but he refused to take advantage of this woman, to use her to satisfy his needs. As much as it would kill him to say no.

He took her hands in his and held her away from him. "What if there's someone else in your life? Being with me won't solve your problem. It won't help you find out who you are."

"There's no one else. I know who and what I am."

The conviction in her voice rattled him. Despite the impossibility of her being his fictional character come to life, he no longer doubted she believed it. In fact, at times he almost considered believing it himself. Would believing make his life easier or harder? He couldn't guess.

"*I* wonder, but either way, this isn't what you need."

She looked into his eyes. "Perhaps not, but it's what I want."

I expected Brandon's protest. I no longer thought of him as a wizard; whatever powers he had, he was also a man—the man I wanted.

I considered my limited experience in these matters, my relationship with Donoval. In my mind, Brandon's resemblance to the king of Shallon had faded. True, both men held themselves to a high standard of honor, but only during Donoval's softer moments, when he relaxed and was more Donnie than monarch, was there any similarity in personality. In more basic attitudes, the two men differed. Where Donoval demanded I submit to him, that I change myself to be what he needed, Brandon was more forgiving and nurturing, even if he claimed I wasn't who I said I was. His humor and gentle nature called to my battered soul. And though Donoval had claimed to love me, with him I could never come first. His people, his country, would always hold that spot. I had not missed the fact that Brandon had repeatedly put me first, and with no proclamations of any feelings.

"You can't want me," Brandon objected.

How wrong he was. He might not be a wizard, but he possessed a powerful magic that made me want to stay with him forever. Honor and duty be damned.

"Why do men feel they know what a woman wants better than she herself does? I want this. I want you."

"But—"

I cut off his objection by brushing my lips across his. "Tonight let me be Seri, a woman of your world. That is who you want me to be, and I want to feel real. Don't deny me."

"You *are* real," he said, cupping my cheek with his hand. "But this is wrong."

"Why?" I pressed a kiss into his palm and ran

my fingers down his chest, stopping just below his navel.

He groaned. "Because . . . I don't know, but . . ."

"If I'm real, allow me the freedom to make my own decisions."

"Yeah, but what about mine?" he asked.

"A wise man once said at the end of our lives we do not regret the things we've done, we regret those that we have not. I wish to die without regrets."

He looked deep into my eyes, searching for assurance. "You're sure about this?"

Was I? Once I gave myself to him, there'd be no going back. Though I claimed I could no longer love, I knew better. Like weather, love couldn't be commanded or controlled. Soft and healing or fierce and devastating, it came as it willed, regardless of what we humans wished, and left us to pay the price. Could I take the physical without yielding to the emotional?

"Yes."

"Wait. Let me get some protection," he said.

"Your words are strange. I need no protection against this." I slid my hand beneath the waistband of the loose undergarment he wore and curled my fingers around his heat. Hard beneath silky skin, forged in the fire of our passion, his cock jumped in my hand.

He sucked in his breath. "What about pregnancy? Are you on the pill?"

"Pill? How can a pill stop conception?" Possibly having a child was one of the reasons I'd resisted bonding with Donoval. As his queen, I would be expected to produce an heir. After the horrific deaths of my siblings, babies I'd nurtured, and, yes, loved with the fervor of one who knew none of that herself, I'd sworn never to expose myself to the pain again. Against reason, a longing so intense it stole my breath slammed into me: to have and hold a child of Brandon's in my body.

"It's a medicine like the herbal tea the healers in Barue give to women to prevent conception, only in pill form," he said. The remembered taste of the bitter brew Donoval had forbidden me to use dissolved my craving for what could never be.

When Brandon leaned over to rummage in the small chest next to the bed, his cock slipped out of my hand. I removed the tunic I wore. Cool air swirled over my damp skin, but it didn't ease the heat growing inside me.

"Got it," he cried, triumphantly holding up a tiny square package. "It's been around for a while. Let's hope it's still . . ." His voice trailed off.

Ignoring his stare, I eyed the package. "What is that?"

"What?" He shook his head. "It's a condom."

"How is it used?"

"I wear it over my . . . over me like this." He shimmied out of his undergarments and rolled the milky colored sheath over his cock. "And it captures my sperm—er, seed—so you don't get pregnant . . . or so we don't transmit any diseases between us."

I nodded. "I understand. I have seen similar objects made of sheep intestine, but none so delicate." I stroked the length of him. The sheath felt slippery beneath my fingers. How would it feel inside me? Donoval had refused to don the sheep-gut kind, forcing me to secretly drink the healers' bitter brew. "Most men would disdain to wear such. Does it not dampen sensation?"

He groaned and shuddered. "Not nearly enough. Keep that up and the damn thing isn't going to be necessary. It's been a long time."

"For me as well." Long, barren, lonely years. I leaned over him. My breasts, heavy with desire, the nipples sensitized, brushed against the firm wall of his chest. Pleasure slid down my spine like honey down my throat, sweet and smooth.

He reached for me.

"No. Let me play." When I pushed his arms above his head, he didn't resist.

Determined to make our encounter last, I began my exploration of his body. I tasted the hollow behind his ear, then circled the tip of my tongue inside the shell. His breath grew short and ragged. Sweat moistened his body. I trailed my lips down his throat to his chest.

"You're killing me." The firm muscles of his chest tensed beneath me as he fisted the bed sheets in his hands. "Let me touch you."

"Not yet." I laved the flat disk of his nipple, then blew gently. It pebbled to a hard nub. I suckled it. The salty taste of him flooded my mouth. Warmth unfolded inside me. Moisture seeped between my thighs, readying my sheath for his sword.

Inch by inch, I stroked, kissed, and licked my way over him, learning his shape, texture, and taste. I knew my dominion over him was an illusion, one he granted me out of consideration. Still, his surrender pleased and amazed me.

Donoval, for all his bedroom skill, had never

allowed me to direct any of our encounters. Our couplings, though they provided physical release, were more battle than love play. They oftentimes left me discontented and angry.

With each touch, Brandon's control stretched nearer the breaking point. Soon the need inside him would burst, and he'd seize command. I anticipated it but wished to delay as long as possible. Being in charge excited me more than I'd believed possible.

Crisp hair tickled my nose as I nuzzled his heavy testicles. Like fresh-mown hay, his warm earthy scent filled my lungs. His sheathed cock bobbed enticingly before my eyes. I captured it in my hand. A slippery substance with a sharp unpleasant odor covered the sheath. Wanting to touch and taste his flesh, I stripped the sheath away. Before he could protest, I took the thick, hot, hard length of him into my mouth.

He gave a strangled groan. His hands clasped my head, whether to hold me to him or push me away I couldn't tell. As his hips began their ancient dance, I followed.

"Seri, have mercy. I can't stop."

Warm and salty, his seed filled my mouth. Enjoying my power over him, I drank in his essence. He shuddered and went limp.

After a few minutes, he pulled me up alongside him and smiled.

Limp and sticky, Brandon's cock lay against his thigh. Breath stuttered through his lips. He'd thought he knew what sex was all about. Damn, he'd written more than a few love scenes, but nothing in his life or fiction came close to what he'd just experienced with Seri. The feel of her hands and mouth on his body had burned away rational thought, left him paradoxically drained and energized.

He wrapped his arms around her. Her breasts pressed flat against his chest, her nipples hard points of pleasure. Laughter lurked in her eyes as she met his gaze; a smug smile hovered on her moist lips. He kissed her and tasted the salty residue of himself.

In moments, to his astonishment, his cock swelled. He felt her lips widen in a grin under his.

He pulled back and smiled at her. "Pleased with yourself, are you?"

She tilted her head and lowered her eyelids as she rubbed herself against him. The moist hair at the juncture of her thighs felt damp and rough against his sensitized flesh.

"Aren't *you* satisfied?" She curled her fingers around him.

Those cool fingers against his heated flesh made him jump. "Not quite."

"So I see." She chuckled.

The feel of her hand alternately squeezing and stroking sent shudders through him. Before he lost it again, he captured and removed it. "My turn," he said as he rolled her beneath him.

"Your turn for what?" Her eyes sparkled with amusement.

"This."

He covered her mouth with his in a long, leisurely kiss of exploration. With the tip of his tongue, he stroked the closed line on her lips, teasing and tasting until they parted on a sigh of surrender, releasing the citrus scent of the orange juice she favored. He delved within, enjoying the tart, sweet flavor, her eager response, and the tension building between them.

While they kissed, his hands ventured lower. Beneath his searching fingers the skin of her throat and shoulders felt like warm suede, smooth and supple, throbbing with vitality. Inch by inch, with hands and mouth he continued his exploration. With the backs of his fingers, he stroked the soft curves of her chest. He cupped the warm, heavy weight of her breasts in his hands. The feel of her nipples pressing into his palms demanded his attention.

She gasped as he sucked one swollen nub into his mouth. He rolled it between his lips, then rasped his tongue across its pebbled areole. To grant him easier access, she arched her back, and when he finally pulled his mouth from her breast, she gave a moan of protest.

With his tongue, he next probed the damp hollow of her navel. She shuddered. He caressed the small swell of her belly, then threaded his fingers through the warm damp curls between her thighs. Beneath his hands, her muscles quivered. Her soft sounds of pleasure urged him on.

When he bent his head to taste her, she squeaked in surprise and tried to clamp her thighs together. He held them apart and used his lips and tongue to explore her intimate secrets. The earthy smell and taste of her filled his nose and mouth. Slick with desire, her body easily accepted the finger he inserted. A flood of warmth flowed over his hand. She made a mewing sound and fine tremors coursed through her, but she no longer tried to stop him. Instead she clutched and twisted the bedding.

Using his finger, he stroked in and out while he

sucked the center of her pleasure. Her fine tremors turned to thrashing. Then she cried out and went rigid as she climaxed. Still, he continued.

"Enough!" She jerked away.

He didn't protest as she pushed him onto his back and straddled his hips. He was more than ready. His cock stood at attention. Without warning, she plunged down and enveloped him.

As much as he wanted to make the moment last, the sight of her flushed cheeks, hungry eyes, and swollen breasts as she rode him hard and fast drove him over the edge. Pleasure grabbed him in its silken talons, ripped him from his precarious perch, and plunged him into an unknown realm of ecstasy far beyond the physical.

From her cry of triumph, he knew she followed.

He also knew his life would never be the same: he loved her.

Drained of passion, we lay together, our bodies spent and content to be so. Brandon slept, but my thoughts kept me awake.

I'd selfishly taken what I wanted: control, power, sex. But had I given him what I sensed he wanted? Commitment? Love? Physical release was easy, but the rest? Could I stay with him? Could I become the real woman he claimed? Was my wanting him enough to justify abandoning the world I knew? Abandoning those that counted on me? Abandoning duty? Abandoning honor?

Though Brandon's passion and the details of this strange transportation to his world suggested that my own reality didn't truly exist, that the people there were not living, breathing beings with existences to live or lose, I discovered my heart did not agree. *I* lived. *I* breathed. How could I believe that they did not do so as well? Donoval? Mauri? How could I not trust my experiences and my relationships? And once again, there was another consideration: if I stayed in this world, would their lives continue or end? I couldn't afford to take the risk. No. Despite what I might desire, honor decreed my destiny lay in Barue, that I return there no matter what. To an existence without true consciousness.

Brandon's eyes opened to regard me with male satisfaction. He stroked his hand down my arm to my hip and tugged me against him. The feel of his arousal pressing into my belly weakened my resolve. What did it matter if I stayed a few more minutes . . . or hours? Barue would wait.

Or would it? How did time elapse there compared to here?

As if he sensed my mental pulling away, Brandon's hand stilled. He searched my face. "What's wrong?" he asked.

I sat up and mustered my nerve. "I don't belong here," I said. "Send me back to my world." My words fell between us, a rain of ice.

"You're wrong." He sat beside me, took my face between his palms, and forced me to meet his gaze. "There is no other world. You're a real person. You've always been a real person. You're not a fictional creation of mine. You have a problem, sure, but we can get you help. I think that—"

I pulled away from him. "Why can't you see the truth?"

"Why can't you?" His tone grew heated. "I won't let you retreat back into your fantasy. Believe me, I know how hard it is not to. I've been trying to escape the real world all my life. It's taken me a long time to realize the truth. It can't be done. This is all there is, all any of us have. Stay here. With me. Deal with real life. I'll help you. I . . ."

He didn't say the one thing that might have swayed me to stay. "Why did you bring me here?" I asked.

He jerked his hands away. Deprived of his heat, my cheeks grew cold, along with my heart.

"For the last time: I'm not a wizard. I didn't bring you here. And you're not a fictional character out of some damned book! You're a living, breathing woman." Anger and exasperation dripped from his voice like blood from a sword. "And you're driving me as nuts as you are."

"I'm not like Wanda or Hillary. I don't belong. I'll never belong," I growled. "Not here." I had to make him see, to understand.

"Well, you're damned well stuck here, because even if I did believe your crazy delusion, I have no idea how to send you anywhere but the loony bin." And with those words, he stomped into the bathing chamber and slammed the door.

I sighed. I'd have to find another way back.

A familiar odor from the past woke Brandon. Wanda's specialty: burnt bacon, scorched eggs, blackened toast, and toxic coffee. He'd lied to Seri. It wasn't that Wanda wouldn't cook; it was that no matter how hard she tried, she *couldn't* cook. And, he admitted grudgingly, she had tried. But during their marriage, her cooking skills never improved.

He buried his face in his pillow to block the

smell and recapture the memory of his night with Seri. Her scent, rich and honeyed, lingered on the bedding. How many times had they made love after he'd returned from the bathroom? Four? Five? He'd lost count. A stupid, macho grin crept over his lips. He pushed aside the thought of how they'd fought, just as they hadn't spoken of it again last night.

"Brandon? Are you awake?" Hillary asked, rapping on the bedroom door.

"Go away. I'm still asleep."

As he spoke, memory dissolved into guilt. And not about his book or Hillary. Despite her willingness, he'd had no right to make love to Seri. And not using protection was more than wrong, it was criminal. What if she got pregnant? Although . . . somehow the thought of Seri's taut belly growing round with his child didn't horrify him the way he thought it should, the way it had with Wanda.

Well, he'd deal with that situation if it happened. First he had to find out who Seri was. Make sure she was free and sane. And convince her to stay.

"Wanda made breakfast." Hillary's voice punched through his musings. His head started to pound.

"I can smell it."

She rapped again. "Come on down. We have business to discuss."

"All right already. Give me a minute."

Five minutes and four aspirin later, he made his way into the kitchen. Seven pairs of eyes, all female—three human, one dog, and three kittens—turned on him. The acrid smell of estrogen hung in the room; or maybe it was smoke from the burnt toast.

"Morning," he muttered.

"Brandon, I'm getting married, but first you need

to sign these." Wanda shoved a sheaf of papers at him.

"I said it on the phone, but the publisher is getting antsy about the delay in your manuscript. And the film company needs your screenplay by the end of next week or the option expires."

Wanda and Hillary spoke together. Seri remained silent. Lips twitching around the edge of the cup she held, she looked up at him. The look of resolve and sadness darkening her eyes set Brandon's already frayed nerves to jangling.

The phone rang. The phone? Seri had destroyed it; how could it ring? Brandon looked around. A new cordless phone sat on the counter. It rang again. He picked it up.

"Hello?"

It was Rich at the garage telling him he'd picked up the SUV. Brandon listened to the details, then said, "I appreciate you letting me know. Thank you." Then he hung up. "Where did this come from?" he asked.

"Wanda and I picked it up last night. You don't get cell phone reception here, and there's no way I can be out of contact," Hillary explained.

The phone rang again.

"Hello," Brandon answered, listened, then handed the phone to Hillary. "It's for you."

She snatched the phone from his hand and began a heated conversation as she headed out into the living room.

"Brandon!" Wanda snatched the papers from where he'd laid them on the counter. "I need you to sign . . ."

"Coffee. First I need coffee." He started toward the coffeemaker. Something sharp pricked his ankle. "Ouch!" He looked down to see two of the kittens, one gray and one black, clinging to his pant leg. The third kitten, the white one who'd crashed his car, sat a few feet away, carefully cleaning its paw and watching him. "It's going to be a long day."

Seri chuckled. His own lips twitched in response.

Two cups of strong, black coffee and ten minutes of silence later, Brandon felt nearly human. His body still ached, but his head no longer throbbed like a pounded bass drum. He sat at the kitchen table. Muffin lay on his bare feet, and the two kittens, the gray and black ones, snoozed in his lap. He absently stroked their soft fur as he sipped his coffee. For one glorious moment, he felt at peace.

Across from him, Wanda fidgeted. He studied her. Though a bit more rounded, with a few extra lines around her mouth and eyes, at thirty-two she didn't look much different from when they'd met and married so many years ago.

Shy and reclusive by nature, he'd been attracted to her zest for life, her ability to charm people. What attracted her in return he'd never been quite sure. They mixed like the proverbial oil and water. He'd hoped being with her would help him blend into the world better; instead, her demands had driven him deeper into himself.

Now he knew her cotton candy looks, her helpless-little-me act, and scatterbrained behavior hid a cunning little cat, too. She used her childlike demeanor to fool people and get what she wanted from life. But in marrying him, she'd miscalculated. He regretted he wasn't capable of giving what she needed.

He finally picked up and read the papers she kept shoving in front of him. Every remnant of peace drained away. The day went from bad to worse.

"Married! We're still married?" Panic-induced sweat beaded his upper lip.

"Just until you sign the papers," she soothed, then went on in a breathless rush. "It's not that bad. Nothing else changes." She wrapped his numb fingers around a pen and guided his hand to the paper. "Just sign. Please."

As much as he wanted to dash his signature off and have her gone from his life, he hesitated. Why was she in such a hurry? She never did anything without a reason. "What's going on, Wanda?"

To his horror, she burst into tears. "I'm getting m-married n-next week," she explained between heaving sobs. "Daniel d-doesn't know about the mix-up with the p-papers. He already thinks I'm s-scatterbrained."

Brandon had to agree with Daniel's assessment. Despite her deviousness, he sometimes wondered how the woman managed to breathe and walk at the same time. She was an odd mix of traits.

"And I'm p-pregnant," she wailed.

Muffin started to bark. The kittens in Brandon's lap woke with a hiss. Tiny claws dug into him as the beasts climbed up his chest. He grabbed one cat in each hand. Without a word, Seri carefully put down her cup and slipped out of the room.

Hillary rushed in from the other room to Wanda's side. "What did you do to her?" she barked.

Great. At some point during the night, the two women had bonded. He deposited both kittens under the table where they proceeded to try and climb up his leg again. Wincing at the prick of their claws, with one hand he tried to shoo them off, and with the other he scribbled his signature on the provided forms, then thrust them into Wanda's hands.

"Oh, thank you, Brandon!" She hurried to his side and enveloped him in a quick hug. The cloying scent of her sweet perfume tickled his nose, making him long for the clean scent of woman and leather that clung to Seri. He wondered how he'd ever fallen for his ex.

"You're welcome. And congratulations." He sneezed and grimaced as the kittens made it up into his lap. Muffin bounced around his legs, yapping.

"This is such a weight off my mind." Wanda gathered the papers to her chest. "I was so afraid Daniel would want to postpone the wedding if he found out."

Brandon shook his head in disbelief. "I'm no marriage counselor, but I think you might want to tell him the truth."

"Thank you again. You're a lifesaver." She didn't respond to his suggestion. "Good-bye."

Typical Wanda. Once she had what she wanted, she left.

After she was gone, Brandon turned to meet Hillary's glare. "What?" he asked in confusion.

She stood, arms crossed over her chest, her

high-heel-clad foot tapping an incessant rhythm.
She sniffed. Muffin nipped at Brandon's foot.

"Hell! Okay, okay! I'll be in my office . . .
writing."

I watched Brandon's bondmate—no, former bondmate, I reminded myself—leave. After the roar of
her vehicle faded, the older woman, Hillary, stomped
into the living room and plopped down on the sofa.
Her little canid jumped into her lap and bared its
teeth at me before curling up for a nap.

"Men. I'll never understand them." Hillary's tone
indicated disgust. "Brandon thought he was divorced from Wanda and claimed he was happy
about it. Now, when she arrives here asking him to
sign a few papers to validate that divorce, he hesi-
tates. What's with that?"

I understood none of her logic. The concept of
dissolving a marriage outside of death made me
uncomfortable, as I suspected it did Brandon. Else,
why would he have made it impossible in the world
he created?

His release from Wanda could mean nothing to
me, either. I wasn't free to claim him. Nonetheless,
I couldn't deny my relief that he was no longer
bound to another woman.

Brandon hung up the phone. The conversation with
Sam had been easier than he feared, as if the time
they hadn't spoken had been days rather than years.
Brandon acknowledged the ease between them was
Sam's doing rather than his. After talking with his
old buddy, Brandon wondered why he'd let the
friendship lapse.

Either way, he'd given Sam the all the information he had about Seri—which, granted, wasn't much—and Sam had promised to get right on it. Until then, as he'd told Hillary, Brandon decided to finish up his last Warrior Woman book.

He slipped upstairs to his office. Though he wasn't 100 percent happy with the story, to get Hillary out of his hair and house and back to New York, he'd turn it in as written. He'd deal with revisions and edits later, when and if his life reverted to normal.

After he forced himself to separate Serilda from Seri in his mind, the words began to flow; his writer's block had dissolved. He let the real world fade away, and he immersed himself in the final, deadly confrontation between Serilda d'Lar and Andre Roark.

As his fingers flew over the keyboard, he saw the bodies. Tasted the blood. Smelled the death. Heard the screams. Felt the pain. Tears of rage and grief streamed unnoticed down his cheeks.

Pulling her sword, Serilda stepped forward into the tempest. The hidden entrance at the back of the castle opened onto a narrow ledge overlooking a deep chasm. Icy rain lashed her cheeks, freezing her hot tears but unable to cool the rage burning inside her.

Mauri lay dying. The girl's innocent blood stained Serilda's sword, but Roark's evil was the cause. She'd taken the girl's life, but Roark had stolen her soul. Now he'd pay.

Lightning flashed. She saw Roark creeping along the castle wall, away from the edge of the cliff.

"Stand and face me, coward!" Against the roar of thunder and the pounding of the rain, her shout was no more audible than a whisper.

Sword in hand, Roark whirled. The wind whipped away his answer. Unmindful of the dangerous footing, she surged forward.

He met her attack. Metal clanged against metal, blade against blade. Sparks flew into the night. Long, breathless minutes passed as they fought their way down the edge of the narrow ledge. One wrong step and they'd tumble into the blackness below.

Serilda lunged. Swords crossed above their heads, and their bodies collided.

"Did you think I'd let you escape my justice?" she snarled in his ear.

With a laugh, he wrenched free. Metal screeched as their swords scraped apart. She circled, looking for an opening. Her feet danced along the slippery rock.

"I had confidence you'd follow." He gripped his sword in both hands and moved in concert with her attack with her.

"Before you die, tell me why?"

"Why what, daughter?"

At the reminder that his blood flowed like acid through her veins, she swallowed in disgust and pressed forward, testing his defense.

He countered her blows. The impact ran through her arms. She staggered back.

"The question is not 'why,' but 'why not?'"

She wiped the rain from her eyes. Or was it

tears? "You were the king's most trusted advisor, his friend and confidant. You had wealth, status, power. His love. Anything you wanted was yours."

Roark shook his head. "It wasn't enough. The people worshipped him like a god when he was just a man. He had more than he deserved—what I deserved. And I had the ability, so I took it."

"You're a fool. You betrayed and killed the royal family, and in the end, it gained you nothing. When the people learned of your treachery, they turned against you."

Above the pounding rain and behind her, she heard the clatter of boots, but she didn't dare turn to look if friend or foe approached; Roark would seize such an advantage and make her pay.

Her enemy glanced over her shoulder, but his face revealed nothing. "I wanted you to reign at my side, daughter. But your misplaced loyalty to a dead king makes that impossible. When you're gone, the people's last hope will fade. They'll return and swear me allegiance."

"My death wouldn't secure their love, only their fear and loathing. But when you're dead, and when the heir to the throne is found, peace and prosperity will return to Barue."

His chuckle chilled her. "Without me, you'll never find him."

"Who is he? Where is he? Tell me and I'll allow you to live."

As she took a step forward, her feet slid on the slick stone. She struggled to regain her balance. Her sword dipped. Roark lunged.

"No!"

Serilda heard Donoval's anguished cry from behind her. She looked down. Roark's sword protruded from her chest. Funny, but she felt nothing more than a slight pressure. Her fingers went numb. Her sword slipped from her hand to the stone wall as she struggled to maintain her balance.

Roark gripped her shoulder and pulled her close, forcing his blade through her to the hilt. Pain stole her breath while his blew warm across her icy cheek. His eyes blazed with triumph—and something more. Surprised, Serilda recognized it as regret.

Their bodies twisted, and over Roark's shoulder she saw Donoval, sword raised, rushing toward them.

"Too late, my love," she mouthed. He shook his head in denial and tried to increase his speed across the treacherous ledge.

She turned her gaze back to Roark and rasped, "Tell me who he is." As her life drained away, and with the last of her strength, she curled her fingers around his upper arms.

"Your dying request? Of course, daughter."

"Who?"

"Young Jole."

In the silence after a peal of thunder, Roark's voice sounded loud and clear. For a brief moment, pleasure wiped away pain and sorrow. Serilda looked up and met Donoval's gaze. His hair whipped around his face. Yards still separated them, but he'd heard. And he knew what she intended.

A sense of peace came over her. Though she'd never trusted Donoval with her heart, she trusted him with everything else—most especially, to see to the welfare of Barue and its rightful young king.

Roark let go of her shoulder and tried to step back, but she held him fast. Her legs buckled, and she swayed toward the ledge.

Panic flared in Roark's eyes. He struggled to pry her fingers loose. "What are you doing? Let me go!"

Even as the world faded from view, she smiled. "I think not, Father." She folded Roark into her embrace and leaned into nothingness.

"Serilda! No!" Over the thunder, Donoval's cry echoed through the night. It was the last word she heard.

Drained of energy, Brandon leaned back in his chair. It was done. Finished. Ended. The book and the series. And he knew it was good. Powerful.

So, why did it feel wrong?

Brandon had left to meet with his friend in a place called Chicago—he'd given me a strange look and explained something had come up expectedly—and Hillary, manuscript in hand, had departed smiling. Alone in the house, I let my feet take me toward

Brandon's office. I peeked in. He'd never said anything about the damage I'd caused, and the desk had been straightened.

The still, humid air that filled the house, heavy with the promise of more rain, matched my mood. Though it wasn't necessary to wear my sword here, I found comfort having a piece of my world on my hip. I knew what I needed to do, what I'd been considering for a while now, but my nerve nearly failed me as I approached the office bookshelves. I reached out and picked out a volume, and settling into Brandon's chair, I began to read. In moments I was transported back to my world—at least, in my mind; my body remained tenaciously planted in Brandon's reality.

Word by word, I relived the horror of my siblings' and parents' murders, the senseless destruction of the gentle monks, my vows of vengeance against Roark, my warrior training, my love affair with Donoval. Against my will I reexperienced every emotion, every sensation. On and on it went until my heart, which I'd believed no longer capable of feeling, seemed to tear apart inside me.

And still, I read. I no longer wondered at Brandon's magic with words, how he'd brought me to life. I read it on the page. He'd captured my isolation, my anguish, my rage, my fear.

Hours passed. The light outside faded to dusk. With each page, I felt myself being sucked back into my world, growing less anchored in Brandon's reality. This was what I'd hoped for, what I wanted.

As I finished the sixth book, the weather reflected my churning emotions. Windblown rain battered the windows. Lightning streaked through rolling black clouds. Thunder growled across the sky.

Yet, nothing I'd read was new to me. I'd lived it all. Felt it all. And my body clung stubbornly to this existence, to hope.

There had to be more. What came next? I had to know. Maybe this would be what I sought.

Beside the board with the keys sat my answer. A stack of paper with neatly printed words beckoned me. The top page read:

WARRIOR WOMAN
THE FINAL BATTLE

This was what Brandon was working on. My hand trembled as I reached for those pages. My future, my fate, lay in the words printed there. Did I have the courage to read them? To know? To leave this world and experience my fate for the sake of those I loved? To leave Brandon?

I read—and learned why Roark hadn't killed me along with my family when I was a child. Why my mother and father hadn't been able to love me. Why Roark had tried so hard to force me to his side. The pages fell to my lap. The answer broke the heart I'd believed I no longer had: Andre Roark was my father. I was his child from the rape of my mother.

Hot tears warmed my frozen cheeks but couldn't touch the ice encasing and crushing my shattered heart. My whole life was a lie! Hysterical laughter bubbled up inside me. Of course it was a lie. I wasn't real. Nothing about me existed. Not my past.

Not my present. Not my future. The future I had yet to read.

As I lifted the pages, darkness blanketed the room. I screamed in frustration. Lightning answered my plea, a series of flashes, and with that intermittent illumination I read on.

"The future is not written in stone; it is shaped by the hearts and minds of men."
—Brother Eldrin, Order of Light

Chapter Nine

Though Brandon found he enjoyed reconnecting with his old friend—he didn't even mind looking at dozens of pictures of Sam's new baby—he returned from his trip to Chicago even more confused than when he'd left.

Despite his best efforts over the last few days, Sam hadn't found out anything about Seri. No birth records. No Social Security number. No missing persons reports. No wanted posters. No airline, train, or bus tickets to Council Falls or any town within walking distance. No cars rented by anyone matching her description. Nothing. Before she'd appeared in Brandon's living room, she hadn't seemed to exist. Sam was baffled.

Few people were capable of leaving no trail. In spite of her wild claims, or perhaps because of them, Brandon didn't believe Seri was one of those few.

In the growing darkness, he pointed his rental car toward home. Wind buffeted his vehicle as he drove, and ahead, lightning streaked the horizon. Rain splattered against his windshield.

Though he and Seri parted with nothing resolved between them, he was eager to be with her again. Being apart had given him more time to consider. Even if they never discovered her true identity, even if she clung to her odd story, somehow he'd find a way to make their relationship work. Whoever she was, wherever she'd come from, he wanted her in his life. He just needed to convince her to stay.

As the miles passed, primal instinct urged him to hurry. Something felt . . . wrong. As if to delay him, the storm increased. Torrents of rain worked the wipers overtime; his car's headlights struggled to pierce the watery gloom.

He hunched forward and peered through the fogged windshield. As the storm's intensity grew, so did his apprehension.

Ahead, his house stood silent and dark. No lights glowed through the windows; there were no sounds but the roaring storm. Brandon ran through the rain and into the house. Breathing hard, he skidded to a halt. Where was Seri? The kittens? Chilled and empty, his home felt as vacant as his heart.

Bolt after bolt of lightning lit the sky, illuminating the rooms through which he passed. Thunder roared, shaking the house, charging the air. His skin prickled with dread as he reached the kitchen.

Over the thrum of the pounding rain he heard it: a low agonized cry. It came from his office.

His final manuscript! No, she couldn't read it! Why had he thoughtlessly left it lying on his desk? There were things about the world he'd created that Seri didn't know, things that would shock her.

Things that would hurt her. Things that might push her over the edge of sanity. He dashed up the stairs and burst into his office.

Head bent, shoulders bowed, Seri stood by the window. The sheaf of papers she held fluttered in a phantom breeze, or from the trembling of her hands. The light of the storm cast her face in unforgiving shades of black and white.

"Seri?"

At the sound of his voice, she looked up. Her face devoid of emotion, she met his gaze.

He started toward her.

"Don't." She shook the papers violently. "How could you? My world. My people. My life. They all mean nothing to you. Toys. Puppets to manipulate. To what purpose? You are indeed a wizard—and if you create worlds and people solely to make them suffer, an evil one."

"Seri." He moved toward her cautiously. "They're just words on a page. They're not real. You are."

He jumped back as she grabbed her sword. Maybe denying her delusion was not the wisest course.

She held the manuscript above her head and pointed her blade at his heart. "For a short time, I almost believed you. I deluded myself that I could be 'Seri.' That I could remain here. That I could abandon my world, my people. That I could . . . be with you." Her voice trembled then grew hard. "But I am Serilda d'Lar of the kingdom of Barue. I will deny that no longer."

She dropped the manuscript, and its pages swirled around her to the floor. Gripping her sword in both hands, she held it above and before her. Almost impossibly, lightning appeared on its tip, glimmering, sizzling. And with a crack of thunder, it streaked downward to encircle her.

Seri's body undulated. Her hair danced around her head, crackling with pinpoints of light. Her mouth opened in a scream that was drowned out by another boom of thunder. For one endless moment, their gazes met. Then, as Brandon watched in helpless horror, she vanished.

He stood alone in the middle of his office. She was gone. Shock made him oblivious to the pain he knew he'd soon feel.

The smell of ozone and burnt paper hung heavy in the air. Scorched sheets of his manuscript fluttered across the floor in another phantom breeze. Outside, the rain fell in heavy sheets, but the windows were closed. Thunder grumbled like ancient plumbing.

With a snap, the power came back on. Brandon heard his computer beep. His desk lamp cast a circle of light over the paper-littered room.

He sagged into his chair. Against all reason, he now believed she was what she claimed: Serilda, his fictional character. Or maybe it was not so unreasonable. Seeing her vanish in a flash of light dispelled all doubt. "If all possible explanations are ruled out, then the impossible must be true," he muttered.

Too late he believed. She was gone.

Another author complaining about suffering from writer's block had once told him that in fiction, the writer was God and all the characters were atheists. At the time, he'd laughed, not entirely sure what the man meant. Brandon didn't consider himself God, and Serilda was no atheist. But she was his creation. Yet, she was gone.

He snatched a sheet of paper out of the air. His own words stabbed into him, shredding his blanket of numbness. *She'd read them.* Discovered the secret of her shrouded past. Learned of his deceit. Accepted her fate, gone back to it willingly. Pain squeezed his chest until his breath came in ragged gasps.

The memory of that look of betrayal, of fear and resignation in her eyes as she disappeared exposed Brandon for what he was: a liar, a cheat, and a coward. For years he'd lied and cheated himself out of living a real life. And was too cowardly to accept Seri for herself. But what could he do? The situation was beyond his understanding, beyond his control, beyond his ability to change.

But was it? The paper crumpled in his fist. He swung around to his desk and attacked the computer, drew up a file and began work. Possessed by a sense of urgency, his fingers flew across the keyboard.

Words were his strength, his weapon, his shield. With words he could do anything. He spilled them upon the screen like blood across a battlefield. He drained them from his body, from his very soul.

Lightning streaked the sky. Thunder crashed. Lights flickered, threatening to go out. The image on the monitor rolled; his heart stuttered, then steadied.

He typed faster, his words coming without thought as he attempted to alter Seri's destiny.

Lightning flashed. Power surged. Pain flared.

Brandon fell into darkness.

Brandon

Chapter Ten

Serilda woke. A dream hovered at the edge of her mind, a warm, sweet, elusive temptation to return to slumber. Then it faded, leaving her feeling as if she'd lost something precious but unsure of what it might be.

Better she not remember. Dreams had no place in her life. Existence in Barue was not for dreamers. Those who stopped fighting in order to dream soon died of harsh reality.

In the three years she'd been fighting Roark, she'd watched many good men die. Too many. But long before that she'd known of his evil. He'd killed her family, murdered the monks who'd raised her. As trusted advisor to the king, he'd murdered the royal family as well, but it took another fifteen years before the government recognized him for what he was. During those years, he'd used his position as head of the ruling council to oppress the people, fatten his coffers, and amass an army. Then, when he felt assured no one could oppose him, he struck, seized control of the government.

He'd misjudged not only his own strength and the strength of the council but also the strength of the people. They hadn't sat placidly. They'd risen up against him, and she was happy to lend her sword arm to the cause.

Though she and her troops had managed to keep Roark from gaining complete control, the devastation he'd wrought with his tyrannical government that he did control had damaged Barue and its people. It was past time to bring Roark's reign of terror to an end. Serilda intended to do so.

She started to stretch. Bruised and battered, her muscles protested the movement. Squeezing her eyes shut, she groaned.

Another memory had her touching her throat to assure herself her head remained attached to her body. Battle the previous day had not gone well. By ignoring Hausic's wise counsel against a frontal assault, she'd led too many good men to unnecessary deaths—another remorse to weigh down a soul already burdened with guilt. Now Roark was forewarned of her presence. He'd retreated inside his castle fortress, and a sneak attack on his encampment was no longer possible.

Sitting up, Serilda shook off her sense of impending doom. One lost battle did not lose a war. As long as she breathed, Barue would not cede completely to her enemy.

The tent lay in shadows. Dawn had yet to break. She pushed aside the bed robes, and, naked, she shivered in the chill morning air. In the small stove, white ash coated the coals and gave off no heat.

As she shifted to rise, her hip bumped a source

of warmth beneath the bed robes. Snatching up her sword, she shot to her feet.

The lump groaned but didn't stir. She used the tip of her sword to shift the bed robes aside.

"Donnie?" she asked. Though he lay with his face turned from her view, she recognized him. Reluctant pleasure mingled with her surprise at his presence in her bed. Since they'd parted, she'd often regretted the lack of his warmth next to her.

He sprawled across her bed on his belly in all his naked splendor.

Despite the white ragged lines of the battle scars marring the perfection of his golden skin, splendid he was. Broad shoulders tapered to a narrow waist, taut buttocks, and trim hips. Muscles corded his arms and legs. Even his feet were well formed. Serilda knew the tangled golden hair framed the face of a seraph.

In the years since she'd kicked him out of her bed, out of her life, out of her heart, she'd forgotten—or told herself she'd forgotten—the beauty of his form. She'd lied. Warmth flooded her belly and lower.

Why was he here? When she'd declined his offer of life bondage in favor of returning to Barue to oppose Roark, he'd given her arms and supplies but refused to send his troops. Had he changed his mind?

Along with the remembered heat, hope unfurled inside her. What would she do to convince him to help? What would she offer him? What would she sacrifice to see Roark defeated?

"Donnie." She prodded his hip with the tip of her sword.

* * *

Something pricked my hip. Damned kittens! I reached out to grab the blasted little varmints and drew back my hand with a yelp.

I bolted upright. My head spun. My vision blurred around the edges. When I tripped over that damn dog, I must have hit my head harder than I thought. Blinking away the spots, I stared in disbelief at the blood welling from the shallow slice across my palm.

"Don't just sit there bleeding all over my bed." Sword in hand, Seri stood over me. She tossed me a piece of cloth.

Confusion and pain flared in my mind and body. Every muscle and bone ached. My head continued to pound. The cut on my hand stung.

What had happened to me? I pushed past the throbbing in my head to think. Fingers of panic unfurled in my belly.

The last thing I remembered was typing frantically to change the ending of my final Warrior Woman book. In my attempt to put an end to the series, the final confrontation between Serilda and Roark had ended in both their deaths. When Seri vanished in front of me, I'd accepted the truth: she was my fictional creation. To save her from the deadly fate I'd written for her, I'd attempted to re-write the ending. Had I finished? I didn't know. A haze clouded my memory.

I must have done something right, because Seri stood in front of me, alive, angry, and gloriously naked. Desire hit me hard and fast. Even in the dim gray light that shadowed and leached the color from the room, her body glowed. At eye level, the crisp hair between her thighs tempted me to lean forward and taste her. I gulped, thankful for the scrap of cloth resting in my lap, and tore my gaze away.

Where was I? I looked around the room—anywhere but at Seri.

Not a room, a tent! Above me, canvas rippled. I sat on a bed. A pile of fur robes softened the simple wooden frame. My head whirled in disorientation.

I reached down to cover myself. The flat side of Seri's sword smacked my hand.

"You'll get blood on the bed robes. Here."

I strangled my shriek of alarm as she used the tip of the sword to lift the cloth from my groin and deposited it across my bleeding palm. Clutching the cloth to my hand, I managed to wrap a fur around my waist and stood. Blood rushed from my brain, leaving me woozy. I tried to blink away the dark spots dancing in front of my eyes.

Seri seemed to have no problem with her nudity. Anger faded from her gaze. A smile played around her lips as she watched me fumbling to preserve my dignity and maintain my precarious balance.

"Why are you here, Donnie?" She laid down her sword and shrugged into a robe.

Once her body was covered, my heart rate settled to near normal. My breathing eased. But my mind and vision didn't clear. Where was I?

"How did you get in here unchallenged? It seems my guards have become lax and lazy." Forehead puckered, she glanced around the small tent. "And where are your things? Your clothes?"

"Good questions," I muttered as I looked around the primitive tent. Where in the hell was I? How had I gotten here, wherever here was? Those fingers of panic closed into tight fists of terror.

Not waiting for my answer, she strode to the tent opening, lifted the flap, and spoke to a man standing guard. I missed what was said because outside the sun peeked over the horizon illuminating a scene straight out of a nightmare, straight out of one of my books.

Stunned, I could only stand and stare at row after row of shabby tents. Weary men dressed in ragged homespun clothing and battered, tarnished armor moved around the encampment, starting their day. Campfires burned low, sending trickles of smoke into the misty morning air. The smell of coffee brewing and meat cooking mingled with the odor of blood-soaked dirt. Somewhere a horse whinnied. Another answered. A dog barked. A man yelled. A thud followed. The dog yelped, then fell silent.

Openmouthed, I stared. Logic told me this couldn't be happening. I couldn't be where I thought I was. Could I? The direction of my thoughts made me question my sanity more than I'd ever questioned Seri's. As much as I wanted to believe I was dreaming, everything felt and smelled much too real for me to fool myself.

Seri let the flap drop, blocking my view of a world gone mad. She turned back to me. "It seems your skill at infiltration has improved." Her grin held a smidgen of dismay. "No one saw you arrive in camp or enter my tent. If you'd had this talent at Dennigon, it would have saved you several months in Alric's dungeon."

Dennigon? Alric? Dungeon? Baffled, I searched my memory. It came to me. She referred to an event in book two of Donoval's adventures when he'd attempted to steal into Lord Alric's castle. In that book, I introduced young Serilda. Growing trepidation kept me silent. Her account of what happened differed from what I wrote. Her world differed from the one I'd created. In my book, Donoval escaped capture without Serilda's help. Still, readers loved her character, and after one more Donoval story, I'd started Serilda's own series of books.

"After the way we parted, I'm surprised at your visit but not displeased. It's been a long time."

She came to stand next to me. The heady scent rising off her sleep-warmed skin distracted me. Her finger stroked down my arm in a wordless promise, leaving a trail of heat.

"I've missed you, Donnie," she continued, her voice pitched low. Her breath caressed my cheek. "Can I hope that you've reconsidered your decision not to back my fight against Roark?"

She thought I was Donoval? Why? I shook my head, not in answer to her question, but in denial. Strands of blond hair caught on the stubble of my beard. My hair. My blond hair. My *long* blond hair.

Hell, no! Donoval's long blond hair. My stomach fell. I didn't want to believe what my senses told me. Here in this world, Seri's world, I *was* Donoval. My thoughts were mine, but it appeared the body was Donoval's.

"If all possible explanations are ruled out, then the impossible must be true," I whispered.

What had happened to my real body in the real world? Was I lying in my office unconscious? Dead?

"No?"

I heard the anger return to her voice. She moved

away, leaving me feeling alone and adrift in a sea of bewilderment.

"Then why are you here? You know I'll not abandon my people to Roark's tender mercies."

Why was I here in Barue? Why was I here in my fictional world? Why was I here in Donoval's body? Why was I here in a nightmare? And more importantly . . . how? The questions made my head spin, my stomach clench, my vision blur. With a groan I sank to the floor.

"Donnie!"

Seri's cry of alarm followed me into blessed oblivion.

Serilda studied the maps spread out before her, but her thoughts focused on the man sleeping behind her. In the three years since she'd last had Donoval in her life, in her bed, much had changed.

She'd grown strong and independent, capable of charting her destiny. Inside, she admitted she owed part of that growth to him. His refusal to back her struggle to free Barue from Roark's tyranny had driven them apart, made her stand on her own. If he'd backed her, the coming victory—or defeat, she allowed—would be his, not hers. But his refusal to support her fight for Barue's freedom was not what had made her leave him. She could fight her own battles. His inability to see her as an equal, a person in her own right rather than a mere woman, an extension of himself, was what had come between them, what had kept her from giving herself to him body and soul. He demanded that she abandon the fight, leaving Barue to whatever fate decreed, while bonding herself to him and doing nothing but serving him and bearing his children.

Leaving him had been painful but necessary. After the murder of her family and then the monks, she'd given up on having any kind of relationship, resigned herself to being alone. But when Donoval entered her life, against her will, her battered heart attached itself to him.

At the tender age of ten and seven, she'd rescued him from Alric's dungeon and joined him in his battle to regain his throne of Shallon. At his side she'd learned how to fight—how to care again. But she'd known if she gave in to his demands, she would lose herself, become nothing more than a possession—though a cherished one—without rights or thoughts of her own. So when Roark made his attempt to seize the throne of Barue, she'd left Shallon and Donoval to fight against him.

She'd believed herself well over her childish infatuation with Donoval for some time now. She refused to consider what she'd felt was love. What did *she* know of love?

Affection. Caring. Concern. These emotions were familiar to her. Hausic, Mauri, and Jole, as well as the people of Barue, stirred her affection. She cared for them. Worried about them, but would not admit to loving them. Loving people made you weak, left you vulnerable. And to defeat Roark she couldn't afford any weakness.

So, why did the sight of Donoval asleep in her bed rouse that long-dead emotion inside her?

Why had he come? And how had he gotten here?

After his appearance, she'd had the camp and the surrounding countryside scoured. There was no sign of his passage. No one had seen him arrive. When he'd collapsed, she'd sent for the healer. Aside from a few bruises, the healer found nothing wrong with the man. She'd dispatched a messenger to Shallon, Donoval's kingdom, but it would be a day or two before a reply came. She could only wait until he woke and explained his presence.

In the meantime, she had a battle to plan. Rousting Roark from the castle was the key to his defeat. During the preceding months, she'd driven him relentlessly through the countryside into retreat. Now, because of her badly executed attack a few days earlier, he'd managed to reach and barricade himself inside this fortress.

She needed to pry him out and crush him. Once winter set in, she'd have to disband her troops; they didn't have the equipment or supplies to stage a siege. And even if they were willing to do so, the ministers and rightful rulers of Barue didn't have the coin to fund one. This long civil war with Roark had drained the country of more than men.

Without provisions, her troops couldn't survive the harsh winter months. Ever ahead of her pursuit, Roark had stripped the surrounding countryside of its crops, livestock, and wildlife. That which he didn't take he destroyed, leaving the few people who escaped his murderous passing nothing to exist on, while he and his men could sit out the winter in comfort. If she didn't roust and defeat him now, come spring he'd begin anew his campaign of terror.

Already the air turned crisp, foliage burst into color; frost touched the ground and iced the edges of the streams. The seer predicted a storm by the end of the week. Once it hit, the war was lost. So in four days time her troops would begin their assault.

All she needed was a plan capable of success. Corrupt blackguard though Roark was, she couldn't deny his genius. No matter how long she studied the maps and diagrams of Roark's stronghold, she could find no chink, no weakness, no crack in his defenses. If she didn't find one, she was defeated before the battle began.

With a cry of frustration, she swept the papers from the table.

"Problem?"

Startled, she whirled around. Donnie sat cross-legged on the bed, a robe draped over his lap. In the light of day, he no longer looked washed out or ill. He looked tough and appealing, a haven of strength and comfort in a storm of chaos. A stubble of beard darkened the hard line of his jaw. He ran a hand through his tangled hair. The motion drew her attention to his well-muscled chest. At her stare, his lips twitched, and his cheeks reddened.

Moisture pooled in her mouth as memories both familiar and strange slammed into her: Copulating atop furs by the flickering light of a fire, their bodies slick with sweat, their passion stoked by the battle for control that ever raged between them. Giving and demanding satisfaction, but never requesting or truly receiving it. Making love on crisp, cool sheets, their bodies growing warm with desire. Pleasure flowing sweet and easy between them . . .

She blinked at the image. Nothing involving herself and Donoval had ever been sweet or easy.

When not fighting for control in bed, they battled for command of each other's lives.

"Problem?" Donoval repeated.

"No. There is clothing for you." She pointed to a neat stack of garments Jole had found at her request. Her scouts had discovered no sign of his guard, horse, weapons, or garments. His appearance in camp and in her bed baffled her.

"Thanks."

Thanks? The word was odd. His voice sounded different, softer. Every word King Donoval spoke came out as a command. Though he generously rewarded those who served him, he rarely expressed gratitude in words. What had happened to change him?

She caught only a glimpse of his pale buttocks as he turned away to dress. Using the bed robe as cover, he struggled into the soft hide trousers and simple cotton shirt and stomped his feet into the boots. His unusual modesty confused her. Donoval took pride in his body and gave no thought to nudity.

Once clothed, he picked up the scattered maps and papers.

"Donnie, why are you here?" She used the nickname he abhorred and waited for his reaction.

Nothing. When she'd used the name before and he hadn't reacted in his normal manner—becoming enraged at being treated with less the than proper dignity and respect he felt he deserved—she'd discounted it because of his strange arrival and disorientation. Now he appeared well and in control. Why didn't he respond to her taunt?

"Seri, I think you need to sit down. I have something to tell you." He placed the papers on the table and pushed her unresisting body into a chair.

His use of the name only Mauri used and his uncharacteristic patience and concern baffled her. Was he bespelled? Or was she?

"I'm not sure where to begin." He ran his hand through his hair, wincing as his fingers caught in the tangled mess. The urge to feel the rough silk of those strands had Serilda curling her fingers into fists.

"I'm not Donnie—er, Donoval."

Chapter Eleven

The skeptical look on Seri's face mirrored my doubts of personal sanity. The coherent, rational explanation I'd formed in my mind dissolved. What I was about to tell her defied belief. And if I didn't believe it, how could I expect her to?

Before my doubts overwhelmed me or she could respond, I hurried on: "It may sound insane, but I'm not who you think I am. I'm not King Donoval."

She regarded me with a mixture of concern and amusement. "Then, who might you be?"

"My name's Brandon Alexander Davis. I'm a writer . . . er, a scribe."

Her brows drew together. "A monk?"

"No." This was going to be harder than I thought. In her world, only monks put pen to paper—or in their case, quill to parchment. Most people were illiterate. Even Donoval could read and write little more than his signature and simple commands. Having been fostered by monks, Seri was an exception.

"I'm a bard, a troubadour, a teller of tales—only I write them down for other people to read."

Her brows drew together, and her lips tightened. "You jest. Why?"

"It's not a joke. I'm not from this world. Your world. I'm from another place."

"You've been injured or ill. Your mind is confused."

"Injured maybe, but my mind is clear. I know who I am, and it's not Donoval. I'm an author. I write books about your world."

"You're a historian? Monks keep—kept—the written history, but since Roark destroyed the Order of Light, none have been penned." Her gaze moved over me. "You look and sound, for the most part, like King Donoval of Shallon."

"I look like Donoval because in this world I inhabit Donoval's body, but my mind is that of Brandon Alexander Davis."

She started to speak.

"Wait, let me finish. I write fiction. What you call history are the books I wrote. I live in a far different world. A world of wonder and, by your standards, magic."

Ignoring the storm brewing in her eyes, I continued, telling her about myself, about Brandon Alexander Davis the neurotic, semihermit author, about my Barbarian King books, my Warrior Woman books. Who she was. How she'd appeared in my office.

When I finished in a breathless rush, for a moment confusion crossed her face as she considered my words; then her lips thinned into a tight, angry slit. "I am no creature of your imagination. I am real. I am Serilda d'Lar. Feel me. I am solid flesh." She grabbed my shoulder in a punishing grip. "As are you."

I flinched as her fingers dug into my flesh, but I welcomed the pain. It grounded me in this world.

If I'd had time to write down my explanation, maybe I could have done better. Trying to speak without a script was a big mistake. Public speaking isn't one of my strengths. The few times I'd agreed to speak at a writers' or fantasy fan convention, I always wrote my speeches ahead of time. And still I'd sounded stiff and stilted.

"I know it sounds crazy." As the words poured out of me, I knew I was mangling everything. "Somehow I've been transported into my fictional world, into Donoval's body."

With each word, the storm in her eyes grew. "For what purpose do you spin this bizarre tale?"

In desperation, I knelt at her feet and clasped her icy fingers in mine. "You have to believe me." As I hadn't believed her. "Your life depends on it."

"Enough!" she roared.

Wrenching her hands from mine, she jumped to her feet. The action knocked me back on my tail-bone. Pain shot up my spine.

"Do you still think me a simpleminded fool? What do you gain by spouting this insane tale?" She paced back and forth.

I eased myself to my feet as she continued her tirade. "Seri—"

"Do not use that ridiculous name. I am Serilda d'Lar. Lady d'Lar to you." She came to a halt; her tone grew harsh and foreboding. "You may be king in Shallon, but here you have no authority. No power. Here, you are just a man. You are Donoval. Not a person of another world." Her tone softened with concern and compassion. "Have a care how you speak. There are those who covet Shallon's riches, King Donoval. You are Shallon's strength. Do not fail her."

I slumped into the chair. I'd bungled this badly. What could I do to convince her of my identity, of the truth? Without her help, we were both trapped. Maybe we were anyway.

I remembered my confusion when she appeared in my home, my failure to believe what she told me, who she was. How could I expect her to believe what even to my ears sounded like the ravings of a madman?

Maybe I was mad, even now locked away in some padded room, babbling insanely.

I considered using her enchanted name. Would using it give me power over her? I wasn't sure, and given her anger, I feared she might run me through if I tried. Probably best to skip it.

I had to find a way back to the real world, and I had to figure out how to take Seri with me before the events I'd written played out to their deadly end. Before I blacked out, I'd been attempting to rewrite that ending, but . . . I couldn't remember if I'd succeeded. When I tried to grasp the memory of what I'd written, the thoughts crumbled like termite-riddled wood.

"Donoval?"

No, I wasn't crazy. This was real. I was real. Seri was hovering over me, looking at me with concern that was real.

"Donoval, talk to me. Tell me how to help you."

She was right. Though my mind might rebel at the idea, in this world I was King Donoval of Shallon. If I wanted to find a way home, it behooved me to play the part. I tried to think how Donoval would handle this situation—as if "perfect in his own mind Donoval" would ever find himself in this fucked-up state of affairs.

I'd created him during a period in my life when I wanted nothing more than to be free of any emotional baggage, to be physically and mentally self-sufficient. A man so sure of who and what he was he needed no one else in his life. Single-minded in his purpose. No inner conflicts or doubts. No flaws.

No heart.

I'd made him perfect, without any resemblance to a real human being—which was probably the reason his character didn't catch on with readers the way Serilda's had. Readers found him one-dimensional and hard to identify with.

It occurred to me that Donoval and I were not so different. Oh, I was far from perfect in any way, but like him, I avoided emotional involvement. To protect myself from the pain of rejection, I kept people at a distance. If I never let them touch me, I couldn't get hurt when they left. I poured all my emotions into building my fictional world but allowed my characters to experience little of it.

It had been over seven years since I wrote the last Barbarian King book, four years since Donoval had even appeared in a Warrior Woman book. The particulars of his personality—aside from his absolute perfection—had faded in my mind, colored by Serilda's impressions, memories, and feelings about him. Unlike some authors, I didn't have a good memory for my stories. I had book bibles to keep track of the characters and details of the worlds I created, but those bibles weren't available to me here. I'd have to rely on my faulty recollections.

In my mind I frantically plotted and discarded idea after idea before an acceptable story line came to me. I prayed that I could be as good an actor as I believed I was a writer.

I leaned forward and groaned.

"Do you need the healer?" Seri asked, alarm replacing anger.

"No!" I straightened. "My head is clear now. Forgive my rantings. On my journey here I was attacked by bandits and took a blow to my head. I spoke of nothing more than a dream."

"The healer mentioned no injury to your head." She looked doubtful of my claim.

I summoned my most autocratic voice. "Then he is a f-fool." My voice cracked as she ran her fingers through my hair searching for lumps.

"She," Serilda corrected. "The healer is a she."

"That explains the oversight."

Her anger stirred again by my chauvinistic attitude, she accepted my less than brilliant explanation. Bristling at my tone, she snatched her hand away. Her fingers caught in my hair, pulling me forward until our faces were a breath apart. Her lips parted on a puff of air. The sweet taste of her breath touched my tongue. This time my groan was real.

A hint of pink touched her cheeks before she scrambled to her feet. "Why have you come?"

"I heard of your siege of Roark's castle."

"And came to revel in my failure?"

"You think so poorly of my character that you believe I'd celebrate your defeat? I'm crushed."

She gave me a puzzled look.

Maintaining Donoval's persona was harder than I thought. He really was a pompous ass. No wonder my readers preferred Seri.

"If not to gloat, why are you here?"

"To ask you once again to give up your quest for vengeance and bond with me," I improvised.

"Vengeance is but a small part of why I fight. I battle not only for myself but also for the people of Barue. I cannot, will not abandon them to Roark and his kind."

Rather than yield to one man, she would devote herself to her people.

Before she could protest further, I pressed a finger to her lips. I gambled that her commitment to her people would overcome her need to be free of obligation to another—to Donoval. "Think before you decide. Give me the right to carry this burden for you. Perhaps you'll defeat Roark without my help, but at what cost? And what of the next power-mad despot? As a protectorate of Shallon, Barue will enjoy peace, prosperity, and freedom from oppression. Is your personal freedom worth the cost of your people's? Let me do what you cannot: free them."

I wanted to say more. As Brandon *and* as Donoval. To tell her she'd more than proven herself. To tell her of my admiration for her strength and courage in the face of overwhelming odds. To tell her I'd never demand she surrender her independence.

To tell her I loved her.

But Donoval would never say those things. And if he did say them, she'd never believe him. I doubt he'd have the sense to think them. Damn his stubborn machismo. And damn me for creating him thus.

Serilda eyed me suspiciously. "If you seek to help me defeat Roark, why have you come alone?"

I searched my Swiss cheese memory for what I'd written before I'd blacked out. Bits of my revised plot came to me. "My troops needed time to prepare. I didn't want to wait."

She crossed her arms over her chest and stared. Since becoming king of Shallon, Donoval was always surrounded by bodyguards. From what I remembered of my revised ending, King Donoval arrived with a full contingent of troops; he didn't appear naked in her bed. It seemed the universe didn't take kindly to my intervention and had decided to stir things up a bit.

Suddenly, I wished I'd listened closer to Grandma's stories. I recalled something about how, by rejecting the real world for a fictional one, a writer summoned it into existence. Once it took physical form, the writer no longer completely controlled it.

Damn. The snatches I remembered weren't much help in figuring out what to do, and I scrambled to come up with an acceptable explanation.

"My guard was killed in the attack."

She didn't look convinced. "We found no evidence of this, no signs of an attack, no bodies."

I shrugged, but didn't offer any further details.

After a few moments she said, "If I agree to your terms, how long before your troops arrive?"

"I need only send a message and they'll come." I could only hope that the message didn't end up delivered to another King Donoval, who'd wonder what the hell was going on. No, I was sure that wouldn't happen. I had Donoval's body. I rubbed my palm over my flat, hard belly and couldn't help but grin at the firm abs. I could get comfortable in this body.

"Dictate your missive." She bent over the desk and picked up a quill.

"Then, you agree to my terms? In exchange for my help, you'll bond with me?"

"With certain stipulations."

She gave me an odd look when I took the quill from her hand. To hide my grin, I bowed my head over the parchment. No wonder Donoval hadn't been able to bend her to his will. With her back against the wall, she still negotiated the terms of her surrender. "Which are?"

"I'll bond with you after Roark is defeated and Barue is free."

"Fair enough," I agreed. If I failed, we'd both be dead anyway.

"And Barue shall remain a protectorate of Shallon only until the rightful heir to the Barue monarchy is found and set on the throne."

"You believe the heir is still alive? It's been eighteen years since Roark murdered the royal family."

During that attack, the newborn heir had been spirited away and hidden.

"Yes. I've been searching for years. My trackers found the nurse who took the infant to safety."

"So, you know who and where the heir is?"

"Not yet. The nurse is old and feeble, her memory spotty. But I will."

Yes, she would. To resolve that ongoing plot thread, the heir would be revealed by Roark just before his and Serilda's final fight. Wouldn't she be surprised and pleased when she learned the identity of the missing heir! Although, with the way it had originally ended . . .

No. I couldn't think that way. Things were going to change.

"And if the heir is never located?" It wouldn't do for me—for Donoval—to capitulate too easily.

"Then Barue will remain under the control and protection of Shallon until you deem otherwise," she granted reluctantly.

"Very well. I agree to your terms."

"Don't count the coins in your coffer too soon. We will find the heir. I'm certain."

"I hope you do. Having Barue as a strong ally on Shallon's southern border is preferable to having her as a weak territory."

She gave me a stunned look. If not for Donoval's insistence on turning Barue into a Shallon colony, rather than granting her independence, Seri would have long ago sacrificed her liberty for Barue's.

I signed my message with a flourish, folded and sealed it with the hot wax she provided, then pressed the heavy royal ring I wore into the wax. Feeling hopeful I could change the fate I'd written for Seri, I leaned back. Now we would see what the day had in store.

As Serilda dispatched her fastest messenger to Shallon, she pondered the Donoval puzzle. He wasn't the man she remembered. He might look the same, all tempting hard muscle and innate sex appeal, but his way of speaking and his attitudes were different. Though in exchange for his help he demanded her as his bondmate, she sensed he no longer wanted to control her every action. His willingness to listen as she spoke, considering and conceding to her logical requests, stirred her, resurrected in her the youthful passion she'd felt for him before she'd discovered his rigid views of a woman's place in the world.

But his bizarre if quickly abandoned story of being from a different world, of Barue and herself being his creations, made her question his reason. What had altered his attitude? Were his delusions merely a result of a blow to the head? Something nagged at her mind, an elusive memory of another place, another time, another existence. When she reached for them, the images dissolved, leaving her head aching and her heart empty.

Unable to decipher the Donoval riddle, she shook off her bemusement. She had no time for hopeless fantasies. Praising Algidar for Donoval's timely assistance in her fight, she summoned Hausic and returned to her tent to plan her battle strategy.

She found Donoval, brows pulled together in concentration, hunched over her maps and diagrams. He scribbled furiously on a piece of parchment. Another anomaly. With a natural instinct for battle tactics, Donoval was a powerful warrior and an authoritative leader, but when they'd met, like most people, he'd been illiterate. After he'd won the throne of Shallon, she'd convinced him a king needed the skills of reading and writing, and he'd reluctantly allowed her to teach him the basics, though he'd been a poor student with little patience for intellectual pursuits. Despite her efforts, he'd found reading difficult and writing nearly impossible.

Her years with the monks had instilled in her a

love of reading, so the thought of being bound to a man who dismissed books as unnecessary frivolities had thrown the first damper on her lust. Now, to see him writing with ease made her speculate what else about him had changed.

Absorbed by his thoughts, he absently tapped the quill against his mouth. She grinned. Splotches of ink stained his fingers and lips, giving him a monkish look at odds with his commanding physical presence.

"What do you write?" She peered over his arm.

"Nothing."

Before she could decipher his scrawl, he crumpled and tossed the parchment into the fire.

"I think I've found a way into Roark's castle."

She dismissed his claim. "Impossible. I've studied the castle diagrams for hours."

"Infiltrating this castle is not impossible. King Aldredge commissioned it built to guard Barue's southernmost border. The castle, main bailey, and surrounding walls were finished just before the royal family was killed. But the moat was never dug, nor is there a village attached to it. After the royal family's deaths it was abandoned, and it has stood empty for nearly twenty years."

"I know the history of Barue," she growled.

Her caustic tone didn't seem to daunt him. He stabbed a finger at the diagram. "The builder now works for me. According to him, the eastern gate had no booby traps. And I doubt Roark has had the time or the skilled craftsmen to install any. The builder also showed me an interesting design feature."

She looked where he pointed at a hidden entrance

she would have sworn was not there before. Though it was camouflaged, it was not invisible. How had she missed it?

"While our troops distract Roark's men, we can gain access to the castle here," he continued. "By the time they realize what's happening, we'll have the gates open and bring the battle inside."

Excitement sizzled through her. "It could work. Since spring we've chased Roark across the country. His men are weary." As were hers. "With your men, we'll outnumber his. Once inside the outer walls, we can defeat them."

Hausic entered the tent. The three of them mapped out a battle plan.

"After Donnie's—er, my troops arrive, while they stage a massive assault on the western gate, Seri and I will take a few men, sneak into the castle, and open the eastern gate."

As he reviewed the plan with Hausic, Hausic's head nodded slowly. A grin spread across his wrinkled features. "It will work. When Roark's troops rush to defend the more vulnerable western gate, he'll not worry overmuch about the eastern gate, believing it to be too strong to fall. Once it's open, our troops will easily overcome the few guards left there, flood in behind him, and overwhelm them while they're trapped in the narrow passage inside the western gate. Brilliant!" He looked at Donoval in approval. "Your strategic skills have greatly improved since we last met, my young king."

"I learned from a master." Before Hausic joined Serilda's fight, he'd been counselor to Donoval. "I've missed your wise counsel, old friend."

At Donoval's praise, the elder man beamed with

pleasure. Serilda knew it had been hard for Hausic to leave Shallon, but he had done so both for his devotion to her and at Donoval's request. Though at the time she hadn't appreciated Donoval's gesture, over the years she'd come to acknowledge the worth of his gift. Without Hausic's counsel, Roark would have crushed her years ago.

What Donoval said about the plan sank into her. Her mouth sagged. "You want me to sneak into Roark's castle with you?"

"Yep. I'll need you to guard my back while I get to the gate."

His use of strange slang didn't mitigate her astonishment. "You trust me to do that?" Never before had Donoval expressed confidence in her fighting abilities. At her insistence he'd trained her, but he'd never believed a woman could be a true warrior. His male arrogance never allowed him to acknowledge her skill—skill she knew surpassed his.

"Who else? You're the best swordsperson I know."

She couldn't shake her feeling of disbelief. This was not the King Donoval she knew. While they were together, he'd done everything he could to keep her off the battlefield. Once, in a misguided attempt to keep her safe, he tied her to his bed. As a result, Roark captured her. After her escape, she'd ended her affair with Donoval and struck out on her own.

No, nothing Donoval had ever said or done erased the pain and humiliation she'd suffered at Roark's hands during that time, but she'd have forgiven him that if he'd accepted her right to be her own person rather than merely an extension of himself. He never had. Sending Hausic had been his only apology for his misjudgment and her resulting ordeal.

The hope shining in Donoval's eyes now irritated her. What more did he want? She'd agreed to his terms. Agreed to be his bondmate. Agreed to give up her freedom. But she hadn't agreed to love him again. That love had died slowly and painfully, as Roark's master torturer applied bloodworms to her naked flesh. She refused to resurrect it now.

"Dono—*my* troops should arrive by the end of the week." Again, he stumbled over his name. "In the meantime, we need to set the stage for our attack. Seri, how do you suggest we proceed?"

Both he and Hausic looked at her. She shook off her anger and bewilderment at his strange behavior and leaned over the maps. "I'll pull almost all my men off the eastern gate and start harassing the western. That will give Roark something to think about."

"Excellent idea. It'll force him to realign his defenses to suit our purpose."

He agreed with her assessment? When he turned to smile at her, his hair brushed against her cheek. Warmth flowed through her to settle in her belly. This is what she'd always wanted from Donoval: a meeting of two minds, two equals, giving and accepting, neither seeking to control or command the other.

She jerked back. This change in Donoval couldn't be real. It couldn't last. She couldn't, wouldn't trust it. To do so would be to relinquish what little was left of her soul.

* * *

After Seri and Hausic left to implement our plan, the wind went out of my sails. Meeting Hausic in person had left me shaken. Inside I knew this world and everyone in it was my creation, figments of my imagination, but until Hausic walked into the tent, I'd kept the reality of my being here from overtaking me. Because Seri had been in the real world, I didn't have a problem accepting her in this one. Believing in Hausic's existence proved more difficult. Doing so made me question my sanity once more.

He was everything and more than I expected: wise, compassionate, humorous, devoted, and ancient. Had I written him so, or had these people and this world taken on an existence beyond the words I put on paper? The answer to that question was beyond my ability to discern. What I'd written before I was transported here seemed to influence what happened, but my control wasn't absolute. There were a myriad of details that differed from my creation. I could only hope that the major factors didn't stray too far from what I wrote. For now I could only deal with what I could see, hear, feel, taste, and smell. For now, this world was my reality. Maybe I could get home again.

"My lord?" A young man hesitated at the entrance of the tent. Jole.

Orphaned as an infant, he was unaware of his true identity. He'd grown up the adopted son of a farmer. When he was fifteen, and his second family was killed by Roark's men, Jole joined Serilda's fight. A handsome youth with dark brown hair and eyes, at eighteen Jole had yet to reach full manhood. His cheeks sported few whiskers, his physique was not fully muscled, but his straight, direct gaze showed the man he'd soon become. A man more than capable of being Barue's rightful king.

"Come in, Jole." I sighed in resignation. His appearance was more evidence that I was no longer in Kansas.

"Lady Serilda bade me bring you armor and weapons."

I could hear his unspoken apology for the items' humble quality.

When I didn't react he added, "The armor is plain but sound." Then he hefted a three-foot long sword. "Though modest in decoration, the blade is balanced and the edge well honed." Watching him made me think of the young man at the weapons booth at the mall. That day seemed a hundred years past, but he added, "They will serve you well in both training and battle."

Sunlight streaming in through the open tent flap glinted off the mirrored surface of the sword. I eyed it with growing unease. The body I inhabited might be Donoval's, but the mind was mine. Writing about swordplay was far different than actually having to do it. If this world was in my head, it felt extremely real. If not . . . I feared the few sword-fighting lessons I'd taken as research wouldn't do me much good on a real battlefield, in a real fight, against a real opponent.

Could I die in this world? And if I did, what would happen to me in the real world? What would happen to Seri and the rest of my creations? The possibilities made my head swim. As did the possibilities of whatever brought me here.

The thought of actually using that sword to

skewer another human being, fictional or otherwise, left me feeling queasy. How in Heaven's name was I going to pull off this insane charade? Jole waited patiently for my response.

I pulled myself together. "Thank you, Jole." When I took the sword and other stuff from him and dumped it on the bed, he gave me a questioning look.

"The men await you on the training field. Do you wish me to help you to don your armor, my lord?"

Training? Another diversion from what I remembered of my revisions. I hadn't made any mention of Donoval training with Serilda's men. I doubted a few hours of practice was going to help but also saw how the men would expect me to train with them.

"Yeah, sure, why not?" I shrugged.

At my answer, Jole's eyebrow quirked upward.

I stood frozen as he fitted the hammered metal breastplate along with the stiff leather arm and leg guards on me. Deciding seeing was more important than whatever protection it might provide; I rejected the helmet with its narrow eye slit. When he strapped the sword scabbard around my waist, I noticed we had company. At some point Mauri had crept unnoticed into the tent. She glanced at me, but her focus centered on Jole. Apart from a touch of color in his cheeks, he gave no indication he noticed her presence.

Her appearance shook me. Like Hausic, in person she was more real than I expected.

Despite the trauma she'd endured during her young life, Mauri retained her innocent spirit. She'd buried the misuse and brutality she'd suffered so deep it rarely surfaced. The shadows in her deep brown eyes hinted at secrets, but she regarded the world with compassion and humor. On the cusp of womanhood, she had blue-black hair that fell straight to her waist, surrounding a face of exotic beauty. Diminutive and lithe, with the hint of budding breasts and narrow hips, she appeared a celestial being, apart from human concerns and cares, as if nothing of the world could touch her inner being.

Seri had rescued the girl at the age of eight from a life of abuse. Since then, Mauri devoted herself to serving her. But she saved her adulation for Jole.

Her heart revealed in her eyes, she stared at the boy. The longer she watched him, the harder it became for him to hide his growing discomfort.

If I'd planned to continue my Warrior Woman series, Mauri and Jole's stories would have been told. But since my decision to end the series and take my writing in a different direction, those plans had been scrapped. Now I wondered: if I didn't write their future, would they have one?

My head started to pound. I must have made some sound of distress, because Jole asked, "Are you ill, my lord? Lady d'Lar told me you were attacked on your way here. Shall I summon the healer?"

"No, I'm fine. Just hungry."

Mauri jumped up. "Shall I fetch you some breakfast?" Ever eager to serve, without waiting for my answer, she dashed out of the tent.

"Oh, great. On top of everything else I'll get food poisoning."

Jole laughed. "Granted, Mauri's domestic skills

are lacking, but she does try, and she has improved with practice since you were last here." He colored at his automatic defense of a girl he generally ignored. "But don't worry; she'll bring you something from the camp cook. After you eat, Lady d'Lar asks that I escort you to meet her by the training field. Before I take my leave, may I render you further service, my lord?"

Yeah, teach me how to be a king—King Donoval of Shallon, I said silently. Out loud I said, "No, I'm doing great. Thanks for lending a hand." I nodded at the armor I now wore with less than comfortable grace. The metal clanged as I moved, chafing my skin.

If I looked as ridiculous as I felt, nothing in his gaze revealed it. He cocked his head to one side to consider my odd choice of words. When understanding dawned on his face, his lips twitched slightly.

"I'll await you outside."

He bowed; then, with an inherent dignity fitting his unknown lineage, he left the tent. I really had to remember to speak more like Donoval or people would realize I wasn't who I claimed to be. If they did, the sword strapped to my waist wasn't going to do me any good.

A few minutes later Mauri returned with a meal for me, a generous helping of roast meat, dark bread, and water laced with cheap wine. She sat on the bed and watched as I ate. The food, while filling, lacked appeal. The meat was tough and dry, the bread coarse and stale, and the water sour.

She cocked her head to one side. "Have you come to take Seri back with you to Shallon?"

Her question caught me by surprise. When I didn't answer, she leaned toward me and continued in an earnest tone.

"You can't take her away. We need her. Without her, Lord Roark and his men will surely gain complete control. You can't allow that to happen." In one blink, shadows clouded the innocence in her eyes, turning her from child to adult. She shuddered, then pinned me with a hard stare. "I won't go back to that life—ever."

Guilt churned inside me. I knew what she remembered. When she was barely eight, one of Roark's men took control of her family's land. For objecting, her father was murdered. Her mother and older siblings were sold into slavery. To satisfy his twisted desires, the man kept Mauri for himself. Until Seri killed him, he'd abused and exploited the girl.

In the book, I hadn't detailed the mistreatment she suffered, but the meaning had been clear. Here, the wine-laced water turned to vinegar in my stomach.

I took her hand. That she didn't flinch at my touch gave evidence of her inner strength. "Seri has agreed to be my bondmate. As such, her people become my people, her battles my battles, her enemies my enemies. We'll not abandon the people of Barue to Andre Roark." The words tumbled out of me unplanned, but they came from my heart. Whatever it took, I'd fix the chaos I'd caused in this world.

"You give your word?"

I pressed her palm against my heart. "As king of Shallon I pledge my word, my heart, my sword, and my life to the protection of Serilda d'Lar and the people of Barue."

"Thank you." The clouds in her eyes parted, and in an instant she became a child again. It was a sight to behold but did little to ease the guilt I felt for the suffering I caused her.

Chapter Twelve

Listening to Donoval reassuring Mauri left Serilda feeling unsettled. Though he'd always been tolerant of the girl's presence and kind in his limited dealings with her, for the most part she'd been beneath his notice. He'd never taken the time to speak with her or listen to her concerns.

She made an involuntary sound. Jole looked up. He stood a few yards away in conversation with another man, but he couldn't have heard Donoval's words. Unwilling to be caught eavesdropping, Serilda hurried away from the tent toward the training field. It would be good to burn off her confusion with physical exertion.

In the past, she'd always been able to predict Donoval's reactions. This new Donoval perplexed her. She had no idea what he might do next.

Now, watching him as he strode ahead of Jole toward where she waited at the edge of the training field, Serilda couldn't take her eyes from him. Dressed in borrowed, ill-fitting armor, he still cut a dashing figure. Strong. Determined. Kingly.

Instead of leaving his long blond hair to flow free around his shoulders as was his usual style, he'd tied it in a neat, more practical manner at the back of his neck. She shook her head. What did she know of his current habits? They'd been apart for over three years. People altered their behavior to suit their circumstances. But did what was inside them ever truly change? Despite growing evidence, she was loath to believe Donoval had altered himself. Doing so left her vulnerable to emotions she had no wish to revive.

The midmorning sun had burned away the dew and warmed the air, and sweat that owed little to that warmth trickled down my spine. As I approached the training field, a crisp blue sky lent an air of reality to the surreal scene that met my eyes.

Spread out over the open field were dozens of men, ranging in age from beardless boys to grizzled veterans, all engaged in exercises and drills. Swords clanged against shields as they fought mock battles. Some wrestled bare-chested. Rolling on the ground, they grunted in exertion. Sweat dripped from their brows, making their sun-darkened skin glisten.

Further away, horses thundered across the ground, the men on their backs swinging swords and mallets. Men, metal, and horseflesh clashed. Close in, the horses leaped and kicked, deliberately missing their opponents by distressingly narrow margins, in a carefully orchestrated dance.

I gasped. The sweet scent of trampled grass and the sour smell of human and animal sweat flooded my nostrils. The thought of joining that chaos made my heart race. Prickles of fear chased up and down my spine. I clenched my fingers over the hilt of the sword hanging from my waist.

To keep from bolting in the opposite direction, I locked my gaze on Seri. An oasis of calm in a raging storm, she kept my panic at bay. Dressed in a simple white shirt covered by a plain brown tunic and snug, dark leather trousers and boots, with a sword strapped to her waist, she looked nothing like the half-naked barbarian warrior woman who graced the covers of my books. When had she started dressing this way? Sunshine turned her hair to a crown of flames and her blue-green eyes to the opaque color of a mountain lake, reflecting everything but revealing nothing. The sight didn't help slow my heart rate.

When I reached her side, activity on the field slowed to a halt. One by one, the men paused their practice and turned to watch me. Their faces showed a myriad of reactions, some hopeful, some resentful, some frightened, some I couldn't read.

Seri stepped forward and seemed to study me. Could she read the growing dread in my eyes?

"Are you ready to train?"

A glance around at the men waiting and watching told me I didn't have much choice. These men fought for their country, their families, their lives, but following a woman strained their sense of rightness, their sense of order, their sense of their place in this world. I'd written them this way, and it wasn't a stretch to accept it as real.

In a universe where women were held in little regard, Serilda's rise to a position of power, her ability to command and lead hardened warriors into battle, showed her strength of mind and body. My appearance threatened her hard-won authority, I now saw. One word from me, King Donoval of Shallon, and they'd abandon her. And she knew it.

If I refused to spar with her, if I disrespected her skill, she'd lose the regard of her men. They'd see it as an indication that I, King Donoval, didn't believe her strong or capable enough to lead them against Roark.

Her willingness to risk losing the loyalty of her troops spoke to her devotion to Barue. She'd give up everything she'd fought for to save the people, the country she loved.

"Are you well enough?" The concern in her softly voiced question shook me from my daze.

"Do I have a choice?" My question came out harsher than I intended.

Her careless shrug couldn't disguise the tension in her body. "Life is full of choices. Make one." She strode through the crowd to an open area and pulled her sword. A half circle formed around her. Silence fell over the field. All eyes turned to me.

Legs spread in a wide stance, she held her sword in both hands, ready to meet my attack. Her eyes challenged me. In theory this was a training session, but she knew it was far more. It was a fight for control that neither of us could win.

The smooth hilt of my sword pressed into my sweaty palm. My muscles clenched. Even if I wanted to seize control from her, which I definitely did not, there was no way could I match her with swords. Though I seemed to inhabit Donoval's muscular, toned body, the mind was mine alone. What if I miscalculated my swing? What if she didn't duck? What if I struck her? Bile burned the back of my throat.

Conversely, I had no doubts about my safety. I had no fear that she'd accidentally strike me.

With trembling fingers, I unbuckled the sheath from my waist and let it and the sword slide to the ground. A low murmur started. As I moved into the ring, the murmur grew to a grumble. When I was a few feet from Seri, the circle closed around us.

"What are you doing?" Her whisper didn't reach the men. Her sword dipped toward the ground.

"Serilda d'Lar's skill with a blade is renowned," my voice rose over the rumble of the men. "As is mine," I added. Donoval wasn't known for his modesty. "There is little need for us to test our mettle against each other. I'll save my arm strength for separating Roark's head from his shoulders."

"Yes!" a man yelled from the crowd, obviously elated that I had joined their force. Someone banged his sword against his shield. Soon the field erupted in clanging and shouting.

Seri sheathed her sword, stepped close to me, and whispered, "I don't know why you refuse to spar with me, but this will not satisfy them for long."

She was right. These men demanded that their leaders train and fight as they did.

"We are equally matched. Our sparring proves nothing," I replied.

Her eyes widened in surprise, then narrowed in suspicion. Donoval had never acknowledged her equal skill with a sword.

"The men will demand to see some contest between us. What do you propose?" Her eyes sparked with blue-green fire, and she watched me warily.

The scent of her, sun-warmed woman, leather and spice, rose on her body heat to surround me. The effect left me dizzy with longing. With difficulty, I gathered my wits.

"A wrestling match?" I spoke loud enough for the crowd to hear. They answered with a cheer of approval.

Color flagged her cheeks, but she nodded in agreement. While I pulled off my armor and shirt, she removed her sword and tunic. Helpful hands took the items.

Wrestling was an inspired idea. With my greater strength, size, and reach, I had the advantage. Being bested by a woman in swordplay would damage Donoval's standing with the men, but her being defeated by me in a wrestling match wouldn't hurt her in their minds. They wouldn't expect her to prevail against a larger, stronger opponent. It was a win-win scenario.

Now all I had to do was win.

Without warning, Serilda lunged. Her shoulder hit my gut. Half the crowd cheered, others groaned.

"Oof!" The air whooshed out of me. I folded in half over her, knocking us both off balance.

In a tangle of arms and legs we went down. I landed on top of her. From knees to waist, her body pressed against mine. My thigh pressed between hers. Her chest heaved with exertion. Moisture sheened the hollow of her throat where her pulse throbbed. Wisps of hair clung to the damp skin of her face. Her warm, musky scent filled my straining lungs. Unbidden, heat unfurled inside me. The circle of men around us faded from my mind.

Resting my weight on one arm, I hovered over her. In the scuffle, my hair came free and flew around my face. Her eyes darkened as my body responded to her nearness.

"Wrestling is more fun than playing with swords, isn't it?" I whispered.

At my quip she scowled.

"Do you yield?"

"Never!"

She wrapped her leg behind mine and twisted. Off balance from holding my weight off her, and unprepared for her sudden move, I flopped onto my back. She was quickly atop me. My head bounced against the ground. Pain exploded behind my eyes. Pinwheels of colored lights spiraled across a black field. She levered herself up. With a gasp, I sucked air back into my collapsed lungs.

"Are you injured?"

Groaning, I blinked away the remaining black spots and peered up at her. A haze of dust from the dry grass filled the air. I coughed. Concern darkened her eyes.

"I'll live, but I think my pride just bit the dust."

Satisfaction sparked in her eyes as she grinned down at me. "Do you yield?"

Now her thigh nestled between mine. Her heat burned my skin.

"No." I wasn't finished quite yet.

I reached up and cupped the back of her head with my hand. My fingers threaded through soft warm curls. She didn't resist as I tugged her face to mine and closed my lips over hers. Beneath mine, her lips felt cool and firm. I slid the tip of my tongue along the seam of hers. With a tiny gasp they parted, and I delved within. The taste of her, like crisp, sweet mint, exploded in my mouth. I lifted my other hand to her face and stroked my thumb along her cheek. A fine tremor ran through her.

The men shouted and stamped their feet. I could feel the vibration against my back. Or was it the rapid pounding of my heart?

"Yield?" I whispered against her lips.

Her lips tightened to a hard line beneath mine. She jerked her head from my hold, jumped to her feet, and strode off the training field.

The fight had lasted less than five minutes. Whichever way you looked at it, I lost.

After Seri left, the training session continued. Against my better judgment, I was roped into sparring and wrestling. The men didn't seem to notice my ineptitude with a sword, or at least none of them mentioned it. I managed not to skewer or be skewered by anyone. I only dropped the blade once.

After being trounced by Seri, to my surprise I did better at wrestling, managing to win several of my matches as I grew more comfortable in the body I now inhabited, Donoval's body. I felt him inside struggling to take over my mind to become me. Part of me wanted to give in, to accept that I was Donoval, not some neurotic writer transported into his fictional world. Despite the insanity of what was happening, I held tight to reality. If I gave in, I'd be lost and Seri along with me. Donoval couldn't, hadn't saved her. Only Brandon could.

When the shadows grew long, training came to a

halt. Josef, an older soldier in charge of training, slapped me on the back. I winced and tried not to stumble at his powerful blow.

"Don't worry, young king, you did well enough." He laughed not unkindly.

His words shattered my hopes that no one had noticed my ineptitude. I let out a groan. "Was I that bad?"

"After being trounced by a woman, you need ask?" This time his laughter boomed. Several men smiled and nodded at the sound. He slapped me on the back again.

When I stumbled, this time he grabbed and hauled me upright.

"But, take heart. The men realize that sitting on a throne of peace makes different demands on a man than leading troops into battle. Your skills are a mite rusty, but your heart is strong. Come, we eat now." Without waiting for my acceptance, he gripped my arm and pulled me toward the encampment.

At the smell of roasting meat, my mouth watered. Campfires lit the growing gloom of evening and warmed the air. Josef led me to a circle of men sitting around one fire. They greeted me with nods.

Though I couldn't put names to every face, I recognized most of them from the training field. These were the commanders, the ones who led the younger men into battle. They were either professional soldiers or men who'd long ago lost any other place they might have held in the world. Older men, seasoned veterans of many wars and battles, they talked quietly among themselves. Their words of battles won and lost, of times and places long gone, of men killing and killed were sad and left me feeling bemused.

At that moment, it was hard to believe I'd created this world, these men. I didn't recognize them as characters with whom I'd peopled my fictional world. As with much of this world I found myself thrust into, they had a presence, a reality that far exceeded my feeble imagination.

No one spoke of the coming battle with Roark, as if to do so would awaken Fate and alter the outcome.

"Here. Eat." Josef handed me a wooden platter loaded high with rare meat dripping with blood and chunks of dark coarse bread. Into my other hand he thrust a cup of what smelled like beer; then he sat down next to me.

Thirst made me imprudent. I took a healthy swallow of the beer and choked at the strong bitter taste.

Laughing Josef tossed back half his own cup without taking a breath. "Weaker than I like, but it'll do, hey, lad?" He nudged my arm with his elbow. Half the contents of my cup sloshed out onto my thigh.

As the men ate and drank, talk turned from battles past to other things: food, drink, and women. Though none spoke directly of Seri, at times when the discussion grew rowdy, they eyed me with curiosity and what might have been envy.

Hunger and thirst overcame my aversion to the tough, gamey meat. Now that I knew what tarak tasted like—awful—I'd have to apologize to Seri. I also wolfed down the coarse, gritty bread and bitter beer. I ate and drank along with the men, taking care to sip slowly. Though foul-tasting, the beer did help ease my aches and pains, leaving me feeling almost human again.

Sitting around the fire, I felt sweat roll down my back. The stench of my perspiration burned my nostrils. Dirt and blood crusted my hands. The skin of my face felt gritty.

When I inquired about where I could bathe, Josef eyed me in surprise. Apparently, I hadn't made bathing a priority among this crew. Only one thing might get these men to do that.

He let out a chuckle and punched a fist into my arm. "Ah, I understand. You share a tent with Lady d'Lar."

Heat rushed up my neck, making me glad of the dirt on my face.

Nodding in what looked like approval, he pointed toward a stand of trees and told me there was a stream I could use if I was crazy enough to wish to do so. Laughter followed me as I strode away from camp.

Aching muscles screaming in protest, I trudged into the woods and followed the scent of water. To my delight, I found a small clearing where a fallen tree had created an even tinier pond. I stripped off my boots, grubby trousers, and shirt and stepped into the water.

Big mistake. The icy water took my breath away. Beneath the canopy of trees, the early evening sunlight filtering through the colorful foliage didn't warm the air. Sweat turned to ice on my skin. Shivering, I jerked back.

I considered heading back to the tent with its warm stove and soft bed furs, but dirt and sweat crusted my skin. If I asked, I knew I'd be provided with hot water to wash, but the thought of making Mauri or Jole or anyone here wait on me didn't sit right in my mind. It would make me feel as if I'd created them solely to serve my needs.

Besides, I wasn't ready to face Seri yet, especially not looking and feeling like something a tarak had dragged back to its den. Next time I faced her, I wanted to be at my best. In control.

In my dreams, seeing her . . . Being within touching distance of her shattered what little control I had.

Gritting my teeth, I splashed into the stream and quickly rinsed the grime from my flesh.

Serilda paced the tent in agitation. Hours had passed since she bested Donoval on the training field. What had she been thinking? He'd be furious with her for making him look the fool in front of the men. She should have stayed and found a way to placate him; instead she'd run away.

Was he even now on his way back to Shallon, leaving her to continue her fight against Roark alone? No. She couldn't believe that of him. Despite all his faults, he'd pledged his word to help Barue.

Perhaps it would be better if he did leave. Something was not right with him. Could three years of ruling Shallon in peace have destroyed his fighting ability? Or had the blow he took to his head scrambled his brain? His strategy seemed sound, his body still muscled and toned, but he lacked the spark of a warrior that she remembered. He even spoke differently. Not to mention being clumsy. If he went into battle as he was now, she feared the outcome.

The tent flap opened. A cold breeze chased across

her skin. She turned to see Donoval entering. Though his shirt and trousers were dirty, his skin was clean. He carried his dusty armor and sword. His hair lay wet against his head, darkened to the color of rich honey. He'd scraped the stubble from his cheeks, leaving them reddened.

Along with the scent of river water, he carried a hint of the strong beer the men preferred.

He didn't say anything as he dropped his armor against the tent wall, but as their eyes met his lips curved in a small smile. Like rain softened the hard ground after a drought, relief softened the hard knot of tension inside her.

"There are clean clothes for you." She pointed to the fresh shirt and trousers lying across the bed. "Have you eaten?"

"Yes, I joined Josef and his men. Tarak really is barely edible, isn't it?"

She forced herself to turn away as he stripped off his soiled garments and pulled on clean ones.

"You can turn around now. I'm decent."

As before, his words made little sense, but she turned to face him. Boots off, he sat on the edge of the bed. He appeared relaxed and unconcerned about what had happened on the training field.

"Are you not angry?" she ventured.

His brows drew together. "About what?"

Instead of easing her mind, his words tightened the coil inside her gut. This was not the Donoval she knew. But if he didn't want to speak of it, she wouldn't press.

"Tomorrow I launch a test assault against Roark to see if he'll take our bait."

"A small foray to draw him out," he added with a grin. "Should be . . . interesting."

She could hear what sounded like a tremor of fear in his voice. It turned another screw in her gut. Donoval was fearless—at times, in her opinion, to the point of stupidity.

"I'll take twenty men and—"

"*We'll* take twenty men," he broke in.

"There's no need for you to fight this battle."

The grin disappeared from his face. He straightened. "After today there's every need. Your men need to know I ride with them. That I'm capable."

"Today was a fluke. You've been injured. No one expects you to lead this charge." Even to her own ears her assurances rang false. If he didn't ride with her and the men, their confidence in him would falter. But if he did, could she keep him safe?

"*I* expect it." His words sounded like a growl. "I ride with you tomorrow."

"As you command, my lord." She inclined her head in curt acknowledgment of the authority she'd granted him by their deal but couldn't keep the anger out of her voice. Let him kill himself if that's what he desired. Who was she to stop him? Unable and unwilling to put her fears into words, she whirled and stalked out of the tent.

"Aw, hell, Seri, come back. I didn't mean . . ." His voiced trailed after her.

Afraid to hear his pleas, afraid she'd succumb, she hurried away.

Serilda stood next to her warhorse, Ryder. Sensing her tension, the big beast pranced restlessly. Behind her, a troop of twenty of her best men awaited the order to ride into battle. Donoval strode up to her and stopped but didn't speak. The bruise she'd put on his cheek while wrestling made her look away in guilt. Hurting him had never been her intention.

Though the men followed her, she knew they instinctively looked to Donoval, to a man, for direction. She quashed her surge of resentment at their unconscious defection. If asked, they'd all swear loyalty to her. But three years couldn't wipe out centuries of male-dominated history and tradition. Even her victory in the wrestling match hadn't swayed them. Most if not all were of the opinion he'd allowed her to pin him.

That she and Donoval knew the truth didn't change her disquiet. He had the strength, but his skills were gone. Though no one else seemed to notice, his refusal to spar with her, his clumsy handling of his sword, along with his strange way of speaking and attitudes left her confused and concerned. In more ways than she cared to count, he wasn't the man she remembered.

The Donoval she knew never backed away from a fight—even one he believed he might lose. His male pride wouldn't allow it. His insistence on riding today should have reassured her that he hadn't changed completely, but it didn't.

She started to hand Donoval Ryder's reins, but he took the reins of the smaller mount instead.

"Ryder's been your horse for the last three years. Let's not confuse him by changing riders," he said softly. Whatever anger he'd harbored toward her the night before was now gone.

"I'm sure he remembers you. You bred and

trained him." She didn't understand her protest, but felt obliged to make it anyway.

As if to confirm her statement, Ryder snuffled Donoval's chest, then rested his massive head on the man's shoulder.

He staggered under the weight. "But I gave him to you."

"As you wish." Refusing to argue with him in front of her men, she swung up into the saddle, then watched in disbelief as he clambered gracelessly onto the smaller horse. Once he was mounted she said, "We await your orders, King Donoval."

He shook his head. "These are your men, Seri. Your battle plan, your command." He spoke for her ears alone. None of her men heard his words.

With each passing moment, her unease grew. Who was this man who claimed to be King Donoval?

The skirmish started well. Serilda led the attack on the western gate. Unable to resist her taunting, Roark opened the small portcullis and dispatched a troop of thirty men. Of course, she'd known he would. By doing so, he risked little and stood to gain much. Roark knew that even if Serilda managed to fight her way to the gate, she'd never be able to penetrate far into the castle walls with this small force. Not since the gate opened to a narrow corridor. Once they were in that corridor, archers on the battlements or in the courtyard could easily pick off her men. Later, when her men breached the eastern gate and gained access to the main yard of the castle fortress, they'd use that same situation against Roark.

Of course, if his troop defeated hers, he could

capture her and end the siege and the war with minimal losses. Not that losing men—allies or foes—ever bothered Roark.

Fear receded to the back of her mind. With a battle cry, she pulled her sword and charged into the fray. Her men followed. In the bright light of day, swords clashed. Men and horses shrieked. Blood flowed.

Answering the press of her knees and his training as a warhorse, Ryder moved as if he was part of her body. They dodged and surged. He reared and lunged, knocking an oncoming attacker from his saddle. Hooves slashed downward, ending the man's scream.

From the corner of her eye, Serilda looked for Donoval. Expecting him to be at her side, she was troubled to see him a distance away, surrounded by four of Roark's men. His sword glinted in the sunlight as he fought, but something wasn't right. It was just as she'd feared: he was barely managing to retain his seat; he moved sluggishly, ineptly, without his usual expertise or fluid style.

His foes moved in for the kill.

Chapter Thirteen

Roark's men poured out of the gate. They attacked swift and hard. Frozen with fear, I watched as Seri led the charge to meet them.

I'd written dozens of battle scenes. I'd written this very scene, in fact, while she was planning strategy in her tent. This small skirmish between Seri and Roark's men—my writing—had been a desperate attempt to take control of this world I'd created but that had now absorbed me. I'd scribbled out what I imagined should happen, what I'd hoped would happen, and I prayed it would truly be the outcome. Seri's men would prevail. If I were to trust my power, I should have no fear, but . . . living it was different. The sights, the sounds, the smells, all overwhelmed my senses. Swords flashed. Men screamed. Metal clanged against metal. Blood. Death. Dying.

I hadn't been able to write every detail, either, or what happened to Donoval; there hadn't been time before Seri became curious about the parchment I used and I had to toss it into the fire. Had that action made a difference? Would I have been able to affect the outcome either way?

Sunlight spilled over the meadow, its warm yellow light a sharp contrast to the dark intensity of the battle being waged. Men fought somberly, the only sounds the ringing metal, the creak of leather, grunts and cries of pain, the muffled thud of hooves against the ground. The smell of fear, that acrid mixture of sweat both human and animal, dirt, and blood, burned my nostrils.

I needed to defend myself, to fight, but at that moment I had an attack of sanity—or insanity. I couldn't accept this situation. Paralyzed, I watched as Roark's men clashed with Seri's troops.

Four of them quickly surrounded me. I drew my sword, but everything I'd ever learned or written about swordplay fled my mind. I reminded myself that this was not a game. This was not fiction, however it had started. This was real. These men meant to kill me. Whatever happened here couldn't be edited, rewritten, or revised.

Something slammed against my back. It was a sword blade, and my metal armor prevented it from cutting me in half, but pain radiated up and down my spine. My horse tossed its head and pranced to one side. A blade thrust past where a second ago my throat had been. Another blade whooshed toward my head. I ducked.

Inside me, the spirit of Donoval swore. I felt him fighting to break free of the restraints I'd placed on him, fighting to return to his body. Which did I fear more, dying in this battle or losing myself?

Losing Seri. That's all I cared about.

Adrenaline coursed through me. I swung my

sword wildly. A cry of pain let me know I'd struck a target. Satisfaction rushed through me as blood sprayed across my face and chest. As I pulled back to see, the man's shocked eyes met mine, then clouded over. He slid limply from his horse. I lost sight of him beneath the milling horses. Hot and metallic, I tasted his blood on my lips.

Horror gripped me. In this reality, I'd killed a man! Sitting in my office writing, I'd thought I understood the emotions of my characters as they lived, laughed, cried, loved, killed, and died. I'd had no clue. Still, the bile clogging my throat couldn't eliminate my gratification at seeing the man fall. He'd meant to kill me and to stop Seri. He would have known no regret had I been the one to die.

Other men entered the fray, distracting my attackers and leaving me alone on the field.

Part of me wanted to flee, to return to the safe, secure world behind my keyboard, where blood and death were mere words on the page. Another part craved something different, something more elemental. That buried part of me reveled in the destruction, gloried in the required strength and skill. That part was Donoval. Like a drug, the urge to strike back, to kill first those who would kill me flooded my veins. But a battle raged between the Brandon I knew myself to be and the character I'd created and whose body I inhabited.

My fingers clutched the hilt of my sword. I held it up. Sunlight glinting off the crimson blood mesmerized me. How easy it would be to let go, to surrender logic, reason, and compassion, to give in to the creature hammering to be released. But if I did, if I became a killing machine, could I ever again be

me: Brandon Alexander Davis? Or would I be forever altered, changed? Would actions in this world
be the same as actions in mine? And even more
troubling, would becoming one with Donoval trap
me in this world?

As I struggled to hold on to myself amidst the
chaos swirling around me, I saw Seri a few yards
away. She fought one man, and another approached
from her rear. She plunged her sword into the first,
but before she could turn and defend herself the
second would be on her. Only I was close enough
to help.

Again, fear rendered me helpless. My scribbles
on paper couldn't save her. I'd tried that already,
and things looked grim.

But I can help, a voice thundered inside me.

In desperation, I surrendered to the power of
Donoval, let his persona seize control of our body.
Without conscious thought, I began to fight, thrust-
ing, cutting, slicing. No longer pausing to see the
results of my blows, I plowed through Roark's men.
I had to reach Seri!

With his hind legs, Ryder lashed out at Seri's attacker and missed. The movement threw her off
balance. She fell forward over the animal's neck. I
came up beside her assailant, who was focused on
her. Before he could strike, I shoved my blade
through his throat. He died with a gurgle.

There was no time for celebration amidst the
melee; the battle raged on, separating me from Seri
almost immediately. And from that moment on,
Donoval's body memory and skill directed me,
fought for me, saved me, saved Seri.

Time stretched out endlessly as I fought and killed.

I took many wounds, but I felt nothing. Only later did I realize the skirmish lasted mere minutes.

At the last moment, Donoval ducked. Serilda breathed a quick sigh of relief. Distracted by his near miss, she almost didn't avoid the next attack against her. A blade ripped through the leather guard on her arm and found her arm.

Behind her, she heard and felt the approach of a rider. Locked in battle with another man, she couldn't turn to look. Ryder lashed out with his hind legs, throwing her off balance for a split second. The man in front of her tried to use the distraction, but she leaned forward and came in under his guard. He died as her sword came up through his chin. When she turned, the other man was gone.

She fought on. Locked in a life-and-death struggle, time ceased to have meaning. Time after time she swung her sword. Bodies spouting blood and gore fell around her. The smell of death, sweat, and human waste stung her nose. Her arms ached. Her mouth went dry. Screams of pain deafened her.

She was pleased to see her men dispatch Roark's. He'd sent out a significant number, but Serilda's soldiers had bested them, and there would clearly be no reinforcements. The skirmish was drawing to an end.

At last, Roark's few remaining men-at-arms turned tail and ran. However, the gate was barred. Their leader didn't tolerate failure.

The men backed up, waiting for the final blow, waiting to be cut down by Serilda's force. Instead, she signaled her men to pull back, leaving the few survivors to face their leader's wrath. If they were smart, they'd run while they had the chance. Roark's anger at losing even a small battle would not be pretty, and he'd take his rage out on those who'd failed but returned.

She'd accomplished her goal. The next time she attacked, Roark would be likely to send a larger force to meet her, leaving the other gate much less guarded. That was the plan.

Eyes averted from the carnage, she sat and waited as her men gathered up their dead and wounded. Of the soldiers she'd started with, she'd lost three. The rest all bore some injury, most minor, a few serious—and there was at least one that would prove fatal. Her battle lust faded, leaving behind the burning acid of regret for lives needlessly lost, for lives destroyed. For lives, both theirs and hers, forever changed by one man's greed and lust for power.

"Lady d'Lar." Hasen, her second-in-command, approached her. "King Donoval has been injured."

"What? How bad?" The last she'd seen him, Donoval had been holding his own. Yet he hadn't fought with his usual skill at any point, and his sword-work was slow and clumsy. Unwilling to admit the cold knot of dread forming in her chest, she searched the milling men for a glimpse of him. His blond head was nowhere in sight.

"I don't know. He refuses to allow anyone to see, and there's much blood."

The battle was over. Donoval retreated, but he stayed part of me, no longer a separate entity; I had let him in.

My thoughts cleared as I came back to myself. My bloodied sword dangled from my hand as I sat atop my horse. Other riderless steeds milled around. Mangled, bloody bodies littered the ground. Some twitched and moaned; others lay still, staring at the cloudless sky with glassy eyes.

Seri's men whooped and yelled at the few survivors of Roark's troop that ran back toward their castle. I searched for her amidst the crowd. Back straight, face blank of emotion, she sat atop her warhorse. Relief slammed into me.

I'd written that she'd survive, and I'd written her standing where she did, but I hadn't written the part about my—Donoval's—intervention. Had my words influenced the outcome of this fight, or was her survival coincidence? Had I any control over what happened in this world? Was Seri's death at Roark's hands already preordained by what I'd written, not to be changed?

I couldn't accept that. My being here altered everything. It had to.

I lifted my arm to gain Seri's attention. A surge of pain caught me by surprise. Through a gash in the leather guard, blood dripped from a cut on my sword arm. The world wavered around me. I swayed in my saddle. A strong hand clasped my shoulder and held me upright.

"My lord, are you injured?" Hasen asked. He had ridden up behind me.

I stared at him in disbelief. Blood caked my body from head to toe, and he wanted to know if I was injured? I took an inventory. The gashes on my cheek, thigh, and calf, though bloody, seemed minor. Wincing, I pressed my palm against the slash just above my groin, below where the armor ended. Hot and sticky, blood seeped through my fingers. It didn't feel like a mortal wound—or at least my guts weren't spilling out—and the pain from this cut was less than some of the others, but in this world, without the aid and assistance of a real doctor, how could I be sure?

When I didn't answer, Hasen tried to pull my hand aside to see.

"I'm fine!" I shoved him away with a bit more force than I intended, and I nearly toppled him off his horse.

He gave me a skeptical look before galloping off to pull up next to Seri. I watched him engage her in conversation; then I groaned as her angry gaze turned to me. What had I done wrong now?

Back in camp, her lips tightly compressed to keep from berating Donoval in front of her men for his carelessness, Serilda waited while he dismounted and preceded her into her large tent. Warmth from the cheery fire blazing near the entrance couldn't touch the chill deep inside her.

Along with clean linen strips, Mauri had left water to boil, a needle and silk thread, and an herbal salve. Fresh bread, fruit, cheese, and wine waited on the table.

Serilda pushed Donoval toward the bed.

"I'll get blood on the bed robes," he protested with a cocky grin.

"Don't argue." She pushed him down and undid his plate armor. Once it was off, she untied and removed the leather guards from his arms and legs.

When the movement pulled open the cut on his arm, moisture beaded his brow. His hand pressed tightly to his abdomen, he winced but said nothing. She saw sweat roll into a cut on his cheek.

The wounds on Donoval's face, chest, and arm appeared minor if painful. The deep gash on his thigh would need stitches. The one he hid beneath his palm, which still seeped blood, concerned her more. If a sword had penetrated his innards, there was little anyone could do for him; he was already dead. She hated the horror she felt, the pain it caused her heart.

After she'd removed all but his leggings, she cleaned and bandaged his injuries, all except the one on his thigh and under his hand. Finally, she had no other choice. She laid her hand over his. "Let me see."

"It's just a scratch. It'll be fine."

"Don't be a fool. Let me see."

"Fine, then. Look." Intentionally misunderstanding which wound she wanted to see first, he wiggled out of his blood-soaked leggings.

She brushed aside his hand and examined both wounds. Looking at the one that had concerned her more, she flinched, then breathed a sigh of relief. A few inches lower and the sword-blow would have unmanned him, but in fact the blade had merely grazed his belly, leaving a ragged tear. It was no worse than the gash on his thigh.

She kept her gaze from confirming that his maleness remained intact, sure that if it had been touched he wouldn't be sitting calmly.

"You were fortunate today." Ignoring his sex,

which rested so near her fingers she could hardly breathe, she spoke while she cleaned and began to stitch the gash on his thigh.

"Damn!" He jumped as the needle pierced his flesh. "That hurts!

To hold him in place, she clamped her hand down on his leg. "Be still, or I might accidentally stitch your cock to your leg." She felt him flinch, and laughed.

Continuing the joke, she jabbed the needle toward his groin, but he caught her wrist in an inflexible grip. "Don't you have anything to numb my skin before you stitch me together?"

She hadn't thought to use numbweed, because in the past Donoval had always refused, considering it a sign of weakness rather than good sense. Unwanted guilt at causing him needless pain made her lash out, that and anger at his changed personality. "We save numbweed for serious injuries. As you said, these are naught but scratches."

He released her hand and nodded. Gritting his teeth he said, "You're right. Proceed."

She shook her head, bemused, but set to.

His muscles twitched and his lips thinned as she stitched his thigh, but he didn't utter another complaint. Each stitch increased her irritation. Averting her gaze from his groin, she cleaned and bandaged the cut on his abdomen.

Once she finished, her fear again morphed into anger. She could no longer contain her scathing censure. "I've never seen such ineptitude in battle. You handled your sword like a beardless boy! Mauri fights better."

When he didn't react with his typical heated dismissal of any criticism, she glanced at his face.

Something was really different here. "Why are you smiling? You could have been killed!"

"I didn't know you cared," he joked.

His humorous tone disconcerted her. The Donoval she knew had little sense of humor, especially concerning his skill. "I don't," she retorted. But her voice didn't carry the ring of conviction. "I need you alive. If you die before your troops arrive, I doubt they'll follow me into battle. Years of peace sitting on Shallon's throne have made you lazy and soft." And to prove her point, she jabbed the muscle of his uninjured arm. It felt solid as ever.

His grin grew, along with another part of him. "Not *so* soft."

Hot and hard, his thrusting manhood brushed against her fingers. She jerked away, but he caught her wrist and placed her hand on his arousal.

She inhaled sharply. The coppery smell of blood, the fresh mint of the herbal salve, and his familiar warm male scent invaded her lungs, stirred her senses, and teased her memories with the times she'd patched, stitched, and bandaged him before. He'd always come back from a battlefield aroused, no matter his wounds, and apparently now was no exception.

For her, the battle, the killing, all left her feeling shattered. Drained. Alone. Numb to any emotion beside rage. Then, as now, she needed to fill the emptiness inside her. Appease the beast. Soothe the flesh. Reaffirm life in the most elemental way. They'd always been good at that.

Yes, then as now, she could take what he offered, use him to fill the chasm in her soul—for the moment.

But things were different now. As before, she feared that being with Donoval offered only a fleeting reprieve to the loneliness inside her. Their encounters, though physically satisfying, left an emotional void. Like cool water poured over sunburn, the feeling couldn't last. Though she knew he cared for her, Donoval could not, would not, give her what she wanted, what she needed above all else. His heart beat only for his country, for his people.

With each gasp she took, his scent invaded her, curled and expanded in her lungs until she couldn't imagine breathing air devoid of his smell. She let her gaze travel down his muscled chest and flat abdomen to where her hand circled his heat. Need overcame common sense. Though it left her wanting, she'd take what he could give. Of their own volition, her fingers caressed the satiny skin covering the steel of his arousal.

"Make love with me?" he asked.

"What of your injuries?" She had never seen him so badly wounded.

She traced a finger along the edge of the gash on his thigh. His cock twitched.

"A scratch. *This* aches more." He touched his chest.

His soft plea startled her. Donoval didn't plead. He commanded. Ordered. Demanded. Occasionally, Donnie might tease and cajole, but he never *asked*. She looked into his eyes and saw . . .

She wasn't sure what she saw. Though this body and voice were Donoval's, the person who stared back at her was a stranger. And yet, he was not. Deep inside her, she felt she knew this man better than she ever had known or would ever know Donoval.

When she was young and vulnerable, she hadn't seen beyond Donoval's physical beauty and strength. Along with her body, she'd tried to give him her heart, but she'd discovered that while he'd share his body with her, he lacked the ability to love a woman—to treat her the way she wanted, to act as she needed, as an equal partner. Their lovemaking, while physically passionate, had never seemed to touch his heart the way his zeal for his people did. No, hours after they finished, she always felt more alone than before.

Though tolerant of her "foibles," he'd never seen her or any woman as a person, an equal, as a being with wants, needs, and desires separate from his. And when he'd had to choose, his heart belonged to his country, Shallon, and to his people. Serilda herself always came last.

Again, fear consumed her. Could she take what he offered without putting her heart at risk?

She didn't protest as he cupped the back of her head with his hand and drew her face to his. His breath caressed her cheek, and his lips hovered a whisper away from her mouth. "Make love with me?" he asked again.

Her body clamored for the release he could provide, but her mind and heart screamed in panic. Giving her heart to him again would destroy her.

"This is not sensible," she managed to say. "We need to focus on the coming battle."

"I don't want to be sensible," he said to cut off her objections. "All my life I've been sensible, careful, cautious. There'll be time enough come morning to plan. Tonight, with you, I want to be wild and crazy. *I want you.* Say yes."

His words made no sense. The Donoval she knew was not a normal, reasonable man. He was not sensible, careful, or cautious. He'd always been, in bed and out, a warrior, ardent and untamed. He claimed and conquered. Took what he wanted.

She returned to her previous concern. "What of your injuries? I've never seen you hurt to this degree. We don't want—"

One hand threaded through her hair, kneading her scalp, and the other drew her closer until her breasts pressed against his chest. "You can take care when you ride me."

The taste of his breath drove rational thought from her mind. *"Donoval."* His name came out on a gasp.

"Call me Donnie."

The sound of the nickname he hated on Donoval's lips shattered her resistance. Donnie was the man she wanted, the dream she'd created in her mind. Tender and loving. Passionate and wild. The man, the lover who valued her above all else. He was everything the king might have been but hadn't shown her.

"Donnie," she whispered against his lips.

With a groan, he covered her mouth with his. He stroked his palms down her body. All clothing fell away, leaving them naked. Skin to skin, they lay atop the bed robes. Warmth that had little to do with the heat radiating off his body surrounded and invaded her.

She pressed her lips to the tender skin behind his

ear. Soft wisps of hair tickled her cheeks and throat. A shudder ran through him. His palms settled over her buttocks and pulled her closer. Hard and heavy, his erection pressed against her belly. Like heat lightning, excitement sizzled through her veins.

Then her belly rasped over the bandage near his groin, reminding her of how close he'd come to dying. She lifted herself away until just the tips of her breasts brushed his chest.

"What's wrong?" he asked.

She trailed a fingertip along the lower edge of the bandage. His skin twitched. "If that blow had gone a hairsbreadth deeper . . ." Unable to continue, her voice trailed off. For the last three years she'd told herself her feelings for Donoval had died, that she no longer cared. Seeing him wounded put that lie to rest. She still questioned what she could and did feel for him but admitted she was far from indifferent.

He wove his fingers through hers and placed their joined hands over his heart. The steady thud soothed her lingering fear.

"But it didn't strike deeper. I'm still here. Alive and in one piece." He shifted so they lay side by side, flinched, then grinned. "Okay, I'm a bit bruised and battered, but mostly in one piece."

Donoval had always discounted his injuries, but he never joked about them. After a battle, his sexual hunger had been ferocious—at times frightening. Though he never revealed his feelings, she felt that only by conquering her could he banish the horror and fear he buried deep within him over the destruction he wrought. At those times, she'd opened her body and heart to him, giving him everything and receiving nothing beyond physical gratification in return.

His new, self-deprecating humor unsettled her. It left her unsure of what to expect.

"I don't wish to injure you further," she said again.

"The only way to do that is to leave me." The fierce hunger in his eyes was familiar, as was his hard cock pressed against her abdomen, but he didn't grab and demand. Instead, he cupped her cheek in his hand and gave her a crooked smile.

"If it'll set your mind at ease, we'll take it slow and easy. We've got all night," he suggested.

Slow and easy were not words Serilda associated with Donoval. Fast and furious. Hard and intense. But never slow and easy.

A memory of a dream teased her mind. Hands stroking. Exploring. Searching. Finding. Lips and tongue kissing. Licking. Tasting. Giving and receiving hours of sweet torturous pleasure . . . What was this dream? What was this memory?

The feel of Donnie's hands moving gently over her breasts dissipated the vaporous visions and replaced them with exquisite reality. Warm and wet, his lips closed over one nipple. Swirling his tongue around that sensitive peak, he coaxed a whimper from her. In a silent offering of surrender, she arched her back.

While he suckled at her breast, he slid his hand down her belly to part her damp curls and stroke the slick, swollen center of her sensation. Her breath caught in her throat, trapped by the eruption building inside her. It had been a long time. Too long since she'd allowed herself to feel anything, physically or emotionally. Too long since need had outweighed duty. She couldn't contain or control herself. She climaxed. Liquid fire surged through her veins. In the heat, reason evaporated. In that moment, the changes in Donoval didn't matter; nothing mattered but the feel of his hands around her, on her, in her.

Minutes passed. Her body shuddered with aftershocks as Donnie continued to stroke her gently.

"So much for slow and easy." He chuckled against her breast, then proceeded to demonstrate what slow and easy really meant.

Hours later, body slick with sweat and sated with pleasure, Serilda lay against Donoval's chest, listening to the rhythmic beat of his strong heart as he slept. She knew she should leave his side but couldn't find the will. Despite her best intentions, she'd fallen under his spell again. She should know better.

Where commands and orders failed to bring her to heel, soft words and tender touches had slipped past her defenses and brought her to her knees. Without a whimper of protest, she'd offered him everything.

Disgust at her weak will burned away physical contentment. She couldn't allow herself to love him. In return for his assistance, she'd promised him her homeland, her people, her body, but *no*, she refused to give him her heart.

She started to rise. Muttering in his sleep, Donnie turned toward her. He draped an arm across her chest and a leg over her thighs, pinning her against him. Despite the anger seething inside her, she told herself he needed rest. If she moved now he'd wake. Tomorrow would be soon enough to put distance between them. She closed her eyes and let sleep steal over her.

Her dreams were tormented. Would he be up to the coming battle?

Chapter Fourteen

The low rumble of the camp coming to life woke me. I opened my eyes to sunlight streaming in through the gaps around the tent flap. The smell of bacon cooking and coffee brewing tickled my nose and set my stomach to growling. Every bone and muscle in my body hurt, but I felt fantastic.

Since the battle, I'd begun to accept the Donoval aspect of myself, and he had begun to accept me. I no longer felt him fighting to break loose. Though I still didn't have complete command of his skills, we'd become one.

Asleep, her head tucked under my chin, her breathing soft and easy, Seri curled against my un-injured side. Memories of our loving sent a shiver of satisfaction through me. Hours of slow and easy had given way to fast and hard, then returned to a more languorous lovemaking, all of which left us exhausted and content.

I'd never considered myself highly sexed. Though in the early stages of our marriage I enjoyed sex with Wanda, when our relationship went bad—it was mostly my fault, I admit—what little desire I'd had for her or any woman died and went unmourned. The years after we split, being celibate never bothered me. The reward just didn't justify the effort.

Seri's appearance had rekindled my passion—and not only for sex but also for existence. She made me realize how isolated and alone I'd become. She'd brought me back to life.

Satisfaction faded as I acknowledged she hadn't made love to me, *Brandon*. She didn't even remember me. She didn't remember being in the real world. She didn't remember being my Seri. Here she was Serilda d'Lar, warrior woman of Barue. And though she denied it even to herself, in this world she loved King Donoval.

Trying to figure out the how and why of her appearance in my world and my transportation to hers made my head pound. Bizarre as they were, Grandma's tales were the most logical explanation. In the end, it didn't matter, though. If this was all a dream, a hallucination, then I was locked away in a padded cell somewhere, and whatever happened couldn't hurt me.

My aching, abused flesh didn't feel imaginary. The heat from the fever I feared I'd developed from my wounds felt real. The cuts and bruises on my body felt real. I felt real. Seri's warm body pressed against me felt real. The memory of making love to her felt exquisitely real.

A new thought process overwhelmed me: what mattered most was how much of Seri's story I'd rewritten before I'd ended up a secondary character in my own book. I searched my mind but couldn't recall. Before I'd blacked out, had I finished revising that final, deadly scene? And if I had managed to make the critical changes, would things happen as I'd written, or did my presence here throw everything up for grabs? None of Grandma's stories mentioned what would happen if the writer ended up inside his fictional world. According to her, my father had never returned to say—assuming I was experiencing something similar to what he had. Yesterday's battle and what happened between Seri and myself hadn't gone exactly as I'd written it, so I just didn't know.

Seri must have felt my tension, because she stirred and opened her eyes. For a moment, I basked in the love shining there; then her body stiffened, and her gaze hardened. Before I could say anything, she sprang to her feet. I shivered, not from the loss of her warmth, but from the ice in her eyes as she threw on her clothing.

"Seri." I sat up, groaning as my body protested.

"I've asked you not to call me that silly name."

Her rejection of what we'd shared triggered an answering anger in me. "You didn't object last night," I goaded.

Her nostrils flared. "Last night was a mistake. One I'll not repeat." Shoulders rigid, she turned her back.

"Get dressed." She tossed me my pants and shirt. "In two days your troops will arrive. We've much planning to do." She strode out of the tent.

Pain, not all of it physical, slammed into me, but anger drove me to my feet. Ignoring the protest of my aching muscles, I dressed and went over to the table. Maybe studying the maps and working on a battle plan would distract me from thinking about this irritating woman. But I doubted it.

Surprisingly, after a few minutes I found myself wrapped up in creating a battle strategy. I guess I'd put more of me in Donoval than I thought—or his shared personality was giving me pointers. But this felt like something that had come from the core of me.

The plan I came up with would require precise timing, but it could work. I thought about attempting to write an easier strategy in novel form, give Seri and myself more options, but given doubts about my ability to change what I'd already written about the layout of Roark's castle, I wasn't confident of the outcome. Better to work with what I knew than depend on hope. Of course, this plan would only work if Donoval's troops showed up.

Looking back, I decided my hasty rewrites from the day before had perhaps yielded partial results. In my original version of the battle, Seri survived, but during the fight young Jole was taken hostage—the action that led to the final confrontation between Seri and Roark where they both died. When I wrote myself/Donoval into the scene, I'd taken out the part about Jole's capture. As far as I knew, the unknowing prince was safe.

Of course, nowhere had I mentioned Donoval being injured or Serilda and him making love.

As the creator of this world, I should have more control! Instead, I felt as if some cosmic editor was redlining my work, making sure I kept the conflict on track even when I wanted to derail it.

No, I couldn't be sure what might happen, even

if I attempted more rewrites. I'd have to live with what I had and hope it worked. Or, more to the point, I'd have to make my plans come to fruition myself.

I leaned over the map. Though outside the weather had turned cold and gray, sweat trickled down my back. The tent flap opened. A breeze blew the parchment across the table. It struck a candle and one corner burst into flame. Swearing in aggravation, I grabbed it and mashed it out.

"Damn it! Be more careful." I shook the parchment at the intruder, grimacing.

"Pardon, my lord."

With his usual composure, Jole took the map from my hand and smoothed it back onto the table. Wide-eyed at the vitriol in my outburst, Mauri peeked around the opening. I sighed and plopped down in a chair.

"Plans not going well, my lord?" Jole asked. He motioned Mauri into the tent, then secured the flap behind her. I had an amusing thought: if he weren't destined to be king, the boy would make a great butler.

Clutching a steaming pot of tea with the edge of her tunic, Mauri scurried over to the small table beside the bed. She carefully poured some tea and handed me a cup. I grimaced at the bitter odor and at the circumstances. I'd hoped Seri would bring this medicinal tea, but she hadn't returned to the tent since morning.

"Drink," Mauri urged.

The pungent smell made my eyes water. "I'd rather have some wine."

"I'll bring some with the evening meal," Jole offered. "But for now you'd best drink the tea."

"And if I don't?" I felt and sounded sullen.

The flap opened again, letting in a blast of frigid air. I looked up into Seri's scowling face.

"I'll hold you down and pour it down your stubborn throat."

"You and what army?"

I tossed the tea out onto the ground and jumped to my feet. We stood nose to nose. Her breath felt cool on my heated skin.

She crossed her arms over her chest and stared. "I need no army. I bested you before. I can do so again."

"Leave us," I told Jole and Mauri. I was fed up with her using them, Hausic, and others to avoid talking to me. This was my chance.

While we faced off, Jole hustled Mauri out of the tent.

"Probably," I said. I snatched up my cup, poured another helping of the noxious brew, and gulped it down. I burned my tongue in the process, and the stuff did little more than make me feel queasy. I doubted it was having any affect on the infection growing inside my wound.

"Probably?" she repeated. Her mouth quirked up on one side.

Ignoring her response, I strode to the table and bent over the map again. "Where have you been all afternoon? There's still a lot to go over before my men arrive."

She came to stand behind me and look over my shoulder. "Seeing to my troops. Giving the commanders their orders. Our plan won't work if they don't know what to do when the time comes."

Her rational explanation left me feeling like a sulky child. "You've been avoiding me."

"I was here all morning."

"Physically, yes—along with Hausic, Josef, and others. But your mind was elsewhere." *And your heart, where was* it? I wanted to ask, but didn't. Any talk of feelings chased her away faster than a tarak did a mouse.

Aside from working with me on laying out a plan of action against Roark, she'd done her best to avoid being alone with me. After our one night together, in the evening when the camp settled down, she disappeared, leaving me in the tent to toss and turn.

"Once Roark is defeated, you won't be able to avoid me any longer. You'll be my bondmate," I taunted.

Judging by the flare of anger in her eyes, I might as well have said *slave*. She dropped the parchment she was holding and stomped out of the tent.

"Nice going, Donoval," I muttered to myself and flopped down on the bed.

Having apparently pushed on through the night, my—no, *Donoval's*—troops arrived a day early. Following the orders I'd given, only a small fraction of the soldiers came into camp. The rest of the men remained out of sight, so as not to give Roark warning of the increase in our ranks.

As I moved among the men—Donoval's and Serilda's—I found myself greeting each commander by name. I laughed and talked with the common soldiers. I gripped their hands, accepted their slaps on the back without wincing, and I managed to make sure none of them saw the effort it took. I hid my pain, refusing to allow the fever sapping my strength to slow my steps. Despite the medicinal brews and the herbal salves, I knew infection had set in. I needed time and rest to regain my strength.

We had neither. Tomorrow, the assault on Roark's castle began. I wasn't going to fail Seri.

Forgotten in the commotion, Serilda stood to the side and watched as long-parted comrades greeted each other. Many of her men had fought with Donoval's in his war to claim the throne of Shallon, and bonds forged between men in battle remained strong.

None of the warriors seemed to notice the strain on Donoval's face, his flushed cheeks and over-bright eyes as he moved through their ranks. But Serilda did.

"Gerhan Esday," she greeted the large bear of a man who served as Donoval's second-in-command.

"Lady d'Lar. A pleasure to see you again." Gerhan bent at the waist in an awkward bow.

Getting the grizzled warrior to follow her into combat wouldn't be easy, but it wouldn't be impossible. Though in his heart he believed women were meant to be wives and mothers, meant to serve men in the kitchen and bedchamber, after she'd defeated him in hand-to-hand combat, he'd ceased to regard her as female. To him, she was a soldier. Devoted to Donoval, Gerhan would soon be on her side if she convinced him his king's life was at risk.

"It's good you're here early," Donnie said around

a ragged cough. "The weather is changing sooner than we'd hoped."

Serilda glanced up at the churning clouds. The recently clear blue sky had changed to pewter gray. A cold gust of wind whipped through the trees, stripping away the remaining leaves that only a few days earlier had burst with red, yellow, and orange color. A drizzle began to fall, and Serilda shivered. Donnie didn't seem to notice the moisture or the drop in temperature. She worried that this was because of his fever.

"Let's go to the tent," she told Gerhan, "and we'll brief you on the battle strategy."

Both he and his king followed.

Serilda watched Donoval walk behind her. As he did, she saw him lean heavily on his second-in-command, an arm thrown across Gerhan's shoulders, though he hid the act as a gesture of affection. She feared if he went into battle ill and still lacking in skill, he'd certainly falter and die. Somehow she had to convince or trick him into remaining behind.

After the crisp outside air, the warmth of the tent felt oppressive. Sweat trickled down my temples and dampened my shirt. Conversely, I shivered. When I wiped my brow, Seri's eyes narrowed. I'd done my best to hide the fever raging in me, but her sharp eyes didn't miss much.

Yes, I was a bit worse for wear, and she watched me like the proverbial hawk, never leaving my side for a moment, waiting to pounce on the slightest sign of weakness. She was planning something. Something I was sure I wasn't going to like.

"The plan is simple," Seri began. "Dawn tomorrow we attack the western gate with the entire force we have in camp. When the majority of Roark's troops rush to its defense, I'll lead a small group through this hidden entrance. Here." She stabbed her dagger into the spot on the map that I'd suggested. "Once inside the fortress, we'll make our way to the eastern gate. There we'll eliminate any remaining guards and open the portcullis for the rest of our troops."

"Your plan may be simple, but it's fraught with danger. What if there is no secret entrance? What if Roark does not reposition his men?" Gerhan, a master of battle tactics, asked the questions we'd so far ignored. We hadn't wanted to send a scout to the secret entrance for fear of attracting attention.

"I know the risks are great," Seri countered. "But we have no choice. If we don't roust Roark from his castle before the snow flies, we'll have lost all opportunity. You know this."

Gerhan looked to me for confirmation of her assessment. It took most of my strength to nod. The room seemed to swim in and out of focus. To keep from falling, I sat on a stool. As they continued to talk, my mind wandered.

"What say you to this mad plan, sire?"

The suspicion in Gerhan's voice roused me from a half dream. King Donoval wasn't known for letting others direct his campaigns. "We'll go with Se-Lady d'Lar's plan," I said.

"Yes, my lord." He didn't look fully persuaded of the wisdom of our plans, but I couldn't summon the energy to argue him around to our way of thinking. Good thing I'd written the man as utterly loyal to his king.

"Inform your lieutenants and see to deployment of the troops. And Gerhan . . ." I stopped him as he turned to leave the tent. "Lady d'Lar's orders are the same as mine. Is that clear?" I summoned all my strength to put the ring of command into my voice. The effort left me drained. "Obey her as you would me."

"As you wish, sire." He bowed and left.

Her back to me, Seri stood at the table. "You have my gratitude."

I moved to her side. "It's not your gratitude I want." I trailed the back of my hand down her cheek.

"What *do* you want from me?"

The question echoed inside me. What did I want, exactly? Her survival? Of course, but it was also possible I could accomplish that without her coop- eration. The arrival of Donoval's troops suggested more that my writing could indeed influence what happened in this world; maybe not in every detail, as my battered body illustrated, but enough to keep her alive. With quill and parchment and time, I could probably rewrite my ending so that she won her battle against Roark, freed Barue, and lived happily ever after. But that wasn't enough. I wanted her to be real. I wanted to take her back with me. I wanted her to accept me for who I was: Brandon Alexander.

I wanted her love.

I must have spoken out loud, because she jerked away.

"I cannot, I will not, love you."

The pain of her rejection lanced through me, until I remembered it was Donoval she denied loving, not me. I'd written this whole sorry mess: their love affair, Donoval's unintentional betrayal. Their split. At the time, it suited my purpose and my state of mind to break them up. The Barbarian King books were done, and I needed Serilda unencumbered by a relationship. If I'd written a happily ever after, the series would have stalled. Plus, in the midst of my breakup with Wanda, I wasn't feeling much of a happily-ever-after vibe.

"You'd go back on your word to be my bond-mate?" I found myself spewing Donoval's nonsense.

She turned to face me. The pain and confusion in her eyes made me want to tell her everything, to explain, to make her believe what I myself had trouble accepting; but I'd tried that route before and it hadn't worked.

"Once Barue is freed from Roark, I will honor my bargain with you. I'll become your bondmate, but I cannot be the woman, the queen you need."

"You're wrong." I reached out to touch her face, to tell her she *was* the woman I needed, the woman I wanted, the queen of my heart.

"Is loving me so difficult?" The question was all me. Donoval would never beg.

Or was it all me? In my fevered brain, Serilda and Seri, Donoval and myself all melted together. I couldn't separate our lives, our histories, couldn't tell what was real, what was fiction.

Seri's lips moved, but I couldn't hear. A roaring in my head drowned out her answer, and the world went black.

* * *

The next morning, the healer straightened from her exam of the sleeping monarch. "The fever has broken. With rest and proper care, King Donoval will fully recover." She handed Serilda several small packets of powder. "Give him one packet mixed in a draught of wine twice a day, and keep him abed for at least a week."

Serilda gripped the healer's arm. "You will say nothing of King Donoval's illness," she ordered. She couldn't risk losing the support of his troops.

"As you wish, my lady." Eyes wide, the healer nodded.

The tight band across Serilda's heart relaxed. She let the woman go. The healer bowed and exited the tent.

Donoval's strength and stamina were legendary. He did not allow himself weakness of either body or mind. No matter his wounds, she'd never before seen him less than wholly in command. Seeing him crumble unnerved her, left her blaming herself. She should have seen he was ill sooner, done something to prevent it. But this man was both more and less than the Donoval she knew. His bumbling performance on the battlefield as well as the difference in his words and manner clearly indicated something amiss. His declaration of love should have warned her all was not right with him.

Still, she had no choice.

"Seri?"

She turned to see Donoval struggling to rise. She rushed to his side. Heat no longer radiated in waves off his body. His eyes blinked open.

"W-water," he rasped.

Lifting his head with her hand, Seri held a cup of

medicinal tea to his parched lips. Beneath her fingers his skin felt cool and dry. His heart beat a strong steady rhythm. She felt his strength and determination.

He swallowed then sputtered. "Damn! What is this swill?"

"Herbal tea. We've been giving it to you all along."

"Well, it smells and tastes like sewer water. Give me some of that wine the doctor ordered."

"You heard the healer?" As she prepared the wine, he sat up.

"Yep, every word. Thanks." He accepted the goblet, took a healthy swallow, then grinned. The color returned to his pale face. "Much better. And that wine was great. Now I'm starved."

Serilda took the empty goblet he held out. Relief eased through her: a dying man didn't demand food.

"What time is it?" Concern flashed in his eyes as he looked around the tent. A lantern provided the only light. Outside, clouds heavy with the threat of rain blanketed the night sky. "How long was I out?"

"Near dawn. You slept through yesterday and most of the night."

"You should have woken me." He attempted to rise, then with a grunt plopped back down. "I need to get ready."

"You need to rest."

Despite the sweat that popped out on his brow, he struggled to his feet and reached for his clothing. "There'll be plenty of time for rest after we take the castle. Help me with this stupid armor."

"You'll rest *now*."

At her response, his gaze shot to the empty goblet, then back to her. Along with the first hint of morning, understanding dawned. "This tastes . . . You drugged me?"

"Yes."

"Why?" He clutched the tent pole to keep from sagging as the drug took effect.

"You're injured and ill. Gerhan agrees you're in no condition to fight," she lied. Gerhan had no idea what she was up to. "I can handle this battle without you. I have no need of your help."

"You're wrong! You need me more than you know. Without me . . . I don't know what will happen. Seri, don't do this. Please," he begged.

Strapping on her sword, Serilda turned away. Donoval's abnormal reaction to being drugged, entreating her rather than raging at her, proved she'd made the right decision. She didn't know what had changed him, but Donoval as he was now had no business on a battlefield. Then why was resisting Donoval's commands easier than Donnie's pleas?

A soft thud made her pause and look back. Half dressed, his arm stretched out toward her, Donnie sprawled across the bed, unconscious. She brushed the hair from his face. Relaxed in sleep as he was, the deep lines of stress around his mouth and eyes were smoothed away, making him appear young and untroubled, different than she'd seen him lately, beset by the concerns of ruling a nation.

No, she couldn't allow him to risk his life for the people of Barue. They were her people. This was her fight, not his. She'd always wanted independence, and he'd never wanted to fight for her. Wasn't this the time to prove her mettle?

Also, if he were killed, Shallon and its people would lose a great leader. Without him, Shallon would flounder and fall back into the barbarity it had known before he took the throne. She couldn't let that happen.

Inside, she knew she lied. If he fell, Shallon would survive; it was she who would not. What she feared most had already happened. She'd given him her heart.

Yet, they had no future together. When he woke, his pride would never allow him to forgive her deceit and betrayal. Would he still demand she be his bondmate? She doubted it. Whatever feelings he held for her would dissolve beneath his fury. Considering his pride, after being drugged and kept out of a battle . . . Even if she succeeded and was victorious over Roark, she'd have to face Donoval's rage. She'd be fortunate if he merely banished her from her country.

"Be safe, my heart," she whispered. Then she shook off her hopeless longings and marched out of the tent.

Chapter Fifteen

I woke to the rumble of thunder and the sound of rain pelting the tent. My body ached, and my mouth tasted like the bottom of Seri's kittens' litter pan smelled. How long had I been out? Prying open my gritty eyes, I stood and walked to the tent flap. Peering out through the torrents of rain, I couldn't determine the hour. I pulled on a shirt, trousers, and boots, but my armor and weapons were missing.

Once I was outside, wind-driven rain soaked me through to my skin in seconds. I shivered.

Except for the sentries guarding the camp, no able-bodied men or warhorses remained. I scanned the horizon. Because the camp lay behind a wooded hill several miles from the fortress, I couldn't see or hear anything of the battle.

As I entered his tent, Hausic looked up from where he huddled by the stove. "My lord. You should not be up." He came to my side and tried to lead me to the chair he'd vacated. "Sit. Warm yourself."

The cheery fire blazing in the stove couldn't dispel the cloud of worry hanging over him, or the fear growing inside me.

I shrugged off his hand. "How long have they been gone?"

"Four hours."

Fortunately for me, in Donoval's first book I'd set him up as resistant to most drugs, so I'd only slept for a short time. Still, by now Seri's troops had attacked the western gate; she was with luck infiltrating the castle, and Donoval's men were in position. If all went according to plan, within the next hour Roark's soldiers would be defeated, Seri would triumph, and the usurper would die. But in order for this to happen, I—Donoval—had to be there. I'd finally recalled how I'd written the ending.

In my original book, when Seri confronted Roark, she slipped, and he plunged his blade through her. In my revised version, at the last moment Donoval stepped in and deflected Roark's blade. If I didn't get there in time, Seri would die.

Of course, things weren't proceeding as I'd rewritten them. Nowhere had I written that Seri drugged me. And Donoval hadn't been injured or sick.

I'd begun the book with Serilda destined to die. Everything in the story led to that final confrontation between her and Roark, led to her tragic death. Now, it seemed, no matter how I rewrote the pages or acted, something insisted on maintaining the integrity of my original concept. Fate was conspiring to keep her alone—alone and likely to die.

I wasn't about to give up. Whatever it took, I was going to be there to save Seri.

"Mauri is gone," Hausic said.

More memory of my book's original ending came back to me. "When?"

"She disappeared shortly after the troops left. I fear she's followed young Jole."

My fears ran in a different direction, one where Mauri was under Roark's control. He'd orchestrated the death of her family shortly after she reached the age of seven and had chosen her enchanted name. Through trickery, he'd learned her enchanted name, then set her in Serilda's path to become his eyes and ears in this camp. During the attack on the castle, Roark finally played his trump card; he'd summoned Mauri and used her.

But was this still the case? I'd looked for hints in the girl since my arrival in Seri's world, and I'd been able to find none. Everything here was a jumble of the versions of this story I'd written; plus things happened that I hadn't written or even imagined. What could I trust? What changes could I effect? And was I more apt to be successful with the sword or the pen?

I decided on a course of action. "I need quill and parchment," I told Hausic. I had to trust who and what I was.

Curiosity burned in his eyes, but he didn't question my request. He quickly produced both items, and I set to work.

Ink splotched both the parchment and my fingers as I scratched out another ending. The writing was horrible, stilted, passive, without my usual attention to detail or flowing language; it was a rough outline rather than a finished draft, but it said what needed to happen. I hoped it would work.

I carefully dried the ink, folded the parchment, and tucked it inside my shirt. Last time I'd destroyed the parchment, and maybe that had affected the outcome. I didn't know, but this time I wasn't taking the chance. And I had more yet to do.

"I need a horse and a sword," I told Hausic.

"Yes, my lord."

Hausic hobbled out of the tent. I followed him into the storm.

Though morning had dawned, pewter rain clouds dropped their loads and churned the world around us to murky soup lit only by bright streaks of lightning dancing across the sky. Wind-whipped rain stung my exposed flesh and blew wet hair into my eyes.

Moving silently, his robes billowing in the tempest, Hausic guided me unseen past the sentries to a tent on the far edge of the encampment. Inside, I found a sword and a dagger but still no armor. I strapped the belt and scabbard around my waist.

"I need a horse or I'll never get to the castle," I shouted over the growing crash of thunder as we moved outside.

"The soldiers took all the warhorses," Hausic replied. "He's not trained for battle, but you can use my mule to get to the castle."

I followed the old man to a corral where Seri kept animals not suited for combat. Oxen and mules used to pull the heavy wagons, along with goats and sheep for milk and meat, all mingled with several horses less massive than the average warhorse. Using the cover of rain and thunder to avoid the sentries' eyes and ears, we sneaked into the pen and retrieved Hausic's mule.

Standing outside the camp perimeter, I eyed the animal with dismay. Every insecurity I possessed now crowded my mind. Though smaller than a warhorse, the mule was a big, rawboned beast. During the fight, the well-trained warhorse had masked my pathetic riding skills. Now I had no such cover. And try as I did, I couldn't tap into Donoval's persona. I'd have to ride this animal alone. Bareback. We couldn't risk alerting the sentry guarding the tack tent.

"Give me a boost," I told Hausic.

Stepping into his cupped hands, I hoisted myself onto the mule's bony back and took the reins.

"He's called Honey." Hausic patted the animal's rangy neck. Drenched by rain, its brown-gray hide looked like mud.

"I hope he's as sweet tempered as his name," I muttered.

At the sound of my voice, Honey's ears flattened against his head. He swiveled around and gave me an evil look.

Hausic shook his head. "He's named for his sweet tooth. He's not pretty, but he's strong. He'll serve you well. King Donoval?"

The old man gripped my hand in his. Through sheets of rain, I met his anxious gaze. Water plastered his robes against his frail body and slicked his parchment-colored hair to his scalp.

"Yes?"

"Bring them all back safely."

After I nodded, he turned and disappeared into the storm.

Against my better judgment, I pushed Honey into a run. It was the right choice. Fleet and surefooted, the beast ran across the uneven plain while I clung precariously to his back. The wounds on my thigh and belly screamed at the abuse. I grimaced as the stitches on my thigh ripped. The rain soaking through my pants swept away the trickle of warmth running down my leg, and I similarly ignored the pain.

In the woods, without direction from me, Honey slowed to a trot. Here the thick trees blocked the howling wind, but the bare branches did nothing to ease the cold rain beating down. Steam rose off Honey's hide. My teeth chattered.

At the edge of the woods, I paused to take stock. Larger and more forbidding than I remembered, Roark's fortress rose before me. Built from blocks of black stone three feet high, five feet wide, and three feet deep, the outer wall stood twenty-five feet high and nearly ten feet deep. Across the top of the wall ran battlements where guards stood watch. The eastern gate opened into the central bailey, which led to the castle proper.

Off to the east, hidden from the battlements' view, I could see Donoval's troops lying in wait. At the western gate, Seri's troops engaged Roark's. Over the roar of thunder, I heard the clash of swords and the screams of men and horses. The shudder running down my spine owed nothing to the cold.

I slid off Honey's back. "Time for me to go on alone," I told the beast. "Thanks for your help."

After turning him toward the camp, I tied the reins across his withers and slapped him on the rump. He sprang forward and quickly disappeared into the woods.

On the battlements, torches sputtered in the downpour. In their flickering light, outlined against the flashes of lightning, I saw the dark shapes of at least four guards moving back and forth, their eyes scanning the ground through the storm. And perhaps there were more. Whatever else Roark was, he was no fool. Though he'd moved the bulk of his men to repel the main attack on the western gate, he hadn't left the eastern gate completely unguarded. If one of those guards sounded the alarm in time, Seri's attack would fail before it began.

Using rocks and shrubs as well as the downpour as cover, I crept across the hundred yards of open land toward the fortress wall. Fortunately for us, the construction had been abandoned before a moat had been dug. Water dripped into my eyes. I wiped it away.

Fifteen feet from the castle wall, I paused and waited for a guard to turn away so I could cross that last open space. This close, despite the storm, I feared my blond hair and white shirt would catch the eye. Another shape rose behind him. The guard . . . went down and didn't get back up.

I watched as the same happened to the other three guards. Seri had made it inside! So the hidden entrance truly existed. It was about time something went right.

"Yes," I whispered, then dashed across those last fifteen feet.

Back pressed against the wall, I knew I was an open target as I moved toward the secret entry. At last I made it. Rough stone tore my skin as I searched the grooves between the blocks for the concealed latch. Something moved beneath my fingers; then, with a creak barely audible above the rain and thunder, a section of stone swung inward. I tumbled backward into darkness.

My backside hit the stone floor with a thud. After the waterlogged air outside, inside the wall smelled dry and dusty. A fine mist drifted through the opening to dampen the grit beneath my palms. I blinked to clear the water from my eyes. Dim light illuminated a short distance along a passageway between courses of stone.

I pushed the stone door closed and immediately wished I hadn't. Complete black surrounded me. In the abrupt silence, the beat of my heart sounded louder than the thunder outside. The weight of the invisible stone walls pressed down. In that dead space, I struggled to breathe.

Resisting the urge to panic, I blinked rapidly. Bit by bit the darkness receded. Ahead, a sliver of light turned the black to gray. I stumbled along the narrow corridor until I reached the source of light, a door that led into the stables. Scuffs and damp boot prints in the dust on the floor indicated someone had been through here recently.

I pushed open the door. The smell of manure burned my nostrils. My eyes watered. Faint sounds of fighting drifted through the pungent air.

In the quiet of the stable, a hungry cow bellowed at an empty manger. Unconcerned with the disputes of men, a handful of scrawny chickens scratched and pecked the dirt, looking for nonexistent grain. A guard, his body covered with dirty straw, lay motionless in a corner.

Though Roark had commandeered the castle, he clearly didn't have the people necessary to maintain it. After standing empty for nearly twenty years and being occupied by Roark's troops for a mere twenty days, it was barely fit for habitation. If things were as bad as they seemed, long before they ran out of food or water, Roark and his men would die of disease.

With one hand I covered my mouth and nose, and with the other hand I drew my sword and moved cautiously through the stable into the main bailey. A quick look around confirmed no guards patrolled nearby. Not a single soul seemed to lurk in the derelict buildings.

In a window high in the keep, a light flickered. Was that Roark waiting inside? It seemed likely. From there, a person could keep watch over the fighting. And though an excellent swordsman, if he could avoid it, Roark preferred not to dirty his hands by engaging the enemy. He'd certainly see no need to venture out in the rain to fend off an attack. Not unless things turned truly dire.

The sounds of fighting grew louder. When and if they broke through the western gate, Seri's troops could only maintain the attack there for a short time without sustaining unacceptable loses. In the narrow corridor beyond, Roark's archers would easily pick them off. Roark would also soon become suspicious of such an ineffective attack and pull his extra forces back to protect the eastern gate—the gate that needed to be open for Donoval's soon-to-arrive troops.

Two thick drawbars barred the eastern gate. It would take at least two men to move them, but Seri and her team were nowhere in sight.

Rain sluiced over me as I moved along the wall toward the gate. A hand clamped on my arm and yanked me off balance. Before I could react, I stumbled backward through a doorway. *Thud!* Where a second before my chest had been, an arrow sank into the wood. A surge of fear-induced adrenaline drove the chill from my body. I looked up in time to see an archer tumble soundless from the battlement to land and lie motionless in the mud of the bailey. Another figure appeared. A torch flared, then sailed out into the storm. The signal had been sent. The figure disappeared from the walkway.

"Fool! What are you doing here?" Seri pressed herself against my back, I could feel her breasts burning into me. "And how did you awaken from the sleeping draught so quickly?"

I turned to face her. Relief at finding her alive and intact rendered me immune from the anger and confusion glittering in her eyes. "Fortunately for you, my body is resistant to most drugs." I sheathed my sword, then grabbed her face between my palms and kissed her. For a moment she resisted; then her lips softened beneath mine.

The world dissolved around me. Nothing existed but the heat flowing between us. Then she jerked free.

"Never mind," she decided. "Come. We have only minutes before your troops reach the gate."

Apparently unaffected by our kiss, she pulled me out of the doorway. I stumbled behind her. Rain washed away any lingering warmth in my body.

Three men appeared from the shadows to join us as we ran toward the eastern gate, and I groaned in horror. Jole was among them. This was another divergence from my rewrite. When I'd changed the ending, I'd had him stay safely behind the troops attacking the western gate.

Along with Seri and Jole, I climbed the stairs to finally reach the drawbar on the gate. On the far side, the three other men attempted to pull the second bar. Swollen with rain, the heavy wood resisted our efforts to drag it through the rusted metal guides. I wondered if these gates ever had been opened since the castle was abandoned.

Shouts rang out. I glanced up from my task. Men streamed out of the narrow corridor from the western gate into the bailey—Roark's men. Did that mean the main attack was succeeding? Outside and beyond the eastern gate I heard Gerhan's voice but couldn't make out his words.

Something rammed into the heavy metal-studded wood, jarring the drawbar under my hands. Gerhan and my men were using a battering ram. Rust from the metal guides flew into the air, and the vibration jolted through me. I lost my hold and stumbled. Seri grabbed my shoulder and kept me from falling.

Arrows thudded into the wood around us. One of Seri's men screamed and tumbled. Apparently some of Roark's archers had spotted us.

"Open the gate!" I grabbed at the drawbar and pulled once more. The muscles in my arms bunched and strained in protest. Despite a rain of arrows, Seri and Jole threw their strength behind mine, while the remaining two men on the other side did the same. The drawbars started to move.

Over the drumming of the rain and rumble of thunder, I barely heard the creaking groan as inch by inch the drawbars slid back. Before the last foot on our side cleared the gate, it flew open. Splinters of wood showered me. The weight of the crumbling gate struck and cracked the rotting supports of the catwalk upon which we stood. It gave way beneath us.

Led by Gerhan, my—Donoval's—troops stormed into the bailey. Swords flashing, they charged on foot and on warhorses toward Roark's men. In seconds, the bailey was a maelstrom of clashing steel and screaming warriors. Blood joined the rain, turning the ground to a pit of steaming mud.

Jole tumbled off the catwalk, but he rolled against the wall, out of the way of the oncoming hooves. Seri caught the top edge of the gate as it swung open. Now she dangled above the fight. I managed to be standing on the only part of the catwalk that didn't collapse, but I couldn't reach her. Nor could she jump to where I was. From the far side of the fighting, several of Roark's archers continued to shoot at us.

"Gerhan!" I shouted.

He looked up and headed toward me.

"No," I yelled, and pointed to Seri. "Help *her*."

With a quick nod he fought his way into position beneath her. "Seri, jump!"

At the sound of his voice, she glanced down. An arrow hit her left arm. Her body jerked. She lost her grip and fell.

"Seri!" Though I knew I couldn't reach, I lunged forward. With an ominous crack, the catwalk collapsed.

Pain and rain blurred Serilda's vision, but as she fell, she saw the catwalk disintegrate. Donnie shouted her name and lunged toward her.

"No!" she screamed as he staggered and fell. His

body disappeared into the crush of oncoming men and warhorses.

She herself landed belly down across Gerhan's saddle. Air whooshed from her lungs.

Through the tangle of men and horses, she caught a glimpse of blond hair on the ground; then it vanished as a warhorse fell. Pain lanced through her heart as she feared the worst. Tears burned her eyes.

Around her, swords continued to clash. Men and horses screamed. Mud and blood spattered her face. Rain sluiced it away.

"Donnie," she gasped, and tried to pull herself upright.

"Be still." With a hand in the middle of her back, Gerhan held her in place. His warhorse whirled and danced beneath her. Each movement pushed more air from her lungs and jarred the arrow protruding from her arm. She gasped for breath. Gritting her teeth against the fiery pain, she pulled it free.

"Let me down," she commanded.

Gerhan moved his warhorse to put more room between them and the battle raging all around. He lifted his hand. Ignoring the hot blood seeping from her arm, she twisted and slipped down the side of the horse to her feet. She pulled her sword and moved around the warhorse. Mud sucked at her boots in the unpaved bailey. Shaking his head but relieved of the need to protect her, Gerhan reentered the fray.

Off to her right, Serilda saw Jole, sword in hand, fighting. Part of her wanted to push him back into the shadows, out of harm's way, to keep him safe. Another part took pride as he fought with skill and courage.

Donnie was nowhere in view. She wasn't sure if he'd been crushed by the fallen horse, but she had to find him. She fought her way toward the base of the wall where he'd disappeared.

With a quick sword blow, she dispatched a man standing in her way. Donnie did not lie amidst the rubble of the catwalk or beneath the dead warhorse. A flower of hope bloomed inside her. Until she saw his cold, dead body, she'd nurture that fragile blossom.

"To the keep!" a man shouted.

Overwhelmed by the unexpected number of foes advancing into the bailey, and by the crush of warhorses, Roark's men ran for the central stronghold. High above, Serilda saw a light. Roark. He sheltered there. She couldn't allow his men to get inside and barricade the doors. In this fortress within a fortress, they could still hold out for weeks. Finding Donnie would have to wait.

"Stop them!" She ran toward the castle door. Rain sheeted down, keeping the world a murky gray.

Shouting directions from the back of his warhorse, Gerhan directed his men. They surged around the fleeing soldiers of the tyrant, barring the path into the castle. Fierce and unremitting, Roark's men fought to reach safety.

Lightning crackled across the sky. Thunder drowned the cries of the wounded and dying as their bodies were trampled into the mud. Again and again, Serilda swung her sword, clearing a path. Blood and gore covered her. Men screamed and fell. Pain and thought receded as training and hours of practice took control.

Suddenly, she was through the keep doors. Inside, she paused. Heavy stone walls muffled the sounds of fighting. In the relative quiet, battle lust subsided. She wiped the rain, mud, and blood from her face and looked around.

Torches flickered as rain trickled through the gaps in the ceiling. The smell of disuse, of rotting wood, mold, and animal droppings, filled the damp air. No rushes covered the stone floor. No fire burned in the massive hearth. No tapestries softened the walls. No servants cowered in corners waiting the outcome of the battle. Aside from the drips of water in the empty hearth, nothing stirred.

Outside, the fighting raged on. None of Roark's men had broken through Donoval's troops.

Her sword arm ached. Blood seeped from her wound and from other numerous cuts.

Where was Roark? A master swordsman, he sometimes fought alongside his men—especially when he needed to make a point. Though he was evil, cruel, and merciless, Serilda didn't believe him a coward. Why did he now hide inside this keep?

Not waiting for answers, she sheathed her sword, closed the heavy wooden door, and dropped the bar. She'd allow nothing and no one to interfere with her justice against this man who'd destroyed her world. Long ago she'd sworn he'd die by her hand and no other. So, why, now that the moment to extract vengeance had come, did she hesitate? Why did the need to find Donnie seem more urgent?

She shook off her doubts and questions. Alive or dead, Donnie would wait.

Pulling her sword, she made her way through the main hall to the stairs leading to the keep's living quarters. To keep her sword arm free in case a defender descended, she kept to the outside edge of the spiral staircase. No one challenged her. But muddy footprints on the stairs told her someone had recently come this way.

Following the prints, she soon reached the top level of the keep. She moved cautiously into the dark hall. No torches burned here, but she smelled the faint scent of a fire.

She rounded a corner and stopped. Ahead, light, warmth, and the aroma of meat and bread leaked from beneath a closed door. She tightened her grip on her sword. Behind that portal Roark awaited. In minutes, one of them would die.

Chapter Sixteen

Serilda stood frozen. In the five years since she'd last been in Roark's presence, she'd buried deep inside the memory of what she'd endured, her terror, her weakness, her guilt. Now, like a tidal wave, it rushed over her, until she couldn't breathe.

The dank torture chamber. Hanging by her wrists, naked, helpless, exposed. The smell of blood, sweat, and feces. Bloodworms burrowing into her flesh. The unceasing agony. Roark, touching her, his fingers trailing gently over the raw wounds. His voice entreating her to end her torment. All she needed do was speak her enchanted name.

Despite the chilled air swirling over her rain-soaked body, sweat dampened her palms and trickled between her breasts. If Jole hadn't infiltrated Roark's troops and found a way to free her, how much longer could she have resisted? The thought of being Roark's puppet, her every thought, action, and emotion controlled by him, sickened her.

She gave a mirthless laugh. Her capture and torture were not the beginning of his bid to control her. From the moment he'd slaughtered the royal family, Roark became the guiding star of her destiny, their fates entwined. Even before he entered her life, she realized she had never controlled her own fate.

An elusive memory of another life, another place, another time teased her. Since she'd nearly—should have, even—died several weeks ago, she'd felt strange. Her life before that moment seemed unreal, a bewildering dream. The here and now took on deeper meaning. Though she remembered everything, recalled every action she'd taken, every emotion she'd felt, every thought she'd had, she no longer connected with that person. She felt different, as if someone else had directed that prior her, the person she used to be. And since Donnie reappeared in her life, the odd feelings had grown stronger.

Though confused by the feelings, she felt herself expanding, becoming more . . . complex, but at the same time, she felt empty, alone, frightened. She needed, wanted, to destroy Roark. Even with his fortress breached, his forces defeated, his reign of terror ended, he was still a force to be feared. He'd built an army once. If allowed to live, he could do so again. For Barue . . . for people to be free, Andre Roark had to die.

Her goals all but reached, Serilda wondered what was left for her. If Donoval lived, her pledge to him would take her far from here. But she knew her warrior skills did not qualify her to rule as queen of Shallon. Perhaps it would be better if she died along with Roark. As long as he died.

With nowhere to go but forward, she approached the door. The latch opened easily under her hand, and she was surprised the tyrant hadn't locked her out. She stood to the side and pushed the door inward to reveal a large chamber. She peered inside. Warmth from the fire burning in the hearth bathed her chilled flesh. The tantalizing aromas of roasted meat and wine hung in the air. Her mouth watered.

She scanned the room. Nothing moved.

Never one to forgo his comfort, Roark had outfitted this chamber with a comfortable bed, thick fur rugs on the stone floor, heavy tapestries on the walls, and several upholstered chairs in front of the hearth.

"Come in, my dear." The voice came from one of the chairs facing the hearth.

Warmth drained from Serilda. Hunger, briefly stirred, turned to nausea. How well she remembered Roark's rich, seductive voice, how he used it to charm and manipulate, terrorize and dominate. Even while he had her tortured, he'd tempted her with assurances of respite while he threatened her with promises of further degradation, all in the same low, soothing tones, until, racked with pain, she nearly succumbed.

Muscles clenched, she stepped into the room and barred the door behind her. This fight was between her and Roark. She'd allow no others to interfere.

Her fingers tightened on the hilt of her sword. To be whole again, she needed to confront him, to deal with her bone-deep fear of his evil. "Face me, villain," she demanded.

He didn't oblige. "In due time. First I have something for you. Come."

"Beyond your death, you have nothing I want," she said as she moved closer.

"Are you sure?"

The amused confidence in his voice worried her. "Your men are defeated. Barue is free of you."

"Sadly, I fear you're correct."

"Then, why do you hesitate? It's time for you to die." She did not voice her fear that he might destroy her instead.

"I think not." He stood and stepped around the chair to face her. He was as she remembered, a tall, handsome man of middle years, with sharp features, thin lips, and emotionless eyes. But it wasn't Roark that held her attention. It was the figure he clasped against his chest, his blade against the fragile expanse of her throat. Eyes open but empty of expression, she stood passive in Roark's hold.

"Mauri!" Instinctively Serilda raised her sword and stepped forward. The girl didn't respond.

"Hold or she dies." Roark fisted his fingers in Mauri's long hair and jerked her head back. His blade nicked her skin. Blood appeared.

"Hurt her, and I'll gut you and strangle you with your entrails."

Roark's laughter boomed throughout the chamber. "Brave words. Do as I bid and she'll live. Disobey and she dies." He pressed the blade deeper. Mauri moaned.

"Don't!" Spreading her arms wide, Serilda lowered her sword. "What do you want?"

"What I've always wanted."

"I'll never tell you my enchanted name." Ice flowed

through her veins. He had to die. She watched and waited for an opening.

"Not even to save her?"

"How did she get here?" Serilda stalled for time.

"Pretty little thing. Pity she has to die. Now that she's grown, she'd have warmed my bed nicely." He stroked his hand down Mauri's unresisting body. "I summoned her."

"How?" *Summoned?* Roark's magic was small, not strong enough to command another without . . . She looked into Mauri's blank eyes and knew the truth before Roark continued.

"The connection between enchanted name and invoker transcends time and space. Long before she came into your hands, she was my creature."

"You know her enchanted name?" She viewed the motionless girl with different eyes.

"Poor lass." He touched Mauri's pale cheek in a mockery of tenderness. "Her parents dead. All alone. When I found her, it didn't take much to coax her enchanted name from her. Once I had it, I placed her in your path. I knew you couldn't resist rescuing her."

"She's been spying for you?"

"She's been my eyes and ears in your camp. Unfortunately, my opportunities to summon her have been few, barely enough to allow me to escape your numerous traps."

No wonder Roark had slipped through her fingers time and time again. Anger warred with pity in Serilda.

"Tsk. Don't blame the child. She has no recall of what she did. Every time I summoned her, she tried to resist giving me information. She fought my commands, so I wiped her memory of our encounters. I couldn't chance her love for you prevailing over her duty to me."

Serilda thanked the heavens that Mauri hadn't known the specific details of their recent attack. "Do as you will. I'll not surrender my soul to you."

Speaking Mauri's death sentence shredded her heart. She'd gladly die for the girl, but giving Roark control over her risked the lives and futures of more than just this one child.

"Why do you resist? Together we could rule Barue."

"I'll never be your consort." The thought of Roark's touch clogged her throat with bile.

"Sweet as it is, I have no desire for your body. You mistake my intentions . . . daughter."

Daughter? Shock rippled through her. "You lie."

"Do I?" He lifted an eyebrow and studied her. "I knew the moment I saw you that you were mine. Your mother thought she escaped me so many years ago, but she carried my seed."

One part of her screamed denial of his words, another accepted them. Now her mother's aversion to touching her, her father's silent dislike, their emotional distance—it all made sense.

"It took me ten years to find her. To find you."

Serilda remembered the attack in the middle of the night. The shouts outside their modest home. Her father grabbing his sword and rushing out the door to face the attackers. Her mother hiding her younger sisters and brothers in the cellar, then pushing her out the back, telling her to run. Cowering in the woods as men on horseback surrounded the house. Seeing the man she called father cut down and trampled, his blood staining the ground red.

She remembered her mother screaming and trying to reach him as men grabbed her. Watching as the leader strode over to her mother. She hadn't heard the words that passed between them, but she'd seen her mother spit in the man's face. He'd slapped her. She sagged limp to the ground.

The crackle of fire when he'd ordered the house torched. Her mother's anguished sobs and pleas as screams began inside the burning house.

She remembered her mother snatching up her father's sword, attacking the man, her strangled cry as the man's blade plunged through her chest. The heat of flames. The screams of her brothers and sisters burning alive. The smell. Her answering cries of grief as she tried to reach them, only to be driven back by the flames' intense heat.

She remembered the look of revelation on the man's face as he caught sight of her. Then she'd been running and running and running, heart pounding, gasping for breath, through the night. Escaping death but never quite escaping the nightmare.

"And when you found her, you killed her, killed them all. Why?"

"She betrayed me. She was mine. What's mine, I keep. Her death was an unfortunate accident." He shrugged. "I meant to take her with me. Her attack surprised me. I reacted badly. I was much younger then," he said, as if that explained it all.

"You truly believed she'd go with you after you murdered everyone she loved?"

"She was supposed to love *me*." The madness in his eyes echoed the insanity of his words.

"Why not kill me as well?"

"You're my blood. My daughter. You're mine. You belong to me."

"I don't belong to you. I belong to no man." But suddenly, she knew she lied. Her heart belonged to Donnie. Not the king who'd dominated and commanded her while satisfying her body, but the new man who'd appeared, who fed her soul, who loved and desired her. Donnie, who'd come to help her in her quest, sacrificing himself and his need to rule his kingdom in order to help her, no matter what. Body and soul, she belonged to him, though he could never be hers. He was like a storybook hero, one created by bards but specifically for her, though her world could know no happy endings.

Horror filled her. Roark's blood flowed in her veins. She wanted to purge the knowledge from her mind, drain the evil taint from her body, cleanse her soul. First, she had to eliminate him from this world.

"Unlike your deceitful mother, you will love me," he was saying.

"I'll never love you. Kill her if you will." Better Mauri died than the girl remain in physical and mental thrall to Roark. "You won't escape my blade."

His smile was a warning, and it came a split second before he spoke. "*I* won't kill her. *You* will." He thrust a dagger into Mauri's hand and shoved her forward, commanding, "Kill Serilda."

Blade poised, Mauri lunged forward. Her eyes were blank.

Seri suffered only a moment of remorse. She

caught the girl's wrist and gave it a sharp twist, heard bones crack. She winced, but the girl's dagger tumbled to the floor. Eyes wild and unfocused, fingers curled like talons and shrieking, Mauri continued her attack, so Seri struck her with the pommel of her sword. With a whimper, the girl crumpled to the floor and lay still.

She bent and quickly checked Mauri's pulse, found it strong and steady. So doing, she stood and looked around for Roark. This was the only chance. Once he died, Mauri would be free of his control.

Her heart stuttered as she surveyed the room. The chamber was empty. The door was still barred behind her, though. Where had he gone?

Next to the hearth, where there was no breeze, a tapestry rippled. She tore it down to expose a gap in the stone wall. Light from the hearth revealed a vanishing secret passageway, a circular stairwell. She couldn't see her foe, but she heard the clatter of Roark's boots as he ran downward. Sheathing her sword, she squeezed through the narrow opening and followed him into oblivion.

I twisted out of the pool of ooze into which I'd been smashed when the warhorse collapsed upon me. Mud caked my body from head to toe, but its consistency had saved me from being crushed. Since I had fallen, the fight had shifted away from the gate, leaving me alone in this corner of the bailey. I stood and let the ceaseless rain rinse the filth from my face and eyes, then looked around. Seri was nowhere to be seen.

In the center of the bailey, Gerhan's mounted soldiers surrounded Roark's remaining men; the fighting here was all but done. Without Roark appearing to lead them, his soldiers had surrendered.

My gaze went upward. High in the keep's tower, the light still burned. In almost every version of my book, I'd set a major confrontation between Roark and Seri in that chamber. They had to be there. But I could see the main door was closed, access to the keep cut off. How could I get in?

Heavy with mud, the parchment inside my garments stuck to my chest. I pulled it out and read. Nothing was going as I'd planned. Ink ran in illegible streaks and smears across the page. Only the last line of what I'd written remained, for all the good it would do. In my gut, I knew the end of Seri's story—the end that I'd always intended. A sense of helplessness came over me.

My presence in this world negated the measly power I wielded with my pen. I couldn't control what happened here any more than I could control the future in my real life—a real life that had always scared me, been out of my grasp. But as my fingers curled around the hilt of the sword hanging at my waist, I realized there were other methods of making a difference than with a pen.

The castle gate opened. Occupied by disarming Roark's soldiers, Gerhan didn't notice the small figure wobbling out into the bailey.

I rushed to her side. She collapsed in my arms.

"Mauri."

"I'm sorry. I tried not to tell him anything, but I couldn't resist," the girl whispered.

"Damn." I felt trapped in a nightmare of my own design. "Mauri, where's Seri? Roark?"

"I don't know," she whimpered. "They went through a secret escape tunnel in the wall."

I searched my memory for the details of my original ending and went cold inside. Roark and Seri had made their way to where the fortress rose along the edge of a steep cliff. Locked in combat, they tumbled to their deaths together.

"My lord. Are you injured?"

I looked up through the rain to see Gerhan. "No. See to the prisoners and the girl," I commanded. *That should keep him occupied.*

But I'd underestimated the old warrior's devotion to Donoval. Gerhan hurried after me as I headed across the bailey. "Where do you go, my lord?"

"Lady d'Lar follows Roark to the cliffs." As I ran, I heard Gerhan shouting commands to his men, but I didn't stop to explain or wait for him. Every second counted.

Torrents of icy rain sluiced over me. Thunder rumbled, shaking the ground. Jagged streaks of lightning flashed across the gray skies, blinding me with their brilliance. Each bolt illuminated a scene of horror. Bodies of men and horses littered the bailey, blood glistening red in puddles of murky water. Thunder drowned out the moans of the injured and dying.

Outside the fortress, I made my way along the wall to the cliff side. In the heavy rain, I couldn't see more than a few feet in front of me. Only the brief flashes of lightning lit my path. Ahead, just as I'd written, the castle had been erected along the edge of a deep chasm.

Keeping a hand on the solid rock of the fortress

wall, I crept forward. Deep mud made a morass all around me. With each step, the ground dipped downward. One misstep and I'd slide right off the edge into the abyss.

Again the question plagued me: if I died as Donoval in this world, would I die in the real world as well? Strangely enough, this didn't concern me as much as Seri's imminent demise. This woman I'd created, this woman I'd believed only a figment of my imagination—whoever and whatever she was, no matter how I'd come here or where I'd go afterward, I only knew I had to save her.

Back pressed to the wall, I eased around the corner. Less than three feet wide, a stony ledge ran along the backside of the castle walls. In front of me, the world fell away into nothingness, a pit of black with no discernable bottom. My stomach flipped as my boots scrambled for purchase on the slick, sloped ground.

With nothing to grab, I slid toward the edge. In desperation I threw myself flat, splayed my body across the ledge, and dug my fingers into the ground. Sharp rocks sliced my palms. My toes hung off the edge, but my slide toward doom ended. Heart pounding in time with the rain, I hugged the ground.

After a few moments, I cautiously rose to my knees, then my feet. How far to the secret tunnel entrance? I'd written so many different descriptions of this stupid castle, I had no clue where the damned thing might be. I peered into the watery gloom. To my left rose the castle wall, its bulk a forbidding barrier. On my right, the world disappeared into a well of nothingness so black and deep even the flares of lightning couldn't reveal its secrets.

I hadn't written or even considered what lay beyond this point. Did this world end here? What would happen if I tumbled into this void? Would I fall forever? Or would I wake with a start, safe in my bed? Questions without answers swirled in my mind. Questions without point. There was only Serilda.

Pulling my sword, I moved forward, step by cautious step. Around the noise of the storm, I heard them.

"Stand and face me, coward!" Against the noise of the storm, Seri's shout sounded like a whisper.

The wind whipped away any answer Roark gave. Above the grumble of thunder, cracks of lightning, and pounding of rain against stone, the clang of metal against metal sounded clear. Fear clutched me like icy fingers, squeezing my lungs of air and hope.

I increased my pace. The clanging stopped. The voices grew louder, but I still couldn't see the speakers.

"Did you think I'd let you escape so easily?" Like the growl of an angry lioness, Seri's voice reached me.

Against the faint glow of light from the open secret entrance, I could see them. Swords raised, they stood at the edge of the cliff. Rain blurred their outlines.

"I had confidence you'd join me here. The child was no match for you. Did you kill her?"

The cold curiosity in Roark's question turned my blood to ice. In that moment, I knew he intended to kill Serilda now, daughter or not.

"You're mad."

"Perhaps I am, daughter." He chuckled, but the sound held no amusement.

"Before you die, tell me why?"

Anguish laced Seri's words. Anguish I'd put there with my words, anguish that had been an eruption of my own unhappiness. Roark's insanity. Seri's pain. All the death and destruction. All were my doing. Nothing Roark said or did would remove my guilt.

"Why? What a strange question, daughter. 'Why not?' is what you should ask. The royal family had power. I wanted it. I had the ability, so I took it."

Cautiously I eased across the loose rock. Stones shifted under my feet and skidded over the edge. But listening to Roark spout the nonsense I'd given him, I swallowed back the bile burning my throat. This was the last scene playing out much as I'd written it. Nothing had changed to match any rewrite.

"As advisor to the king, you had wealth, status, power. You held his trust and affection. Anything you wanted was yours."

"It wasn't enough. I wanted more. I would have it all—position and power. I would have had the people worship me as they did him."

"So you betrayed and killed them . . . but you gained nothing. You're a fool. At your treachery, the people turned from you."

"Once their last hope lies dead, their hope will fade. They'll come back to me."

"My death will not give you their love. The heir yet lives. He'll be found, and Barue will return to its former glory. You'll be forgotten."

Roark's laughter echoed over the thunder. "Without me, the heir will never be found."

Seri stepped forward. Her sword dipped. "You know where he is? Tell me and I'll let you live."

Distracted by his revelation, she didn't react as Roark lifted his sword.

"No!" The wind whipped away my scream of denial. Slipping and sliding, I charged forward. The mud made it all but impossible.

Roark lunged. His blade found Seri's chest and pierced it. Her eyes widened in shock. Her sword clattered to the ground.

Roark gripped Seri's shoulder and pulled her close, forcing his blade through her to the hilt. Over his shoulder, her gaze met mine. I read her intent. Yards still separated us.

"No, Seri, don't," I whispered. I was still too far away.

"Before I die, tell me," she rasped. "Who is he?" Her fingers curled around Roark's upper arms.

"Why, young Jole, of course!" He let go of Seri's shoulder and his sword, and he started to step away, but he couldn't. She held him fast.

Pleasure and surprise lit her face as she looked at me. "Take care of him."

Her words were for me, for King Donoval. Despite all her fears and anger, she trusted me to see to the welfare of Barue and its rightful king. Her hands remained locked on Roark's arms. Her body swayed.

"What are you doing? Let me go!" Roark tried to pry her fingers loose.

Her smile lit up the pale oval of her face, even as the light in her eyes dimmed. "I think not . . . Father."

Arriving just too late, I watched helpless as she

folded Roark in her embrace and stepped over the edge—into the nothingness.

I stood at the edge of the chasm. No sound or light revealed the passage of these two epic enemies, enemies I had created and ultimately destroyed. Like the blackness meeting my gaze, my heart was empty.

Shoulders bowed in grief, I sank to my knees. My sword dropped uselessly from my fingers. Rain washed away the meager warmth of the tears running down my cheeks. I'd failed Seri. As surely as if I'd run the sword through her heart and pushed her off the cliff myself, I'd killed her.

It was over, the villain vanquished, the heir to the throne discovered, the heroine sacrificed for the good of all; the story of Warrior Woman was finished. All tied up in a neat, satisfying bundle. Readers could rail against fate, revel in the tragedy. All I could do was sob.

I ground my fists into the jagged stones on the ground, threw back my head, and howled. This wasn't right. This was as I'd written it, but it wasn't what I wanted.

"Your power with words will demand great sacrifice. And if you're not careful, it will destroy you." My grandmother's words came back to me. If only I'd heeded them, perhaps believed in the warning of my vanished father, would Seri still be alive?

No. I wasn't going to let it stand. Losing her would destroy me. Whatever entity directed this universe had miscalculated. I was still here. My doubts had let Serilda die, but no more. No matter the sacrifice demanded of me, I would change her fate. I felt Donoval's agreement.

Parchment and quill. I needed parchment and quill.

I scrambled to my feet and darted up the secret passage and into the keep.

Seri & Brandon

"Reality is the garden of our imagination."
—Brother Eldrin, Order of the Light

Chapter Seventeen

I burst out of the door onto the ledge just behind
Roark. Confused, I stopped and blinked against the
rain dripping down my face. Was I dead? I touched
my chest. No blade protruded. No blood gushed
around my fingers. No pain stole my breath. Lightning crackled overhead. Thunder rumbled, shaking
the ground beneath my feet.

As had happened many times on the battlefield,
once very recently in fact, I'd been plucked away a
moment before death claimed me. Only this time I
was back where I started, not in some gray place
shrouded in mist.

Like the rain drenching my body, memories
poured through my mind. Again, that endless gray
void. A strange world of mechanical carriages without horses to pull them. Donoval . . . no, a wizard
named Brandon. One after another, images, thoughts,
emotions too numerous to sort, and understanding
rushed over me. I could no longer separate this world
from the other, tell the real from the unreal.

Donnie's claim of being another man, from

another world, another reality, none of it seemed bizarre any longer.

Beneath the onslaught, I staggered. In front of me, beyond the narrow ledge, the world disappeared into a black so deep not even lightning revealed any hint of what lay within.

Roark moved along the ledge away from me. Whatever or whoever had brought me back, I couldn't let him escape. I ran after him. "Stand and face me, Father!" I cried.

At my call, he glanced back but didn't stop. With the brief turn of his head, he missed seeing the lightning illuminate the figure racing toward him. Donnie! Sword held aloft, his golden hair flying, Donnie attacked.

At the last second, Roark raised his sword and deflected Donnie's blow. Sparks flew off their clashing blades. Arms raised, their bodies slammed together, then bounced apart.

Lightning struck the ledge in front of me. The force of the strike knocked me on my backside and sent a tingle of energy through me. I felt the ledge crack at the castle wall and shift beneath me.

As if unaware of the danger, Roark circled Donnie. I held my breath as Donnie's feet moved closer to the tilting edge. Chunks crumbled and fell away. Their collapse made no sound over the crashes of thunder reverberating through the air.

As the ground buckled, Donnie staggered, arms pinwheeling, body teetering over the edge. Roark's manic laugh of triumph was chilling. Blade upraised for the killing blow, he surged forward.

I scrambled to my feet and tried to move to help. The ledge rocked beneath me.

At the last moment, Donnie ducked beneath Roark's blade, twisted, and came up behind him. Roark whirled. His blade caught Donnie's sword arm, slicing through the leather guard. Blood spurted forth. Donnie's arm sagged; the point of his sword dipped. Then, through the rain and between the flashes of lightning, unable to move for fear of distracting Donnie or sending the unstable ledge tumbling into the void, I could only watch in horror. Roark plunged his sword into Donnie's chest.

Donnie fell to the ground. But as Roark leaned forward to push the blade home, Donnie lifted his feet against Roark's chest and threw him.

Roark's feet left the ground. His scream of rage turned to terror. Arms flailing, he twisted midair, searching for some way to return to the loose rock. Then he was over the edge, gone. His shrieks, which should have echoed as he fell, vanished.

I peered into the darkness but could see nothing.

"Donnie?" I picked my way across the ledge to his side.

Dead? My heart ached at the impossible thought. He couldn't be dead! I loved him.

"I love you, too," he rasped.

Had I spoken aloud? It didn't matter. I'd shout my love to the heavens if it would keep him with me.

"Stay with me." To keep the rain from his face, I leaned over him.

"I'd really like to, but . . ." He coughed. Blood gushed from his lips. "As usual, things didn't go quite the way I wrote them. He wasn't supposed to stab me. Damn, it hurts." He reached inside his shirt and pulled out a folded piece of parchment. "Take this. Read it."

"Don't talk. I'll get the healer." I ignored the parchment and started to rise.

He grabbed my arm; his grasp was weak. "It's no use."

"You'll not die. I won't allow it!" Tears made hot streams down my rain-chilled cheeks.

"It doesn't matter. I did what I meant to do: I saved you." I had to bend my head to his lips to hear his words.

"Without you," I sobbed, "my life matters not. What will I do without you?" I realized it was true. Everything I'd fought for, everything I'd desired, it was nothing without him to share it.

He chuckled softly. "It matters. The people of Barue. Jole. Mauri. And you managed without me for years. You'll do so again." His chuckle turned to choking coughs.

I wrapped my arm around him and braced his back against my shoulder, as if by loving him I could lift and carry him to safety, perhaps keep death at bay. But I knew it was useless. My love hadn't saved my family or the monks. It wouldn't save this man I loved.

"There's something you need to know," he gasped. "Young Jole is the missing heir. I can't tell you how I know, but . . . at the base of his spine, he has the royal birthmark as proof. He'll need you to help him bring peace and order back to Barue."

Burgeoning grief drowned my pleasure in the news. Jole would make a fine king.

Donnie took my hand and closed my fingers around the damp parchment. "Read it and you'll understand," he said. "Knowledge will set you free. Believe. I love you."

Then his eyes closed, and he sagged in my arms. Dead.

I raised my face to the rain. None of this made sense. Not my scattered memories, nor Donnie's strange claims. How could anything be the answer to this puzzle?

Sitting in the rain, tears streaming down my face, I unfolded his parchment. Wet with Donnie's blood, most of the script was smudged; only one line in Donnie's ragged scrawl remained crisp and clear.

The power of love opened her eyes, and she believed.

Against all possibility, in that instant, everything crystallized in my mind, even as the parchment crumpled in my grip. My nails dug into my palms.

"You can't be dead! I love you!" The tempest swallowed my scream.

I loved him, all the parts of him. King Donoval, strong, brave, and exasperating. Donnie, sweet, caring, and lovable. But most of all I loved Brandon, clumsy, unsure, and endearing, and the genesis of it all. Too late, I remembered. Too late, I believed. Too late, I understood. Our time together was ended.

In grief, I clutched his limp body to my chest. I shook but not with cold. Tears scalded my eyes but refused to fall. Around me the storm raged on, the thunder and lightning a contrast to the quiet emptiness expanding inside me.

Lightning struck the wall. Energy sizzled through me. Stones pelted my face. I knew I should move, flee, especially as the ledge shifted beneath me. Soon it would collapse. But as I didn't have the strength or the heart to move Donnie's body, nor could I leave him to plunge alone into the void, I refused to move. We would stay together. Our fates were linked.

I whispered the words Brandon had written, "The power of love opened my eyes, and I believed."

Yes, I believed. I believed in Brandon's world. I believed in my world. I believed in the magic and power of love. And though he believed we were through, that I would continue on as he had once written me, I believed in my own autonomy—in the power I wielded as well. I was no longer a pawn to be controlled by bards or scribes, kings or tyrants. And I believed somewhere, sometime, someplace Donnie and I would be together once more.

Lightning struck again. The ledge crumbled beneath me. My stomach rose in my throat, but I held Donnie tight as we tumbled into oblivion.

> *"Though the world is dark, we each can light
> the candle our own happy ending."*
> —Brother Eldrin, Order of the Light

Chapter Eighteen

Hard lumps dug painfully into my spine. I reached under me and pulled out a . . . pen? I tried to shift away, but a warm, wet weight lay across my chest. Blinking water from my eyes, I tried to focus on the ceiling of my office.

The ceiling?

My office!

I was alive! At least, I felt alive.

Cautiously, I moved. No pain seared through me. No sword protruded from the center of my chest. No blood stained the garments I wore, but they were indeed drenched—from the rain-swept cliff from which I'd come? My muscles ached, my skin felt damp and raw, but all my parts seemed to be intact and in working order.

I collected my scattered thoughts.

I remembered dying. I recalled Roark's sword plunging through me, the pain, the anguish in Seri's eyes as she watched me slip away into the unknown. What happened after that remained a blank. No brilliant white light or scorching flames. No loved ones welcoming me to the other side. No red beast with horns and a tail dancing in glee. No one telling me to go back. No memories. Just . . . nothingness. Then I'd woken up here and now.

"Seri?" I gasped. I looked at the woman draped across me. Spiked with moisture, her dark eyelashes lay against her pale cheeks. With each breath, her parted lips blew warm air against my skin. One hand rested on my thigh. At the sound of my voice, her fingers curled into my flesh. My instant reaction was unexpected but not unwelcome. I couldn't suppress my grin at the knowledge that *part* of me was definitely in working order.

In her hand, she clutched a soggy piece of parchment. Ink smeared the crumpled folds. One word remained legible:

believe

She stirred, lifting her head from my chest. Slicked with water against her skull, her reddish-blonde curls were crimson shot with gold. Her thoughts veiled in her green eyes, nonetheless her gaze met mine.

"We're alive?" she asked in a hushed tone.

"It seems like it." I wanted to grin, to laugh and shout, but unsure of her reaction to returning to the real world, I held back.

She snatched her hand from my thigh and sat up. Her fingers curled and uncurled around the hilt of her sword, which had apparently come with her. Mine was gone, lost in the oblivion between our worlds.

Cool air swirled over me. I missed the warmth

and comfort of her chest and face pressed against mine. I scooted up until my back rested against the desk and waited for her reaction.

I followed her gaze as she looked around my office. Papers littered the floor. The desk lamp cast a mellow glow over the chaos. For a long time, she stared at the mural on my wall, then turned her gaze to the view outside the windows. A light rain pattered softly against the house, its sound a comforting rhythm. Lightning no longer lit the sky, and shafts of sunlight peeked between the dissolving clouds. The river below flowed swiftly, its surface like a stream of raw silver.

"What do you remember?" I asked.

Confusion turned her eyes the grayish green color of a stormy sea. "I remember I died. Then I lived again." She touched the center of her chest then looked up. "Then you died." Pain darkened her eyes. "Now we're alive. Back in your world. I don't understand how these things have happened."

"I'm not sure, either, but we're alive and safe. Do you remember being here before?"

She dipped her head. "I remember it all. Are we here to stay? Will I return to Barue?"

From the moment she'd first appeared, her goal had been to return to her world. To save her people. To live free. Was there anything that could convince her to stay with me now?

"I'm not sure. Do you want to?"

When I lay dying, she'd whispered words of love, but what did she mean by it? Was her love for me strong enough to anchor her in this world? Had she known what she was effecting? Could she be happy here? If she wanted to return to the world of Barue,

I couldn't keep her with me. I wasn't sure of the how or why of her appearance in my life, or how I'd ended up in her world, but somehow I knew if she didn't want to stay, she shouldn't. And I knew that whatever I had to do, I would find a way to send her back. And I knew I had the power to do it.

Though it pained me to offer, I said, "I don't know how, but if you want to go back, I'll find a way to get you there." It was a promise.

"Are you so eager to be rid of me?"

"No, of course not!" I said. "I—"

She pressed her fingers against my lips. "The how and why do not matter. What is important is that we are here, together. Roark's death . . ." She paused. "He *is* dead, isn't he?"

I nodded vigorously, knowing it to be true.

She smiled and continued, "Thank heavens. But I wish to remain here with you, no matter what."

"You're sure?" I asked.

"I do not say what I do not mean."

Though I dreaded the answer, I had to ask. "What about Barue? Your life there? Mauri and Jole? Can you leave them?" Afraid to see the answer in her eyes, I looked away.

She cupped my cheek in her palm and met my gaze. "With Barue and Mauri free of Roark's yoke, I'm no longer needed there. You are the architect of their lives. I trust you to keep them safe." She threaded her fingers through mine.

I lifted our joined hands to her cheek. The uncertainty in her eyes reflected my own.

"Your world is a strange and wonderful place," she said after a moment. "I realize that I started as naught but a creature of your imagination, but . . . I am more. I swear it. I don't know if I can be as *real* as the other people in your life, Hillary and Wanda, but I'm willing to try and fit in. Do not send me back. I love you . . . Brandon."

All of my doubt vanished. Hillary was going to be thrilled when she got the revisions on my latest book. I smiled and wrapped my arms around Seri. "There's more to you than anything I ever created. Your world is more real than I ever intended. In fact, maybe I didn't even create it. Maybe it exists in some parallel universe as real as this one, and I simply tapped into it. Whatever I've done, I don't know anymore. But I do know you've always been real to me, more real than Hillary or Wanda and a better person than any I know. I know without you my life will be empty. And I know without any reservations that I love you. Stay with me."

"Forever," she agreed.

Autumn Dawn

WHEN SPARKS FLY

Polaris just got a little hotter.

"Dawn injects a fresh new energy into the futuristic romance genre... Brava!"
—*RT BOOKreviews*

WHERE FIRES RISE

Perhaps it was his wild black hair and indigo eyes, or maybe it was his enigmatic aura, but there was something about Hyna Blue that drew Gem. The man had clearly done hard labor, his cybernetic implants gave him increased strength, but he was no longer whole...and now he was getting drunk in her tavern. Yes, Hyna Blue aroused instincts both carnal and nurturing. Gem's blood had been fiery to start with. Blue heated it even more.

Of course, since the planet of Polaris discovered its trainum mine, things were hot all over. Prosperity had blown in on a solar wind, along with many disreputable types, the least deceptive of which were some shape-shifting aliens. The ruined beauty of one patron and his drunken proposals were the least of Gem's worries—and perhaps her one solace. Like her father had named it long ago, this inn was The Spark. Gem had to survive the blaze.

ISBN 13: 978-0-505-52802-5

TEKGRRL

A DARK SEED...

When she was 12, Mindy asked to go to the School like other gifted girls. Her parents sent her to another planet.

...HAS GROWN TO FRUITION

Today, Mindy's back on Earth. She's a mechanical genius with the Elite Hands of Justice, America's premier superhero squad. She's been having headaches, though, and not just because her longtime crush is flirting with a teammate. It's not because she's pushing thirty. It's also not because of the contrary actions of the new Secretary for Superhero Affairs, ex-ally Simon Leasure. No, what's burning her brain is a past she can't remember, a past that has been erased. It's a memory surging closer—in flying saucers. Her worst nightmare is returning, big-time, and only she and her friends can stop it.

A. J. MENDEN

ISBN 13: 978-0-505-52787-5

KATHRYNE KENNEDY

Author of *Double Enchantment*

Enchanting the Beast

~Relics of Merlin~

"Really fun and imaginative." —Eloisa James

Grimspell castle. With its dark, imposing stone walls, it certainly looked haunted. As a ghost-hunter, Lady Philomena was accustomed to restless spirits. But she found the dark, imposing nature of the castle's owner far more haunting than any specter. London Society might not approve of shape-shifters such as Sir Nicodemus Wulfson, but firmly-on-the-shelf Philomena rather enjoyed the young baronet's sudden interest in sniffing around her skirts. She'd even consider giving in to him altogether if not for a murderer on the loose—a beast that might just be Nico himself.

"Simply delightful."
—*Publishers Weekly* on *Enchanting the Lady*

ISBN 13: 978-0-505-52764-6

☐ **YES!**

Sign me up for the Love Spell Book Club and send my
FREE BOOKS! If I choose to stay in the club, I will pay
only $8.50* each month, a savings of $6.48!

NAME: _____

ADDRESS: _____

TELEPHONE: _____

EMAIL: _____

☐ I want to pay by credit card.

☐ **VISA**   ☐ **MasterCard**   ☐ **DISCOVER**

ACCOUNT #: _____

EXPIRATION DATE: _____

SIGNATURE: _____

Mail this page along with $2.00 shipping and handling to:
Love Spell Book Club
PO Box 6640
Wayne, PA 19087
Or fax (must include credit card information) to:
610-995-9274
You can also sign up online at **www.dorchesterpub.com**.
*Plus $2.00 for shipping. Offer open to residents of the U.S. and Canada only.
Canadian residents please call 1-800-481-9191 for pricing information.
If under 18, a parent or guardian must sign. Terms, prices and conditions subject to
change. Subscription subject to acceptance. Dorchester Publishing reserves the right
to reject any order or cancel any subscription.